"They are full-fleshed, full-blown entries in each of the series of stories. Full of the action, setting, and character that have made each of these writers, as the title boldly states, modern legends in their genre. There isn't a misfire in the bunch, a rarity in anthologies, and very much a rarity in the fantasy field. This is a collection of grace, style, and substance.

"So, if you are a follower of any of these series, you need this book. And if you've never tried modern fantasy, this is a wonderful place to be introduced to its masters."
— *The Statesman Journal* (Salem, Oregon)

"This is an excellent way to visit old friends, or get clued in on some multivolumed epics." — *The Denver Post*

"A collection of short novels by some of the biggest names in fantasy, all set in their best-known secondary worlds. There are delights aplenty in this huge volume."
— *Edmonton Journal*

"A fascinating assortment of short novels by fantasy's power-house authors, set in the most-loved world each created. Each tale stands alone, which is an added bonus for those readers who may not have read every series represented. Every tale in *Legends* is original, high-quality, and adds gloriously to the world in which it is set. Some are amusing and charming, others tragic, but all reflect the nobility of the human spirit."
— *The Herald* (Rock Hills, South Carolina)

"In addition to its obvious appeal to confirmed series readers, this tour de force serves as a superb introduction to the genre's most memorable sagas. A priority purchase."
— *Library Journal*

"This is an altogether impressive volume, completely approachable. The illustrations and maps included throughout are certainly a lovely bonus, but quite unnecessary in a volume that sells itself by the fifth page and holds to its early promise all the way through." — *VOYA*

"An essential for every fantasy fan." — *SFX*

Legends

Volume 2

Short Novels by the Masters of Modern Fantasy

edited by

Robert Silverberg

TOR®

A TOM DOHERTY ASSOCIATES BOOK
NEW YORK

This is a work of fiction. All the characters and events portrayed in this book are either products of the author's imagination or are used fictitiously.

LEGENDS: VOLUME 2

Copyright © 1998 by Agberg, Ltd.

A Tor Book
Published by Tom Doherty Associates, LLC
175 Fifth Avenue
New York, NY 10010

www.tor.com

Tor® is a registered trademark of Tom Doherty Associates, LLC.

ISBN: 0-812-57523-7
Library of Congress Catalog Card Number: 98-23593

First edition: October 1998
First mass market edition: November 1999

Printed in the United States of America

0 9 8 7 6 5 4 3 2 1

FOR MARTY AND RALPH
who certainly know why

CONTENTS

INTRODUCTION

❧

Here is a book of visions and miracles—the second volume in a set of three containing eleven rich, robust new stories by the best-known and most accomplished modern creators of fantasy fiction, each one set in the special universe of the imagination that made that writer famous throughout the world.

Fantasy is the oldest branch of imaginative literature—as old as the human imagination itself. It is not difficult to believe that the same artistic impulse that produced the extraordinary cave paintings of Altamira and Chauvet, fifteen and twenty and even thirty thousand years ago, also probably produced astounding tales of gods and demons, of talismans and spells, of dragons and werewolves, of wondrous lands beyond the horizon—tales that fur-clad shamans recited to fascinated audiences around the campfires of Ice Age Europe. So, too, in torrid Africa, in the China of prehistory, in ancient India, in the Americas: everywhere, in fact, on and on back through time for thousands or even hundreds of thousands of years. I like to think that the storytelling impulse is universal—that there have been storytellers as long as there have been beings in this world that could be spoken of as "human"—and that those storytellers have in particular devoted their skills and energies and talents, throughout our long evolutionary path, to the creation of extraordinary marvels and wonders.

We will never know, of course, what tales the Cro-Magnon storytellers told their spellbound audiences on those frosty nights in ancient France. But surely there were strong components of the fantastic in them. The evidence of the oldest stories that *have* survived argues in favor of that. If fantasy can be defined as literature that depicts the world beyond that of mundane reality, and mankind's struggle to assert dominance over that world, then the most ancient story that *has* come down to us— the Sumerian tale of the hero Gilgamesh, which dates from about 2500 B.C.—is fantasy, for its theme is Gilgamesh's quest for eternal life.

Homer's *Odyssey,* abounding as it does in shapeshifters and wizards and sorceresses, in Cyclopses and many-headed man-eating creatures, is rich with fantastic elements, too, as are any number of other Greek and Roman tales. As we come closer to our own times we meet the dread monster Grendel of the Anglo-Saxon *Beowulf*, the Midgard serpent and the dragon Fafnir and the apocalyptic Fenris-wolf of the Norse sagas, the hapless immortality-craving Dr. Faustus of German legend, the myriad enchanters of *The Thousand and One Nights*, the far-larger-than-life heroes of the Welsh *Mabinogion* and the Persian *Shah-Nameh,* and an infinity of other strange and wonderful creations.

Nor did the impulse toward the creation of the fantastic disappear as the modern era, the era of microscopes and telescopes, of steam engines and railway systems, of telegraphs and phonographs and electric light, came into being. Our fascination with the unseen and the unseeable did not end simply because so many things previously thought impossible now had become realities. What is more fantastic, after all, than having the sound of an entire symphony orchestra rise up out of a flat disk of plastic? Or to speak into a device that one holds in one's hand, and be heard and understood ten thousand miles away? But the same century that gave us the inventions of Thomas Alva Edison and Alexander Graham Bell gave us Lewis Carroll's two incomparable tales of Alice's adventures in other realities, H. Rider Haggard's innumerable novels of lost civilizations, and Mary Wollstonecraft Shelley's *Frankenstein*.

Nor did the twentieth century—the century of air travel and atomic energy, of television and computers, of open-heart surgery and sex-change operations—see us losing our taste for tales of the extraordinary. A host of machine-age fantasists—James Branch Cabell and A. Merritt and Lord Dunsany, E. R. Eddison and Mervyn Peake and L. Frank Baum, H. P. Lovecraft and Robert E. Howard and J. R. R. Tolkien, to name a few of the best-known ones—kept the world well supplied with wondrous tales of the fantastic.

One change of tone did occur in the twentieth century, though, with the rise to popularity of science fiction—the branch of fantasy that applies immense ingenuity to the task of making the impossible, or at least the implausible, seem altogether probable. As science fiction—which was given its essential nature well over a hundred years ago by Jules Verne and H. G. Wells, and developed in modern times by such writers as Robert A. Heinlein, Isaac Asimov, and Aldous Huxley—came to exert its immense appeal on the atomic-age reading public, "pure" fantasy fiction (that is, fantasy that makes no attempt at empirical explanation of its wonders) came to be thought of as something largely reserved for children, like myths and fairy tales.

The older kind of fantasy never disappeared, of course. But in the United States, at least, it went into eclipse for nearly fifty years. Science fiction, meanwhile, manifested itself to the reading public in the form of magazines with names like *Amazing Stories* and *Astounding Science Fiction* and readerships composed largely of boys and earnest young men with an interest in gadgets and scientific disputation. The only American magazine dealing in the material we define as fantasy fiction was *Weird Tales*, founded in 1923, but that magazine published not only fantasy but a great many other kinds of genre fiction that might not be thought of as fantasy today—tales of pure terror, for example, with no speculative content.

The separation between fantasy and science fiction is not always easy to locate, but some distinctions are fairly clear-cut, if not entirely rigid. Stories that deal with androids and robots, spaceships, alien beings, time machines, viruses from outer space, galactic empires, and the like usually can be described as science fiction. These are all matters that are *conceptually possible* within the framework of scientific law as we currently understand it. (Although such things as time machines and faster-than-light vehicles certainly stretch that framework to its limits, and perhaps beyond them.) Fantasy, meanwhile, uses as its material that which is *generally believed to be impossible or nonexistent* in our culture: wizards and warlocks, elves and goblins, werewolves and vampires, unicorns and enchanted princesses, efficacious incantations and spells.

Fantasy fiction per se did not have a real magazine of its own until 1939, when John W. Campbell, Jr., the foremost science fiction editor of his time, brought *Unknown* (later called *Unknown Worlds*) into being in order to allow his writers greater imaginative latitude than his definitions of science fiction would permit. Many of the same writers who had turned Campbell's *Astounding Science Fiction* into the most notable magazine of its type yet published—Robert A. Heinlein, L. Sprague de Camp, Theodore Sturgeon, Lester del Rey, Jack Williamson—also became mainstays of *Unknown*, and the general structural approach was similar: postulate a far-out idea and develop all its consequences to a logical conclusion. The stories about being nasty to water gnomes or selling your soul to the devil wound up in *Unknown*; those about traveling in time or voyaging to distant planets were published in *Astounding*.

But *Unknown,* though it was cherished with great

fondness by its readers and writers, never attained much of a public following, and when wartime paper shortages forced Campbell to choose between his two magazines in 1943, *Unknown* was swiftly killed, never to reappear. Postwar attempts by nostalgic ex-contributors to *Unknown* to recapture its special flavor were largely unsuccessful; H. L. Gold's *Beyond* lasted ten issues, Lester del Rey's *Fantasy Fiction* managed only four. Only *The Magazine of Fantasy,* edited by Anthony Boucher and J. Francis McComas, succeeded in establishing itself as a permanent entity, and even that magazine found it wisest to change its name to *Fantasy and Science Fiction* with its second issue. When science fiction became a fixture of paperback publishing in the 1950s, fantasy once again lagged behind: few fantasy novels were paperbacked, and most of them—Jack Vance's *The Dying Earth* and the early reprints of H. P. Lovecraft and Robert E. Howard are good examples—quickly vanished from view and became collector's items.

It all began to change in the late 1960s, when the sudden availability of paperback editions of J. R. R. Tolkien's *Lord of the Rings* trilogy (previously kept from paperback by an unwilling hardcover publisher) aroused a hunger for fantasy fiction in millions of readers that has, so far, been insatiable. Tolkien's books were such an emphatic commercial success that publishers rushed to find writers who could produce imitative trilogies, and the world was flooded with huge Hobbitesque novels, many of which sold in extraordinary quantities themselves. Robert Howard's *Conan* novels, once admired only by a small band of ardent cultists, began to win vast new readers about the same time. And a few years later Ballantine Books, Tolkien's paperback publisher, brought out an extraordinary series of books in its Adult Fantasy series, edited by Lin Carter, which made all the elegant classic masterpieces of such fantasists as E. R. Eddison, James Branch Cabell, Lord Dunsany, and Mervyn Peake available to modern readers. And, ever since, fantasy has been a dominant factor in modern publishing. What was a neglected stepsibling of science fiction fifty years ago is, today, an immensely popular genre.

In the wake of the great success of the Tolkien trilogy, newer writers have come along with their own deeply imagined worlds of fantasy, and have captured large and enthusiastic audiences themselves. In the late 1960s, Ursula K. Le Guin began her searching and sensitive Earthsea series, and Anne McCaffrey co-opted the ancient fantastic theme of the dragon for her Pern novels, which live on the borderline between fantasy and science fiction. Stephen King, some years later, won a readership of astounding magnitude by plumbing the archetypical fears of humanity and transforming them into powerful novels that occupied fantasy's darker terrain. Terry Pratchett, on the other hand, has magnificently demonstrated the comic power of satiric fantasy. Such writers as Orson Scott Card and Raymond E. Feist have won huge followings for their Alvin Maker and Riftwar books. More recently, Robert Jordan's mammoth Wheel of Time series, George R. R. Martin's Song of Ice and Fire books, and Terry Goodkind's Sword of Truth tales have taken their place in the pantheon of modern fantasy, as has Tad Williams' Memory, Sorrow and Thorn series.

And here is the whole bunch of them, brought together in one huge three-volume collection in which fantasy enthusiasts can revel for weeks. A new Earthsea story, a new tale of Pern, a new Dark Tower adventure, a new segment in Pratchett's playful Discworld series, and all the rest that you'll find herein—there has never been a book like this before. Gathering such an elite collection of first-magnitude stars into a single volume has not been an easy task. My gratitude herewith for the special assistance of Martin H. Greenberg, Ralph Vicinanza, Stephen King, John Helfers, and Virginia Kidd, who in one way or another made my editorial task immensely less difficult than it otherwise would have been. And, too, although it goes without saying that I'm grateful to my wife, Karen, for her inestimable help in every phase of this intricate project, I think I'll say it anyway—not just because she's a terrific person, but because she came up with what unquestionably was the smartest idea of the whole enterprise.

—Robert Silverberg
December, 1997

THE SWORD OF TRUTH

OF TRUTH

Terry Goodkind

WIZARD'S FIRST RULE (1994)
STONE OF TEARS (1995)
BLOOD OF THE FOLD (1996)
TEMPLE OF THE WINDS (1997)

Terry Goodkind burst onto the fantasy scene in 1994 with the publication of *Wizard's First Rule*, which tells the story of Richard Cypher, a young man who learns that he is the key to defeating the evil sorcerer Darken Rahl, who threatens to subjugate all lands and peoples. Three succeeding novels in the series have brought Goodkind to the bestseller lists.

Little does Richard know when he happens across Kahlan, an alluring but secretive woman being chased by four assassins, that his life as a woods guide is about to be forever altered. Richard, a man with his own troubling secrets, helps Kahlan find the wizard she seeks but, as the boundary between the lands begins to fail, discovers himself caught up not only in a strange new world, but in Kahlan's quest for a way to stop Darken Rahl, the charismatic and cunning leader of the far-off land of D'Hara. Darken Rahl has launched a war of arms as well as persuasion against the people of the Midlands as he searches for the power to control them entirely. Richard and Kahlan are running out of time to find the repository of this power before Darken Rahl can impose a merciless fate on them. Richard, who comes to care deeply for Kahlan, must confront timeless lessons about the encroachment of evil on an unsuspecting world. The series becomes an inner quest as much as it is a struggle for destiny and freedom. In the course of obtaining the essential weapon—the Sword of Truth—he learns that the stakes are higher than simple life and death, and that the dividing line between moral choices and evil ones is often shrouded by apathy, ignorance, and greed.

In *Stone of Tears,* Richard strives to master the magic power that is his birthright, but finds that the effort of wielding such magic threatens his life. To save him, Kahlan, in desperation, sends him away with the Sisters of the Light. The Sisters, who promise to teach him to control his power, spirit him away beyond the Valley of the Lost to the Palace of the Prophets in the Old World. Kahlan undertakes an arduous journey to find their friend and mentor, Zedd, the First Wizard. Along the way she discovers the people of a city that has been attacked by the Imperial Order, and must forge an army of young recruits into a force that will not only stop this new threat to the Midlands but will extract vengeance. Richard's teachers turn out to include some who are sworn to the Keeper of the Underworld and intend to use Richard to free their master. Richard has already unwittingly helped them by using his gift, which tore the veil that separates the realm of the dead from the world of the living. Richard's only hope to save everyone is to find the Stone of Tears, but to do that, he must escape his imprisonment at the Palace of the Prophets. And to have any hope of escape, he must learn to use his gift before the Sisters of the Dark, who would destroy him, can turn him to their purposes.

In *Blood of the Fold,* the third novel, the emperor of the Imperial Order in the Old World lusts to conquer the Midlands. To that end, he tries to use an army of antimagic zealots to purge the Midlands of those born with the gift of magic. The emperor, a dream-walker with magic of his own, captures the Sisters of the Dark and uses them against Richard and Kahlan, while the people who call themselves the Blood of the Fold plot their own conquest of the Midlands. Unless Richard can seize power and mold the fragmented Midlands into one, the Imperial Order will sweep across the land, shadowing the Midlands in an age of slavery, and freedom's last flames will die forever.

In *Temple of the Winds,* Emperor Jagang sends an assassin to kill Richard, and in the process unleashes a deadly plague. The conflagration of disease claims more people with each passing day as Richard and Kahlan desperately search for a cure. Trust and love are tested in a twisting trail of devotion and betrayal. With hundreds and then thousands of their people perishing each day, Richard and Kahlan must find the Temple of the Winds, and then decide if they will pay the terrible price required to enter.

The present story takes place a number of years prior to the events of *Wizard's First Rule.*

DEBT OF BONES

⟨⟨⟨⟩⟩⟩

Terry Goodkind

What do you got in the sack, dearie?"
Abby was watching a distant flock of whistling swans, graceful white specks against the dark soaring walls of the Keep, as they made their interminable journey past ramparts, bastions, towers, and bridges lit by the low sun. The sinister specter of the Keep had seemed to be staring back the whole of the day as Abby had waited. She turned to the hunched old woman in front of her.

"I'm sorry, did you ask me something?"

"I asked what you got in your sack." As the woman peered up, she licked the tip of her tongue through the slot where a tooth was missing. "Something precious?"

Abby clutched the burlap sack to herself as she shrank a little from the grinning woman. "Just some of my things, that's all."

An officer, trailed by a troop of assistants, aides, and guards, marched out from under the massive portcullis that loomed nearby. Abby and the rest of the supplicants waiting at the head of the stone bridge moved tighter to the side, even though the soldiers had ample room to pass. The officer, his grim gaze unseeing as he swept by, didn't return the salute as the bridge guards clapped fists to the armor over their hearts.

All day soldiers from different lands, as well as the Home Guard from the vast city of Aydindril below, had been coming and going from the Keep. Some had looked travel-sore. Some wore uniforms still filthy with dirt, soot, and blood from recent battles. Abby had even seen two officers from her homeland of Pendisan Reach. They had looked to her to be little more than boys, but boys with the thin veneer of youth shedding too soon, like a snake casting off its skin before its time, leaving the emerging maturity scarred.

Abby had also seen such an array of important people as she could scarcely believe: sorceresses, councilors, and even a Confessor had come up from the Confessor's Palace down in the city. On her way up to the Keep, there was rarely a turn in the winding road that hadn't offered Abby a view of the sprawling splendor in white stone that was the Confessor's Palace. The alliance of the Midlands, headed by the Mother Confessor herself, held council in the palace, and there, too, lived the Confessors.

In her whole life, Abby had seen a Confessor only once before. The woman had come to see Abby's mother and Abby, not ten years at the time, had been unable to keep from staring at the Confessor's long hair. Other than her mother, no woman in Abby's small town of Coney Crossing was sufficiently important to have hair long enough to touch the shoulders. Abby's own fine, dark brown hair covered her ears but no more.

Coming through the city on the way to the Keep, it had been hard for her not to gape at noblewomen with hair to their shoulders and even a little beyond. But the Confessor going up to the Keep, dressed in the simple, satiny black dress of a Confessor, had hair that reached halfway down her back.

She wished she could have had a better look at the rare sight of such long luxuriant hair and the woman important enough to possess it, but Abby had gone to a knee with the rest of the company at the bridge, and like the rest of them feared to raise her bowed head to look up lest she meet the gaze of the other. It was said that to meet the gaze of a Confessor could cost you your mind if you were lucky, and your soul if you weren't. Even though Abby's mother had said that it was untrue, that only the deliberate touch of such a woman could effect such a thing, Abby feared, this day of all days, to test the stories.

The old woman in front of her, clothed in layered skirts topped with one dyed with henna, and mantled with a dark draping shawl, watched the soldiers pass and then leaned closer. "Do better to bring a bone, dearie. I hear that there be those in the city who will sell a bone such as you need—for the right price. Wizards don't take no salt pork for a need. They got salt pork." She glanced past Abby to the others to see them occupied with their own interests. "Better to sell your things and hope you have enough to buy a bone. Wizards don't want what some country girl brung 'em. Favors from wizards don't come easy." She glanced to the backs of the soldiers as they reached the far side of the bridge. "Not even for those doing their bidding, it would seem."

"I just want to talk to them. That's all."

"Salt pork won't get you a talk, neither, as I hear tell." She eyed Abby's hand trying to cover the smooth round shape beneath the burlap. "Or a jug you made. That what it is, dearie?" Her brown eyes, set in a wrinkled leathery mask, turned up, peering with sudden, humorless intent. "A jug?"

"Yes," Abby said. "A jug I made."

The woman smiled her skepticism and fingered a lick of short gray hair back under her wool head wrap. Her gnarled fingers closed around the smocking on the forearm of Abby's crimson dress, pulling the arm up a bit to have a look.

"Maybe you could get the price of a proper bone for your bracelet."

Abby glanced down at the bracelet made of two wires twisted together in interlocking circles. "My mother gave me this. It has no value but to me."

A slow smile came to the woman's weather-cracked lips. "The spirits believe that there is no stronger power than a mother's want to protect her child."

Abby gently pulled her arm away. "The spirits know the truth of that."

Uncomfortable under the scrutiny of the suddenly talkative woman, Abby searched for a safe place to settle her gaze. It made her dizzy to look down into the yawning chasm beneath the bridge, and she was weary of watching the Wizard's Keep, so she pretended that her attention had been caught as an excuse to turn back toward the collection of people, mostly men, waiting with her at the head of the bridge. She busied herself with nibbling on the last crust of bread from the loaf she had bought down in the market before coming up to the Keep.

Abby felt awkward talking to strangers. In her whole life she had never seen so many people, much less people she didn't know. She knew every person in Coney Crossing. The city made her apprehensive, but not as apprehensive as the Keep towering on the mountain above it, and that not as much as her reason for being there.

She just wanted to go home. But there would be no home, at least nothing to go home to, if she didn't do this.

All eyes turned up at the rattle of hooves coming out under the portcullis. Huge horses, all dusky brown or black and bigger than any Abby had ever seen, came thundering toward them. Men bedecked with polished breastplates, chain mail, and leather, and most carrying lances or poles topped with long flags of high office and rank, urged their mounts onward. They raised dust and gravel as they gathered speed crossing the bridge, in a wild rush of color and sparkles of light from metal flashing past. Sandarian lancers, from the descriptions Abby had heard. She had trouble imagining the enemy with the nerve to go up against men such as these.

Her stomach roiled. She realized she had no need to imagine, and no reason to put her hope in brave men such as those lancers. Her only hope was the wizard, and that hope was slipping away as she stood waiting. There was nothing for it but to wait.

Abby turned back to the Keep just in time to see a statuesque woman in simple robes stride out through the opening in the massive stone wall. Her fair skin stood out all the more against straight dark hair parted in the middle and readily reaching her shoulders. Some of the men had been whispering about the sight of the Sanderian officers, but at the sight of the woman, everyone fell to silence. The four soldiers at the head of the stone bridge made way for the woman as she approached the supplicants.

"Sorceress," the old woman whispered to Abby.

Abby hardly needed the old woman's counsel to know it was a sorceress. Abby recognized the simple flaxen robes, decorated at the neck with yellow and red beads sewn in the ancient symbols of the profession. Some of her earliest memories were of being held in her mother's arms and touching beads like those she saw now.

The sorceress bowed her head to the people and then offered a smile. "Please forgive us for keeping you waiting out here the whole of the day. It is not from lack of respect or something we customarily do, but with the war on our hands such precautions are regrettably unavoidable. We hope none took offense at the delay."

The crowd mumbled that they didn't. Abby doubted there was one among them bold enough to claim otherwise.

"How goes the war?" a man behind asked.

The sorceress's even gaze turned to him. "With the blessings of the good spirits, it will end soon."

"May the spirits will that D'Hara is crushed," beseeched the man.

Without response, the sorceress appraised the faces watching her, waiting to see if anyone else would speak or ask a question. None did.

"Please, come with me, then. The council meeting has ended, and a couple of the wizards will take the time to see you all."

As the sorceress turned back to the Keep and started out, three men strode up along the supplicants and put themselves at the head of the line, right in front of the old woman. The woman snatched a velvet sleeve.

"Who do you think you are," she snapped, "taking a place before me, when I've been here the whole of the day?"

The oldest of the three, dressed in rich robes of dark purple with contrasting red sewn inside the length of the slits up the sleeves, looked to be a noble with his two advisors, or perhaps guards. He turned a glare on the woman. "You don't mind, do you?"

It didn't sound to Abby at all like a question.

The old woman took her hand back and fell mute.

The man, the ends of his gray hair coiled on his shoulders, glanced at Abby. His hooded eyes gleamed with challenge. She swallowed and remained silent. She didn't have any objection, either, at least none she was willing to voice. For all she knew, the noble was important enough to see to it that she was denied an audience. She couldn't afford to take that chance now that she was this close.

Abby was distracted by a tingling sensation from the bracelet. Blindly, her fingers glided over the wrist of the hand holding the sack. The wire bracelet felt warm. It hadn't done that since her mother had died. In the presence of so much magic as was at a place such as this, it didn't really surprise her. The crowd moved out to follow the sorceress.

"Mean, they are," the woman whispered over her shoulder. "Mean as a winter night, and just as cold."

"Those men?" Abby whispered back.

"No." The woman tilted her head. "Sorceresses. Wizards, too. That's who. All those born with the gift of magic. You better have something important in that sack, or the wizards might turn you to dust for no other reason than that they'd enjoy it."

Abby pulled her sack tight in her arms. The meanest thing her mother had done in the whole of her life was to die before she could see her granddaughter.

Abby swallowed back the urge to cry and prayed to the dear spirits that the old woman was wrong about wizards, and that they were as understanding as sorceresses. She prayed fervently that this wizard would help her. She prayed for forgiveness, too—that the good spirits would understand.

Abby worked at holding a calm countenance even though her insides were in turmoil. She pressed a fist to her stomach. She prayed for strength. Even in this, she prayed for strength.

The sorceress, the three men, the old woman, Abby, and then the rest of the supplicants passed under the huge iron portcullis and onto the Keep grounds. Inside the massive outer wall Abby was surprised to discover the air warm. Outside it had been a chill autumn day, but inside the air was spring-fresh and pleasant.

The road up the mountain, the stone bridge over the chasm, and then the opening under the portcullis appeared to be the only way into the Keep, unless you were a bird. Soaring walls of dark stone with high windows surrounded the gravel courtyard inside. There were a number of doors around the courtyard, and ahead a roadway tunneled deeper into the Keep.

Despite the warmth of the air, Abby was chilled to the bone by the place. She wasn't sure that the old woman wasn't right about wizards. Life in Coney Crossing was far removed from matters of wizards.

Abby had never seen a wizard before, nor did she know anyone who had, except for her mother, and her mother had never spoken of them except to caution that where wizards were concerned, you couldn't trust even what you saw with your own eyes.

The sorceress led them up four granite steps worn smooth over the ages by countless footsteps, through a doorway set back under a lintel of pink-flecked black granite, and into the Keep proper. The sorceress lifted an arm into the darkness, sweeping it to the side. Lamps along the wall sprang to flame.

It had been simple magic—not a very impressive display of the gift—but several of the people behind fell to worried whispering as they passed on through the wide hall. It occurred to Abby that if this little bit of conjuring would frighten them, then they had no business going to see wizards.

They wended their way across the sunken floor of an imposing anteroom the likes of which Abby could never even have imagined. Red marble columns all around supported arches below balconies.

In the center of the room a fountain sprayed water high overhead. The water fell back to cascade down through a succession of ever larger scalloped bowls. Officers, sorceresses, and a variety of others sat about on white marble benches or huddled in small groups, all engaged in seemingly earnest conversation masked by the sound of the water.

In a much smaller room beyond, the sorceress gestured for them to be seated at a line of carved oak benches along one wall. Abby was bone-weary and relieved to sit at last.

Light from windows above the benches lit three tapestries hanging on the high far wall. The three together covered nearly the entire wall and made up one scene of a grand procession through a city. Abby had never seen anything like it, but with the way her dreads careered through her thoughts, she could summon little pleasure in seeing even such a majestic tableau.

In the center of the cream-colored marble floor, inset in brass lines, was a circle with a square inside it, its corners touching the circle. Inside the square sat another circle just large enough to touch the insides of the square. The center circle held an eight-pointed star. Lines radiated out from the points of the star, piercing all the way through both circles, every other line bisecting a corner of the square.

The design, called a Grace, was often drawn by those with the gift. The outer circle represented the beginnings of the infinity of the spirit world out beyond. The square represented the boundary separating the spirit world—the underworld, the world of the dead—from the inner circle, which represented the limits of the world of life. In the center of it all was the star, representing the Light—the Creator.

It was a depiction of the continuum of the gift: from the Creator, through life, and at death crossing the boundary to eternity with the spirits in the Keeper's realm of the underworld. But it represented a hope, too—a hope to remain in the Creator's Light from birth, through life, and beyond, in the underworld.

It was said that only the spirits of those who did great wickedness in life would be denied the Creator's Light in the underworld. Abby knew she would be condemned to an eternity with the Keeper of darkness in the underworld. She had no choice.

The sorceress folded her hands. "An aide will come to get you each in turn. A wizard will see each of you. The war burns hot; please keep your petition brief." She gazed down the line of people. "It is out of a sincere obligation to those we serve that the wizards see supplicants, but please try to understand that individual desires are often detrimental to the greater good. By pausing to help one, then many are denied help. Thus, denial of a request is not a denial of your need, but acceptance of greater need. In times of peace it is rare for wizards to grant the narrow wants of supplicants. At a time like this, a time of a great war, it is almost unheard of. Please understand that it has not to do with what we would wish, but is a matter of necessity."

She watched the line of supplicants, but saw none willing to abandon their purpose. Abby certainly would not.

"Very well then. We have two wizards able to take supplicants at this time. We will bring you each to one of them."

The sorceress turned to leave. Abby rose to her feet.

"Please, mistress, a word if I may?"

The sorceress settled an unsettling gaze on Abby. "Speak."

Abby stepped forward. "I must see the First Wizard himself. Wizard Zorander."

One eyebrow arched. "The First Wizard is a very busy man."

Abby reached into her sack and pulled out the neck band from her mother's robes. She stepped into the center of the Grace and kissed the red and yellow beads on the neck band.

"I am Abigail, born of Helsa. On the Grace and my mother's soul, I must see Wizard Zorander. Please. It is no trivial journey I have made. Lives are at stake."

The sorceress watched the beaded band being returned to the sack. "Abigail, born of Helsa." Her gaze rose to meet Abby's. "I will take your words to the First Wizard."

"Mistress." Abby turned to see the old woman on her feet. "I would be well pleased to see the First Wizard, too."

The three men rose up. The oldest, the one apparently in charge of the three, gave the sorceress a look so barren of timidity that it bordered on contempt. His long gray hair fell forward over his velvet robes as he glanced down the line of seated people, seeming to dare them to stand. When none did, he returned his attention to the sorceress.

"I will see Wizard Zorander."

The sorceress appraised those on their feet and then looked down the line of supplicants on the bench. "The First Wizard has earned a name: the wind of death. He is feared no less by many of us than by our enemies. Anyone else who would bait fate?"

None of those on the bench had the courage to gaze into her fierce stare. To the last they all silently shook their heads. "Please wait," she said to those seated. "Someone will shortly be out to take you to a wizard." She looked once more to the five people standing. "Are you all very, very sure of this?"

Abby nodded. The old woman nodded. The noble glared.

"Very well then. Come with me."

The noble and his two men stepped in front of Abby. The old woman seemed content to take a station at the end of the line. They were led deeper into the Keep, through narrow halls and wide corridors, some dark and austere and some of astounding grandeur. Everywhere there were soldiers of the Home Guard, their breastplates or chain mail covered with red tunics banded around their edges in black. All were heavily armed with swords or battle-axes, all had knives, and many additionally carried pikes tipped with winged and barbed steel.

At the top of a broad white marble stairway the stone railings spiraled at the ends to open wide onto a room of warm oak paneling. Several of the raised panels held lamps with polished silver reflectors. Atop a three-legged table sat a double-bowl cut-glass lamp with twin chimneys, their flames adding to the mellow light from the reflector lamps. A thick carpet of ornate blue patterns covered nearly the entire wood floor.

To each side of a double door stood one of the

meticulously dressed Home Guard. Both men were equally huge. They looked to be men more than able to handle any trouble that might come up the stairs.

The sorceress nodded toward a dozen thickly tufted leather chairs set in four groups. Abby waited until the others had seated themselves in two of the groupings and then sat by herself in another. She placed the sack in her lap and rested her hands over its contents.

The sorceress stiffened her back. "I will tell the First Wizard that he has supplicants who wish to see him."

A guard opened one of the double doors for her. As she was swallowed into the great room beyond, Abby was able to snatch a quick glimpse. She could see that it was well lighted by glassed skylights. There were other doors in the gray stone of the walls. Before the door closed, Abby was also able to see a number of people, men and women both, all rushing hither and yon.

Abby sat turned away from the old woman and the three men as with one hand she idly stroked the sack in her lap. She had little fear that the men would talk to her, but she didn't want to talk to the woman; it was a distraction. She passed the time going over in her mind what she planned to say to Wizard Zorander.

At least she tried to go over it in her mind. Mostly, all she could think about was what the sorceress had said, that the First Wizard was called the wind of death, not only by the D'Harans, but also by his own people of the Midlands. Abby knew it was no tale to scare off supplicants from a busy man. Abby herself had heard people whisper of their great wizard, "The wind of death." Those whispered words were uttered in dread.

The lands of D'Hara had sound reason to fear this man as their enemy; he had destroyed countless of their troops, from what Abby had heard. Of course, if they hadn't invaded the Midlands, bent on conquest, they would not have felt the hot wind of death.

Had they not invaded, Abby wouldn't be sitting there in the Wizard's Keep—she would be at home, and everyone she loved would be safe.

Abby marked again the odd tingling sensation from the bracelet. She ran her fingers over it, testing its unusual warmth. This close to a person of such power it didn't surprise her that the bracelet was warming. Her mother had told her to wear it always, and that someday it would be of value. Abby didn't know how, and her mother had died without ever explaining.

Sorceresses were known for the way they kept secrets, even from their own daughters. Perhaps if Abby had been born gifted . . .

She sneaked a peek over her shoulder at the others. The old woman was leaning back in her chair, staring at the doors. The noble's attendants sat with their hands folded as they casually eyed the room.

The noble was doing the oddest thing. He had a lock of sandy-colored hair wound around a finger. He stroked his thumb over the lock of hair as he glared at the doors.

Abby wanted the wizard to hurry up and see her, but time stubbornly dragged by. In a way, she wished he would refuse. No, she told herself, that was unacceptable. No matter her fear, no matter her revulsion, she must do this. Abruptly, the door opened. The sorceress strode out toward Abby.

The noble surged to his feet. "I will see him first." His voice was cold threat. "That is not a request."

"It is our right to see him first," Abby said without forethought. When the sorceress folded her hands, Abby decided she had best go on. "I've waited since dawn. This woman was the only one waiting before me. These men came at the last of the day."

Abby started when the old woman's gnarled fingers gripped her forearm. "Why don't we let these men go first, dearie? It matters not who arrived first, but who has the most important business."

Abby wanted to scream that her business was

important, but she realized that the old woman might be saving her from serious trouble in accomplishing her business. Reluctantly, she gave the sorceress a nod. As the sorceress led the three men through the door, Abby could feel the old woman's eyes on her back. Abby hugged the sack against the burning anxiety in her abdomen and told herself that it wouldn't be long, and then she would see him.

As they waited, the old woman remained silent, and Abby was glad for that. Occasionally, she glanced at the door, imploring the good spirits to help her. But she realized it was futile; the good spirits wouldn't be disposed to help her in this.

A roar came from the room beyond the doors. It was like the sound of an arrow zipping through the air, or a long switch whipping, but much louder, intensifying rapidly. It ended with a shrill crack accompanied by a flash of light coming under the doors and around their edges. The doors shuddered on their hinges.

Sudden silence rang in Abby's ears. She found herself gripping the arms of the chair.

Both doors opened. The noble's two attendants marched out, followed by the sorceress. The three stopped in the waiting room. Abby sucked a breath.

One of the two men was cradling the noble's head in the crook of an arm. The wan features of the face were frozen in a mute scream. Thick strings of blood dripped onto the carpet.

"Show them out," the sorceress hissed through gritted teeth to one of the two guards at the door.

The guard dipped his pike toward the stairs, ordering them ahead, and then followed the two men down. Crimson drops splattered onto the white marble of the steps as they descended. Abby sat in stiff, wide-eyed shock.

The sorceress wheeled back to Abby and the old woman.

The woman rose to her feet. "I believe that I would rather not bother the First Wizard today. I will return another day, if need be."

She hunched lower toward Abby. "I am called Mariska." Her brow drew down. "May the good spirits grant that you succeed."

She shuffled to the stairs, rested a hand on the marble railing, and started down. The sorceress snapped her fingers and gestured. The remaining guard rushed to accompany the woman, as the sorceress turned back to Abby.

"The First Wizard will see you now."

Abby gulped air, trying to get her breath as she lurched to her feet.

"What happened? Why did the First Wizard do that?"

"The man was sent on behalf of another to ask a question of the First Wizard. The First Wizard gave his answer."

Abby clutched her sack to herself for dear life as she gaped at the blood on the floor. "Might that be the answer to my question, if I ask it?"

"I don't know the question you would ask." For the first time, the sorceress's expression softened just a bit. "Would you like me to see you out? You could see another wizard or, perhaps, after you've given more thought to your petition, return another day, if you still wish it."

Abby fought back tears of desperation. There was no choice. She shook her head. "I must see him."

The sorceress let out a deep breath. "Very well." She put a hand under Abby's arm as if to keep her on her feet. "The First Wizard will see you now."

Abby hugged the contents of her sack as she was led into the chamber where waited the wind of death. Torches in iron sconces were not yet burning. The late-afternoon light from the glassed roof windows was still strong enough to illuminate the room. It smelled of pitch, lamp oil, roasted meat, wet stone, and stale sweat.

Inside, confusion and commotion reigned. There were people everywhere, and they all seemed to be talking at once. Stout tables set about the room in no discernible pattern were covered with books, scrolls, maps, chalk, unlit oil lamps, burning candles, partially eaten meals, sealing wax, pens, and a clutter of every sort of odd object, from balls of knotted string to half-spilled sacks of sand. People stood about the tables, engaged in conversations or arguments, as others tapped passages in books, pored over scrolls, or moved little painted weights about on maps. Others rolled slices of roasted meat plucked from platters and nibbled as they watched or offered opinions between swallows.

The sorceress, still holding Abby under her arm, leaned closer as they proceeded. "You will have the First Wizard's divided attention. There will be other people talking to him at the same time. Don't be distracted. He will be listening to you as he also listens to or talks to others. Just ignore the others who are speaking and ask what you have come to ask. He will hear you."

Abby was dumbfounded. "While he's talking to other people?"

"Yes." Abby felt the hand squeeze her arm ever so slightly. "Try to be calm, and not to judge by what has come before you."

The killing. That was what she meant. That a man had come to speak to the First Wizard, and he had been killed for it. She was simply supposed to put that from her thoughts? When she glanced down, she saw that she was walking through a trail of blood. She didn't see the headless body anywhere.

Her bracelet tingled and she looked down at it. The hand under her arm halted her. When Abby looked up, she saw a confusing knot of people before her. Some rushed in from the sides as others rushed away. Some flailed their arms as they spoke with great conviction. So many were talking that Abby could scarcely understand a word of it. At the same time, others were leaning in, nearly whispering. She felt as if she were confronting a human beehive.

Abby's attention was snagged by a form in white to the side. The instant she saw the long fall of hair and the violet eyes looking right at her, Abby went rigid. A small cry escaped her throat as she fell to her knees and bowed over until her back protested. She trembled and shuddered, fearing the worst.

In the instant before she dropped to her knees, she had seen that the elegant, satiny white dress was cut square at the neck, the same as the black dresses had been. The long flag of hair was unmistakable. Abby had never seen the woman before, but without doubt knew who she was. There could be no mistaking this woman. Only one of them wore the white dress.

It was the Mother Confessor herself.

She heard muttering above her, but feared to listen, lest it was death being summoned.

"Rise, my child," came a clear voice.

Abby recognized it as the formal response of the Mother Confessor to one of her people. It took a moment for Abby to realize that it represented no threat, but simple acknowledgment. She stared at a smear of blood on the floor as she debated what to do next. Her mother had never instructed her as to how to conduct herself should she ever meet the Mother Confessor. As far as she knew, no one from Coney Crossing had ever seen the Mother Confessor, much less met her. Then again, none of them had ever seen a wizard, either.

Overhead, the sorceress whispered a growl. "Rise."

Abby scrambled to her feet, but kept her eyes to the floor, even though the smear of blood was making her sick. She could smell it, like a fresh butchering of one of their animals. From the long trail, it looked as if the body had been dragged away to one of the doors in the back of the room.

The sorceress spoke calmly into the chaos. "Wizard Zorander, this is Abigail, born of Helsa. She wishes a word with you. Abigail, this is First Wizard Zeddicus Zu'l Zorander."

Abby dared to cautiously lift her gaze. Hazel eyes gazed back.

To each side before her were knots of people: big, forbidding officers—some of them looked as if they might be generals; several old men in robes, some simple and some ornate; several middle-aged men, some in robes and some in livery; three women—sorceresses all; a variety of other men and women; and the Mother Confessor.

The man at the center of the turmoil, the man with the hazel eyes, was not what Abby had been expecting. She had expected some grizzled, gruff old man. This man was young—perhaps as young as she. Lean but sinewy, he wore the simplest of robes, hardly better made than Abby's burlap sack—the mark of his high office.

Abby had not anticipated this sort of man in such an office as that of First Wizard. She remembered what her mother had told her—not to trust what your eyes told you where wizards were concerned.

All about, people spoke to him, argued at him, a few even shouted, but the wizard was silent as he looked into her eyes. His face was pleasing enough to look upon, gentle in appearance, even though his wavy brown hair looked ungovernable, but his eyes . . . Abby had never seen the likes of those eyes. They seemed to see all, to know all, to understand all. At the same time they were blood-shot and weary looking, as if sleep eluded him. They had, too, the slightest glaze of distress. Even so, he was calm at the center of the storm. For that moment that his attention was on her, it was as if no one else were in the room.

The lock of hair Abby had seen around the noble's finger was now held wrapped around the First Wizard's finger. He brushed it to his lips before lowering his arm.

"I am told you are the daughter of a sorceress." His voice was placid water flowing through the tumult raging all about. "Are you gifted, child?"

"No, sir . . ."

Even as she answered, he was turning to another who had just finished speaking. "I told you, if you do, we chance losing them. Send word that I want him to cut south."

The tall officer to whom the wizard spoke threw his hands up. "But he said they've reliable scouting information that the D'Harans went east on him."

"That's not the point," the wizard said. "I want that pass to the south sealed. That's where their main force went; they have gifted among them. They are the ones we must kill."

The tall officer was saluting with a fist to his heart as the wizard turned to an old sorceress. "Yes, that's right, three invocations before attempting the transposition. I found the reference last night."

The old sorceress departed to be replaced by a man jabbering in a foreign tongue as he opened a scroll and held it up for the wizard to see. The wizard squinted toward it, reading a moment before waving the man away, while giving orders in the same foreign language.

The wizard turned to Abby. "You're a skip?"

Abby felt her face heat and her ears burn. "Yes, Wizard Zorander."

"Nothing to be ashamed of, child," he said while the Mother Confessor herself was whispering confidentially in his ear.

But it *was* something to be ashamed of. The gift hadn't passed on to her from her mother—it had skipped her.

The people of Coney Crossing had depended on Abby's mother. She helped with those who were ill or hurt. She advised people on matters of community and those of family. For some she arranged marriages. For some she meted out discipline. For some she bestowed favors available only through magic. She was a sorceress; she protected the people of Coney Crossing.

She was revered openly. By some, she was feared and loathed privately.

She was revered for the good she did for the people of Coney Crossing. By some, she had been feared and loathed because she had the gift—

because she wielded magic. Others wanted nothing so much as to live their lives without any magic about.

Abby had no magic and couldn't help with illness or injury or shapeless fears. She dearly wished she could, but she couldn't. When Abby had asked her mother why she would abide all the thankless resentment, her mother told her that helping was its own reward and you should not expect gratitude for it. She said that if you went through life expecting gratitude for the help you provided, you might end up leading a miserable life.

When her mother was alive, Abby had been shunned in subtle ways; after her mother died, the shunning became more overt. It had been expected by the people of Coney Crossing that she would serve as her mother had served. People didn't understand about the gift, how it often wasn't passed on to an offspring; instead they thought Abby selfish.

The wizard was explaining something to a sorceress about the casting of a spell. When he finished, his gaze swept past Abby on its way to someone else. She needed his help, now.

"What is it you wanted to ask me, Abigail?"

Abby's fingers tightened on the sack. "It's about my home of Coney Crossing." She paused while the wizard pointed in a book being held out to him.

He rolled his hand at her, gesturing for her to go on as a man was explaining an intricacy to do with inverting a duplex spell. "There's terrible trouble there," Abby said. "D'Haran troops came through the Crossing . . ."

The First Wizard turned to an older man with a long white beard. By his simple robes, Abby guessed him to be a wizard, too.

"I'm telling you, Thomas, it can be done," Wizard Zorander insisted. "I'm not saying I agree with the council, I'm just telling you what I found and their unanimous decision that it be done. I'm not claiming to understand the details of just how it works, but I've studied it; it can be done. As I told the council, I can activate it. I have yet to decide if I agree with them that I should."

The man, Thomas, wiped a hand across his face. "You mean what I heard is true, then? That you really do think it's possible? Are you out of your mind, Zorander?"

"I found it in a book in the First Wizard's private enclave. A book from before the war with the Old World. I've seen it with my own eyes. I've cast a whole series of verification webs to test it." He turned his attention to Abby. "Yes, that would be Anargo's legion. Coney Crossing is in Pendisan Reach."

"That's right," Abby said. "And so then this

D'Haran army swept through there and—"

"Pendisan Reach refused to join with the rest of the Midlands under central command to resist the invasion from D'Hara. Standing by their sovereignty, they chose to fight the enemy in their own way. They have to live with the consequences of their actions."

The old man was tugging on his beard. "Still, do you know if it's real? All proven out? I mean, that book would have to be thousands of years old. It might have been conjecture. Verification webs don't always confirm the entire structure of such a thing."

"I know that as well as you, Thomas, but I'm telling you, it's real," Wizard Zorander said. His voice lowered to a whisper. "The spirits preserve us, it's genuine."

Abby's heart was pounding. She wanted to tell him her story, but she couldn't seem to get a word in. He had to help her. It was the only way.

An army officer rushed in from one of the back doors. He pushed his way into the crowd around the First Wizard.

"Wizard Zorander! I've just gotten word! When we unleashed the horns you sent, they worked! Urdland's force turned tail!"

Several voices fell silent. Others didn't.

"At least three thousand years old," the First

Wizard said to the man with the beard. He put a hand on the newly arrived officer's shoulder and leaned close. "Tell General Brainard to hold short at the Kern River. Don't burn the bridges, but hold them. Tell him to split his men. Leave half to keep Urdland's force from changing their mind; hopefully they won't be able to replace their field wizard. Have Brainard take the rest of his men north to help cut Anargo's escape route; that's where our concern lies, but we may still need the bridges to go after Urdland."

One of the other officers, an older man looking possibly to be a general himself, went red in the face. "Halt at the river? When the horns have done their job, and we have them on the run? But why! We can take them down before they have a chance to regroup and join up with another force to come back at us!"

Hazel eyes turned toward the man. "And do you know what waits over the border? How many men will die if Panis Rahl has something waiting that the horns can't turn away? How many innocent lives has it already cost us? How many of our men will die to bleed them on their own land—land we don't know as they do?"

"And how many of our people will die if we don't eliminate their ability to come back at us another day! We must pursue them. Panis Rahl will

never rest. He'll be working to conj⋯
thing else to gut us all in our sleep. We mu⋯
them down and kill every last one!''

"I'm working on that," the First Wizard said
cryptically.

The old man twisted his beard and made a sar-
castic face. "Yes, he thinks he can unleash the underworld itself on them."

Several officers, two of the sorceresses, and a
couple of the men in robes paused to stare in open
disbelief.

The sorceress who had brought Abby to the audience leaned close. "You wanted to talk to the
First Wizard. Talk. If you have lost your nerve,
then I will see you out."

Abby wet her lips. She didn't know how she
could talk into the middle of such a roundabout
conversation, but she knew she must, so she just
started back in.

"Sir, I don't know anything about what my
homeland of Pendisan Reach has done. I know
little of the king. I don't know anything about the
council, or the war, or any of it. I'm from a small
place, and I only know that the people there are in
grave trouble. Our defenders were overrun by the
enemy. There is an army of Midlands men who
drive toward the D'Harans."

She felt foolish talking to a man who was carrying on a half dozen conversations all at once. Mostly, though, she felt anger and frustration. Those people were going to die if she couldn't convince him to help.

"How many D'Harans?" the wizard asked.

Abby opened her mouth, but an officer spoke in her place. "We're not sure how many are left in Anargo's legion. They may be wounded, but they're an enraged wounded bull. Now they're in sight of their homeland. They can only come back at us, or escape us. We've got Sanderson sweeping down from the north and Mardale cutting up from the southwest. Anargo made a mistake going into the Crossing; in there he must fight us or run for home. We have to finish them. This may be our only chance."

The First Wizard drew a finger and thumb down his smooth jaw. "Still, we aren't sure of their numbers. The scouts were dependable, but they never returned. We can only assume they're dead. And why would Anargo do such a thing?"

"Well," the officer said, "it's the shortest escape route back to D'Hara."

The First Wizard turned to a sorceress to answer a question she had just finished. "I can't see how we can afford it. Tell them I said no. I'll not cast that kind of web for them and I'll not give them the means to it for no more offered than a 'maybe.' "

The sorceress nodded before rushing off.

Abby knew that a web was the spell cast by a sorceress. Apparently the spell cast by a wizard was called the same.

"Well, if such a thing is possible," the bearded man was saying, "then I'd like to see your exegesis of the text. A three-thousand-year-old book is a lot of risk. We've no clue as to how the wizards of that time could do most of what they did."

The First Wizard, for the first time, cast a hot glare toward the man. "Thomas, do you want to see exactly what I'm talking about? The spell-form?"

Some of the people had fallen silent at the tone in his voice. The First Wizard threw open his arms, urging everyone back out of his way. The Mother Confessor stayed close behind his left shoulder. The sorceress beside Abby pulled her back a step.

The First Wizard motioned. A man snatched a small sack off the table and handed it to him. Abby noticed that some of the sand on the tables wasn't simply spilled, but had been used to draw symbols. Abby's mother had occasionally drawn spells with sand, but mostly used a variety of other things, from ground bone to dried herbs. Abby's mother used sand for practice; spells, real spells, had to be drawn in proper order and without error.

The First Wizard squatted down and took a

handful of sand from the sack. He drew on the floor by letting the sand dribble from the side of his fist.

Wizard Zorander's hand moved with practiced precision. His arm swept around, drawing a circle. He returned for a handful of sand and drew an inner circle. It appeared he was drawing a Grace.

Abby's mother had always drawn the square second; everything in order inward and then the rays back out. Wizard Zorander drew the eight-pointed star inside the smaller circle. He drew the lines radiating outward, through both circles, but left one absent.

He had yet to draw the square, representing the boundary between worlds. He was the First Wizard, so Abby guessed that it wasn't improper to do it in a different order than a sorceress in a little place like Coney Crossing did. But several of the men Abby took as wizards, and the two sorceress behind him, were turning grave glances to one another.

Wizard Zorander laid down the lines of sand for two sides of the square. He scooped up more sand from the sack and began the last two sides.

Instead of a straight line, he drew an arc that dipped well into the edge of the inner circle—the one representing the world of life. The arc, instead of ending at the outer circle, crossed it. He drew the last side, likewise arced, so that it too crossed into the inner circle. He brought the line to meet the other where the ray from the Light was missing. Unlike the other three points of the square, this last point ended outside the larger circle—in the world of the dead.

People gasped. A hush fell over the room for a moment before worried whispers spread among those gifted.

Wizard Zorander rose. "Satisfied, Thomas?"

Thomas's face had gone as white as his beard. "The Creator preserve us." His eyes turned to Wizard Zorander. "The council doesn't truly understand this. It would be madness to unleash it."

Wizard Zorander ignored him and turned toward Abby. "How many D'Harans did you see?"

"Three years past, the locust swarms came. The hills of the Crossing were brown with them. I think I saw more D'Harans than I saw locusts."

Wizard Zorander grunted his discontent. He looked down at the Grace he had drawn. "Panis Rahl won't give up. How long, Thomas? How long until he finds something new to conjure and sends Anargo back on us?" His gaze swept among the people around him. "How many years have we thought we would be annihilated by the invading horde from D'Hara? How many of our people have been killed by Rahl's magic? How many thousands have died of the fevers he sent? How many thousands have blistered and bled to death from the touch of the shadow people he conjured? How many villages, towns, and cities has he wiped from existence?"

When no one spoke, Wizard Zorander went on.

"It has taken us years to come back from the brink. The war has finally turned; the enemy is running. We now have three choices. The first choice is to let him run for home and hope he never comes back to again visit us with his brutality. I think it would only be a matter of time until he tried again. That leaves two realistic options. We can either pursue him into his lair and kill him for good at the cost of tens, perhaps hundreds of thousands of our men—or I can end it."

Those gifted among the crowd cast uneasy glances to the Grace drawn on the floor.

"We still have other magic," another wizard said. "We can use it to the same effect without unleashing such a cataclysm."

"Wizard Zorander is right," another said, "and so is the council. The enemy has earned this fate. We must set it upon them."

The room fell again to arguing. As it did, Wizard Zorander looked into Abby's eyes. It was a clear instruction to finish her supplication.

"My people—the people in Coney Crossing— have been taken by the D'Harans. There are others, too, who they've captured. They have a sorceress holding the captives with a spell. Please, Wizard Zorander, you must help me.

"When I was hiding, I heard the sorceress talking to their officers. The D'Harans plan to use the captives as shields. They will use the captives to blunt the deadly magic you send against them, or to blunt the spears and arrows the Midlands army sends against them. If they decide to turn and attack, they plan to drive the captives ahead. They called it 'dulling the enemies' weapons on their own women and children.' "

No one looked at her. They were all once again engaged in their mass talking and arguing. It was as if the lives of all those people were beneath their consideration.

Tears stung at Abby's eyes. "Either way all those innocent people will die. Please, Wizard Zorander, we must have your help. Otherwise they'll all die."

He looked her way briefly. "There is nothing we can do for them."

Abby panted, trying to hold back the tears. "My father was captured, along with others of my kin. My husband is among the captives. My daughter is among them. She is not yet five. If you send magic, they will be killed. If you attack, they will be killed. You must rescue them, or hold the attack."

He looked genuinely saddened. "I'm sorry. I can't help them. May the good spirits watch over them and take their souls to the Light." He began turning away.

"No!" Abby screamed. Some of the people fell silent. Others only glanced her way as they went on. "My child! You can't!" She thrust a hand into the sack. "I've a bone—"

"Doesn't everyone," he grumbled, cutting her off. "I can't help you."

"But you must!"

"We would have to abandon our cause. We must take the D'Haran force down—one way or another. Innocent though those people are, they are in the way. I can't allow the D'Harans to succeed in such a scheme or it would encourage its widespread use, and then even more innocents would die. The enemy must be shown that it will not deter us from our course."

"NO!" Abby wailed. "She's only a child! You're condemning my baby to death! There are other children! What kind of monster are you?"

No one but the wizard was even listening to her any more as they all went on with their talking.

The First Wizard's voice cut through the din and fell on her ears as clearly as the knell of death. "I am a man who must make choices such as this one. I must deny your petition."

Abby screamed with the agony of failure. She wasn't even to be allowed to show him.

"But it's a debt!" she cried. "A solemn debt!"

"And it cannot be paid now."

Abby screamed hysterically. The sorceress began pulling her away. Abby broke from the woman and ran out of the room. She staggered down the stone steps, unable to see through the tears.

At the bottom of the steps she buckled to the floor in helpless sobbing. He wouldn't help her. He wouldn't help a helpless child. Her daughter was going to die.

Abby, convulsing in sobs, felt a hand on her shoulder. Gentle arms pulled her closer. Tender fingers brushed back her hair as she wept into a woman's lap. Another person's hand touched her back and she felt the warm comfort of magic seeping into her.

"He's killing my daughter," she cried. "I hate him."

"It's all right, Abigail," the voice above said. "It's all right to weep for such a pain as this."

Abby wiped at her eyes, but couldn't stop the tears. The sorceress was there, beside her, at the bottom of the steps.

Abby looked up at the woman in whose arms she lay. It was the Mother Confessor herself. She could do her worst, for all Abby cared. What did it matter, what did any of it matter, now?

"He's a monster," she sobbed. "He is truly named. He is the ill wind of death. This time it's my baby he's killing, not the enemy."

"I understand why you feel that way, Abigail," the Mother Confessor said, "but it is not true."

"How can you say that! My daughter has not yet had a chance to live, and he will kill her! My husband will die. My father, too, but he has had a chance to live a life. My baby hasn't!"

She fell to hysterical wailing again, and the Mother Confessor once again drew her into comforting arms. Comfort was not what Abby wanted.

"You have just the one child?" the sorceress asked.

Abby nodded as she sucked a breath. "I had another, a boy, but he died at birth. The midwife said I will have no more. My little Jana is all I will ever have." The wild agony of it ripped through her. "And he will kill her. Just as he killed that man before me. Wizard Zorander is a monster. May the good spirits strike him dead!"

With a poignant expression, the sorceress smoothed Abby's hair back from her forehead "You don't understand. You see only a part of it. You don't mean what you say."

But she did. "If you had—"

"Delora understands," the Mother Confessor said, gesturing toward the sorceress. "She has a daughter of ten years, and a son, too."

Abby peered up at the sorceress. She gave Abby a sympathetic smile and a nod to confirm the truth of it.

"I, too, have a daughter," the Mother Confessor said. "She is twelve. Delora and I both understand your pain. So does the First Wizard."

Abby's fists tightened. "He couldn't! He's hardly more than a boy himself, and he wants to kill my baby. He is the wind of death and that's all he cares about—killing people!"

The Mother Confessor patted the stone step beside her. "Abigail, sit up here beside me. Let me tell you about the man in there."

Still weeping, Abby pushed herself up and slid onto the step. The Mother Confessor was older by maybe twelve or fourteen years, and pleasant-looking, with those violet eyes. Her mass of long hair reached her waist. She had a warm smile. It had never occurred to Abby to think of a Confessor as a woman, but that was what she saw now. She didn't fear this woman as she had before; nothing she did could be worse than what already had been done.

"I sometimes minded Zeddicus when he was but a toddler and I was still coming into womanhood."

The Mother Confessor gazed off with a wistful smile. "I swatted his bottom when he misbehaved, and later twisted his ear to make him sit at a lesson. He was mischief on two legs, driven not by guile but by curiosity. He grew into a fine man.

"For a long time, when the war with D'Hara started, Wizard Zorander wouldn't help us. He didn't want to fight, to hurt people. But in the end, when Panis Rahl, the leader of D'Hara, started using magic to slaughter our people, Zedd knew that the only hope to save more lives in the end was to fight.

"Zeddicus Zu'l Zorander may look young to you, as he did to many of us, but he is a special wizard, born of a wizard and a sorceress. Zedd was a prodigy. Even those other wizards in there, some of them his teachers, don't always understand how he is able to unravel some of the enigmas in the books or how he uses his gift to bring so much power to bear, but we do understand that he has heart. He uses his heart, as well as his head. He was named First Wizard for all these things and more."

"Yes," Abby said, "he is very talented at being the wind of death."

The Mother Confessor smiled a small smile. She tapped her chest. "Among ourselves, those of us who really know him call him the trickster. The trickster is the name he has truly earned. We named him the wind of death for others to hear, so as to strike terror into the hearts of the enemy. Some people on our side take that name to heart. Perhaps, since your mother was gifted, you can understand how people sometimes unreasonably fear those with magic?"

"And sometimes," Abby argued, "those with magic really are monsters who care nothing for the life they destroy."

The Mother Confessor appraised Abby's eyes a moment, and then held up a cautionary finger. "In confidence, I am going to tell you about Zeddicus Zu'l Zorander. If you ever repeat this story, I will never forgive you for betraying my confidence."

"I won't, but I don't see—"

"Just listen."

After Abby remained silent the Mother Confessor began. "Zedd married Erilyn. She was a wonderful woman. We all loved her very much, but not as much as did he. They had a daughter."

Abby's curiosity got the best of her. "How old is she?"

"About the age of your daughter," Delora said.

Abby swallowed. "I see."

"When Zedd became First Wizard, things were grim. Panis Rahl had conjured the shadow people."

"I'm from Coney Crossing. I've never heard of such a thing."

"Well, the war had been bad enough, but then Panis Rahl taught his wizards to conjure shadow people." The Mother Confessor sighed at the anguish of retelling the story. "They are so called because they are like shadows in the air. They have no precise shape or form. They are not living, but created out of magic. Weapons have no more effect on them than they would have on smoke.

"You can't hide from the shadow people. They drift toward you across fields, or through the woods. They find you.

"When they touch someone, the person's whole body blisters and swells until their flesh splits open. They die in screaming agony. Not even the gift can heal one touched by a shadow person.

"As the enemy attacked, their wizards would send the shadow people out ahead. In the beginning whole battalions of our brave young soldiers were found killed to a man. We saw no hope. It was our darkest hour."

"And Wizard Zorander was able to stop them?" Abby asked.

The Mother Confessor nodded. "He studied the problem and then conjured battle horns. Their magic swept the shadow people away like smoke in the wind. The magic coming from the horns also traced its way back through the spell, to seek out the one who cast it, and kill them. The horns aren't foolproof, though, and Zedd must constantly alter their magic to keep up with the way the enemy changes their conjuring.

"Panis Rahl summoned other magic, too: fevers and sickness, wasting illnesses, fogs that caused blindness—all sorts of horrors. Zedd worked day and night, and managed to counter them all. While Panis Rahl's magic was being checked, our troops were once again able to fight on even terms. Because of Wizard Zorander, the tide of battle turned."

"Well, that much of it is good, but—"

The Mother Confessor again lifted her finger, commanding silence. Abby held her tongue as the woman lowered her hand and went on.

"Panis Rahl was enraged at what Zedd had done. He tried and failed to kill him, so he instead sent a quad to kill Erilyn."

"A quad? What's a quad?"

"A quad," the sorceress answered, "is a unit of four special assassins sent with the protection of a spell from the one who sent them: Panis Rahl. It is their assignment not only to kill the victim, but to make it unimaginably torturous and brutal."

Abby swallowed. "And did they . . . murder his wife?"

The Mother Confessor leaned closer. "Worse. They left her, her legs and arms all broken, to be found still alive."

"Alive?" Abby whispered. "Why would they leave her alive, if it was their mission to kill her?"

"So that Zedd would find her all broken and bleeding and in inconceivable agony. She was able only to whisper his name in love." The Mother Confessor leaned even closer. Abby could feel the breath of the woman's whispered words against her own face. "When he used his gift to try to heal her, it activated the worm spell."

Abby had to force herself to blink. "Worm spell . . . ?"

"No wizard would have been able to detect it." The Mother Confessor clawed her fingers and, in front of Abby's stomach, spread her hands outward, in a tearing gesture. "The spell ripped her insides apart. Because he had used his loving touch of magic, she died in screaming pain as he knelt helpless beside her."

Wincing, Abby touched her own stomach, almost feeling the wound. "That's terrible."

The Mother Confessor's violet eyes held an iron look. "The quad also took their daughter. Their daughter, who had seen everything those men had done to her mother."

Abby felt tears burning her eyes again. "They did that to his daughter, too?"

"No," the Mother Confessor said. "They hold her captive."

"Then she still lives? There is still hope?"

The Mother Confessor's satiny white dress rustled softly as she leaned back against the white marble balustrade and nested her hands in her lap. "Zedd went after the quad. He found them, but his daughter had been given to others, and they passed her on to yet others, and so on, so they had no idea who had her, or where she might be."

Abby looked to the sorceress and back to the Mother Confessor. "What did Wizard Zorander do to the quad?"

"No less than I myself would have done." The Mother Confessor stared back through a mask of cold rage. "He made them regret ever being born. For a very long time he made them regret it."

Abby shrank back. "I see."

As the Mother Confessor drew a calming breath, the sorceress took up the story. "As we speak, Wizard Zorander uses a spell that none of us understands; it holds Panis Rahl at his palace in D'Hara. It helps blunt the magic Rahl is able to conjure against us, and enables our men to drive his troops back whence they came.

"But Panis Rahl is consumed with wrath for the man who has thwarted his conquest of the Midlands. Hardly a week passes that an attempt is not made on Wizard Zorander's life. Rahl sends dangerous and vile people of all sort. Even the Mord-Sith."

Abby's breath caught. That was a word she had heard. "What are Mord-Sith?"

The sorceress smoothed back her glossy black hair as she glared with a venomous expression. "Mord-Sith are women who, along with their red leather uniform, wear a single long braid as the mark of their profession. They are trained in the torture and killing of those with the gift. If a gifted person tries to use their magic against a Mord-Sith, she is able to capture their magic and use it against them. There is no escaping a Mord-Sith."

"But surely, a person as strong in the gift as Wizard Zorander—"

"Even he would be lost if he tried to use magic against a Mord-Sith," the Mother Confessor said. "A Mord-Sith can be defeated with common weapons—but not with magic. Only the magic of a Confessor works against them. I have killed two.

"In part because of the brutal nature of the training of Mord-Sith, they have been outlawed for as long as anyone knows, but in D'Hara the ghastly tradition of taking young women to be indoctrinated as Mord-Sith continues to this day. D'Hara is a distant and secretive land. We don't know much about it, except what we have learned through unfortunate experience.

"Mord-Sith have captured several of our wizards and sorceresses. Once captured, they cannot kill themselves, nor can they escape. Before they die, they give over everything they know. Panis Rahl knows of our plans.

"We, in turn, have managed to get our hands on several high-ranking D'Harans, and through the touch of Confessors we know the extent of how we have been compromised. Time works against us."

Abby wiped the palms of her hands on her thighs. "And that man who was killed just before I went in to see the First Wizard, he couldn't have been an assassin; the two with him were allowed to leave."

"No, he was not an assassin." The Mother Confessor folded her hands. "I believe Panis Rahl knows of the spell Wizard Zorander discovered, that it has the potential to obliterate all of D'Hara. Panis Rahl is desperate to rid himself of Wizard Zorander."

The Mother Confessor's violet eyes seemed to glisten with a keen intellect. Abby looked away and picked at a stray thread on her sack. "But I don't see what this has to do with denying me help to save my daughter. He has a daughter. Wouldn't he do anything to get her back? Wouldn't he do whatever he must to have his daughter back and safe?"

The Mother Confessor's head lowered and she stroked her fingers over her brow, as if trying to rub at a grievous ache. "The man who came before you was a messenger. His message had been passed through many hands so that it could not be traced back to its source."

Abby felt cold goose bumps running up her arms. "What was the message?"

"The lock of hair he brought was from Zedd's daughter. Panis Rahl offered the life of Zedd's daughter if Zedd would surrender himself to Panis Rahl to be executed."

Abby clutched her sack. "But wouldn't a father who loved his daughter do even this to save her life?"

"At what cost?" the Mother Confessor whispered. "At the cost of the lives of all those who will die without his help?

"He couldn't do such a selfish thing, even to save the life of one he loves more than any other. Before he denied your daughter help, he had just refused the offer, thus sentencing his own innocent daughter to death."

Abby felt her hopes again tumbling into blackness. The thought of Jana's terror, of her being hurt, made Abby dizzy and sick. Tears began running down her cheeks again.

"But I'm not asking him to sacrifice everyone else to save her."

The sorceress gently touched Abby's shoulder. "He believes that sparing those people harm would mean letting the D'Harans escape to kill more people in the end.''

Abby snatched desperately for a solution. ''But I have a bone.''

The sorceress sighed. ''Abigail, half the people who come to see a wizard bring a bone. Hucksters convince supplicants that they are true bones. Desperate people, just like you, buy them.''

''Most of them come seeking a wizard to somehow give them a life free of magic,'' the Mother Confessor said. ''Most people fear magic, but I'm afraid that with the way it's been used by D'Hara, they now want nothing so much as to never again see magic. An ironic reason to buy a bone, and doubly ironic that they buy sham bones, thinking they have magic, in order to petition to be free of magic.''

Abby blinked. ''But I bought no bone. This is a debt true. On my mother's deathbed she told me of it. She said it was Wizard Zorander himself bound in it.''

The sorceress squinted her skepticism. ''Abigail, true debts of this nature are exceedingly rare. Perhaps it was a bone she had and you only thought . . .''

Abby held her sack open for the sorceress to see. The sorceress glanced in and fell silent. The Mother Confessor looked in the sack for herself.

"I know what my mother told me," Abby insisted. "She also told me that if there was any doubt, he had but to test it; then he would know it true, for the debt was passed down to him from his father."

The sorceress stroked the beads at her throat. "He could test it. If it is true, he would know. Still, solemn debt though it may be, that doesn't mean that the debt must be paid now."

Abby leaned boldly toward the sorceress. "My mother said it is a debt true, and that it had to be paid. Please, Delora, you know the nature of such things. I was so confused when I met with him, with all those people shouting. I foolishly failed to press my case by asking that he test it." She turned and clutched the Mother Confessor's arm. "Please, help me? Tell him what I have and ask that he test it?"

The Mother Confessor considered behind a blank expression. At last she spoke. "This involves a debt bound in magic. Such a thing must be considered seriously. I will speak to Wizard Zorander on your behalf and request that you be given a private audience."

Abby squeezed her eyes shut as tears sprang anew. "Thank you." She put her face in both hands and began to weep with relief at the flame of hope rekindled.

———

The Mother Confessor gripped Abby's shoulders. "I said I will try. He may deny my request."

The sorceress snorted a humorless laugh. "Not likely. I will twist his ear, too. But Abigail, that does not mean that we can convince him to help you—bone or no bone."

Abby wiped her cheek. "I understand. Thank you both. Thank you both for understanding."

With a thumb, the sorceress wiped a tear from Abby's chin. "It is said that the daughter of a sorceress is a daughter to all sorceresses."

The Mother Confessor stood and smoothed her white dress. "Delora, perhaps you could take Abigail to a rooming house for women travelers. She should get some rest. Do you have money, child?"

"Yes, Mother Confessor."

"Good. Delora will take you to a room for the night. Return to the Keep just before sunrise. We will meet you and let you know if we were able to convince Zedd to test your bone."

"I will pray to the good spirits that Wizard Zorander will see me and help my daughter," Abby felt sudden shame at her own words. "And I will pray, too, for his daughter."

The Mother Confessor cupped Abby's cheek. "Pray for all of us, child. Pray that Wizard Zorander unleashes the magic against D'Hara, before it is too late for all the children of the Midlands— old and young alike."

*   *   *

On their walk down to the city, Delora kept the conversation from Abby's worries and hopes, and what magic might contribute to either. In some ways, talking with the sorceress was reminiscent of talking with her mother. Sorceresses evaded talk of magic with one not gifted, daughter or not. Abby got the feeling that it was as uncomfortable for them as it had been for Abby when Jana asked how a mother came to have a child in her tummy.

Even though it was late, the streets were teeming with people. Worried gossip of the war floated to Abby's ears from every direction. At one corner a knot of women murmured tearfully of menfolk gone for months with no word of their fate.

Delora took Abby down a market street and had her buy a small loaf of bread with meats and olives baked right inside. Abby wasn't really hungry. The sorceress made her promise that she would eat. Not wanting to do anything to cause disfavor, Abby promised.

The rooming house was up a side street among tightly packed buildings. The racket of the market carried up the narrow street and flittered around buildings and through tiny courtyards with the ease of a chickadee through a dense wood. Abby wondered how people could stand to live so close together and with nothing to see but other houses and people. She wondered, too, how she was going to be able to sleep with all the strange sounds and noise, but then, sleep had rarely come since she had left home, despite the dead-quiet nights in the countryside.

The sorceress bid Abby a good night, putting her in the hands of a sullen-looking woman of few words who led her to a room at the end of a long hall and left her to her night's rest, after collecting a silver coin. Abby sat on the edge of the bed and, by the light of a single lamp sitting on a shelf by the bed, eyed the small room as she nibbled at the loaf of bread. The meat inside was tough and stringy, but had an agreeable flavor, spiced with salt and garlic.

Without a window, the room wasn't as noisy as Abby had feared it might be. The door had no bolt, but the woman who kept the house had said in a mumble for her not to fret, that no men were allowed in the establishment. Abby set the bread aside and, at a basin atop a simple stand two strides across the room, washed her face. She was surprised at how dirty it left the water.

She twisted the lever stem on the lamp, lowering the wick as far as it would go without snuffing the flame; she didn't like sleeping in the dark in a strange place. Lying in bed, staring up at the water-stained ceiling, she prayed earnestly to the good spirits, despite knowing that they would ignore a request such as she made. She closed her eyes and prayed for Wizard Zorander's daughter, too. Her prayers were fragmented by intruding fears that felt as if they clawed her insides raw.

She didn't know how long she had lain in the bed, wishing for sleep to take her, wishing for morning to come, when the door slowly squeaked open. A shadow climbed the far wall.

Abby froze, eyes wide, breath held tight, as she watched a crouched figure move toward the bed. It wasn't the woman of the house. She would be taller. Abby's fingers tightened on the scratchy blanket, thinking that maybe she could throw it over the intruder and then run for the door.

"Don't be alarmed, dearie. I've just come to see if you had success up at the Keep."

Abby gulped air and she sat up in the bed. "Mariska?" It was the old woman who had waited with her in the keep all day. "You frightened the wits out of me!"

The small flame from the lamp reflected in a sharp shimmer in the woman's eye as she surveyed Abby's face. "Worse things to fear than your own safety."

"What do you mean?"

Mariska smiled. It was not a reassuring smile. "Did you get what you wanted?"

"I saw the First Wizard, if that's what you mean."

"And what did he say, dearie?"

Abby swung her feet down off the bed. "That's my business."

The sly smile widened. "Oh, no, dearie, it's our business."

"What do you mean by that?"

"Answer the question. You've not much time left. Your family has not much time left."

Abby shot to her feet. "How do you—"

The old woman seized Abby's wrist and twisted until Abby was forced to sit. "What say the First Wizard?"

"He said he couldn't help me. Please, that hurts. Let me go."

"Oh, dearie, that's too bad, it is. Too bad for your little Jana."

"How . . . how do you know about her? I never—"

"So, Wizard Zorander denied your petition. Such sad news." She clicked her tongue. "Poor, unfortunate, little Jana. You were warned. You knew the price of failure."

She released Abby's wrist and turned away. Abby's mind raced in hot panic as the woman shuffled toward the door.

"No! Please! I'm to see him again, tomorrow. At sunrise."

Mariska peered back over her shoulder. "Why? Why would he agree to see you again, after he has denied you? Lying will buy your daughter no more time. It will buy her nothing."

"It's true. I swear it on my mother's soul. I talked to the sorceress, the one who took us in. I talked to her and the Mother Confessor, after Wizard Zorander denied my petition. They agreed to convince him to give me a private audience."

Her brow bunched. "Why would they do this?"

Abby pointed to her sack sitting on the end of the bed. "I showed them what I brought."

With one gnarled finger, Mariska lifted open the sack. She looked for a moment and then glided closer to Abby.

"You have yet to show this to Wizard Zorander?"

"That's right. They will get me an audience with him. I'm sure of it. Tomorrow, he will see me."

From her bulky waistband, Mariska drew a knife. She waved it slowly back and forth before Abby's face. "We grow weary of waiting for you."

Abby licked her lips. "But I—"

"In the morning I leave for Coney Crossing. I leave to see your frightened little Jana." Her hand slid behind Abby's neck. Fingers like oak roots gripped Abby's hair, holding her head fast. "If you bring him right behind me, she will go free, as you were promised."

Abby couldn't nod. "I will. I swear. I'll convince him. He is bound by a debt."

Mariska put the point of the knife so close to Abby's eye that it brushed her eyelashes. Abby feared to blink.

"Arrive late, and I will stab my knife in little Jana's eye. Stab it through. I will leave her the other so that she can watch as I cut out her father's heart, just so that she will know how much it will hurt when I do her. Do you understand, dearie?"

Abby could only whine that she did, as tears streamed down her cheeks.

"There's a good girl," Mariska whispered from so close that Abby was forced to breathe the spicy stink of the woman's sausage dinner. "If we even suspect any tricks, they will all die."

"No tricks. I'll hurry. I'll bring him."

Mariska kissed Abby's forehead. "You're a good mother." She released Abby's hair. "Jana loves you. She cries for you day and night."

After Mariska closed the door, Abby curled into a trembling ball in the bed and wept against her knuckles.

Delora leaned closer as they marched across the broad rampart. "Are you sure you're all right, Abigail?"

Wind snatched at her hair, flicking it across her face. Brushing it from her eyes, Abby looked out at the sprawl of the city below beginning to coalesce out of the gloom. She had been saying a silent prayer to her mother's spirit.

"Yes. I just had a bad night. I couldn't sleep."

The Mother Confessor's shoulder pressed against Abby's from the other side. "We understand. At least he agreed to see you. Take heart in that. He's a good man, he really is."

"Thank you," Abby whispered in shame. "Thank you both for helping me."

The people waiting along the rampart—wizards, sorceresses, officers, and others—all momentarily fell silent and bowed toward the Mother Confessor as the three women passed. Among several people she recognized from the day before, Abby saw the wizard Thomas, grumbling to himself and looking hugely impatient and vexed as he shuffled through a handful of papers covered in what Abby recognized as magical symbols.

At the end of the rampart they came to the stone face of a round turret. A steep roof overhead protruded down low above a round-topped door. The sorceress rapped on the door and opened it without waiting for a reply. She caught the twitch of Abby's brow.

"He rarely hears the knock," she explained in a hushed tone.

The stone room was small, but had a cozy feel to it. A round window to the right overlooked the city below, and another on the opposite side looked up on soaring walls of the Keep, the distant highest ones glowing pink in the first faint rays of dawn. An elaborate iron candelabrum held a small army of candles that provided a warm glow to the room.

Wizard Zorander, his unruly wavy brown hair hanging down around his face as he leaned on his hands, was absorbed in studying a book lying open on the table. The three women came to a halt.

"Wizard Zorander," the sorceress announced, "we bring Abigail, born of Helsa."

"Bags, woman," the wizard grouched without looking up, "I heard your knock, as I always do."

"Don't you curse at me, Zeddicus Zu'l Zorander," Delora grumbled back.

He ignored the sorceress, rubbing his smooth chin as he considered the book before him. "Welcome, Abigail."

Abby's fingers fumbled at the sack. But then she remembered herself and curtsied. "Thank you for seeing me, Wizard Zorander. It is of vital importance that I have your help. As I've already told you, the lives of innocent children are at stake."

Wizard Zorander finally peered up. After appraising her a long moment he straightened. "Where does the line lie?"

Abby glanced to the sorceress on one side of her and then the Mother Confessor on the other side. Neither looked back.

"Excuse me, Wizard Zorander? The line?"

The wizard's brow drew down. "You imply a higher value to a life because of a young age. The line, my dear child, across which the value of life becomes petty. Where is the line?"

"But a child—"

He held up a cautionary finger. "Do not think to play on my emotions by plying me with the value of the life of a child, as if a higher value can be placed on life because of age. When is life worth less? Where is the line? At what age? Who decides?

"All life is dear. Dead is dead, no matter the age. Don't think to produce a suspension of my reason with a callous, calculated twisting of emotion, like some slippery officeholder stirring the passions of a mindless mob."

Abby was struck speechless by such an admonition. The wizard turned his attention to the Mother Confessor.

"Speaking of bureaucrats, what did the council have to say for themselves?"

The Mother Confessor clasped her hands and sighed. "I told them your words. Simply put, they didn't care. They want it done."

He grunted his discontent. "Do they, now?" His hazel eyes turned to Abby. "Seems the council doesn't care about the lives of even children, when the children are D'Haran." He wiped a hand across his tired-looking eyes. "I can't say I don't comprehend their reasoning, or that I disagree with them, but dear spirits, they are not the ones to do it. It is not by their hand. It will be by mine."

"I understand, Zedd," the Mother Confessor murmured.

Once again he seemed to notice Abby standing before him. He considered her as if pondering some profound notion. It made her fidget. He held out his hand and waggled his fingers. "Let me see it, then."

Abby stepped closer to the table as she reached in her sack.

"If you cannot be persuaded to help innocent people, then maybe this will mean something more to you."

She drew her mother's skull from the sack and placed it in the wizard's upturned palm. "It is a debt of bones. I declare it due."

One eyebrow lifted. "It is customary to bring only a tiny fragment of bone, child."

Abby felt her face flush. "I didn't know," she stammered. "I wanted to be sure there was enough to test . . . to be sure you would believe me."

He smoothed a gentle hand over the top of the skull. "A piece smaller than a grain of sand is enough." He watched Abby's eyes. "Didn't your mother tell you?"

Abby shook her head. "She said only that it was a debt passed to you from your father. She said the debt must be paid if it was called due."

"Indeed it must," he whispered.

Even as he spoke, his hand was gliding back and forth over the skull. The bone was dull and stained by the dirt from which Abby had pulled it, not at all the pristine white she had fancied it would be. It had horrified her to have to uncover her mother's bones, but the alternative horrified her more.

Beneath the wizard's fingers, the bone of the skull began to glow with soft amber light. Abby's breathing nearly stilled when the air hummed, as if the spirits themselves whispered to the wizard. The sorceress fussed with the beads at her neck. The Mother Confessor chewed her lower lip. Abby prayed.

Wizard Zorander set the skull on the table and turned his back on them. The amber glow faded away.

When he said nothing, Abby spoke into the thick silence. "Well? Are you satisfied? Did your test prove it a debt true?"

"Oh yes," he said quietly without turning to-

ward them. "It is a debt of bones true, bound by the magic invoked until the debt is paid."

Abby's fingers worried at the frayed edge of her sack. "I told you. My mother wouldn't have lied to me. She told me that if not paid while she was alive, it became a debt of bones upon her death."

The wizard slowly rounded to face her. "And did she tell you anything of the engendering of the debt?"

"No." Abby cast a furtive, sidelong glance at Delora before going on. "Sorceresses hold secrets close, and reveal only that which serves their purposes."

With a slight, fleeting smile, he grunted his concurrence.

"She said only that it was your father and she who were bound in it, and that until paid it would continue to pass on to the descendants of each."

"Your mother spoke the truth. But that does not mean that it must be paid now."

"It is a solemn debt of bones." Abby's frustration and fear erupted with venom. "I declare it due! You will yield to the obligation!"

Both the sorceress and the Mother Confessor gazed off at the walls, uneasy at a woman, an ungifted woman, raising her voice to the First Wizard himself. Abby suddenly wondered if she might be struck dead for such insolence. But if he didn't help her, it wouldn't matter.

The Mother Confessor diverted the possible results of Abby's outburst with a question. "Zedd, did your reading tell you of the nature of the engendering of the debt?"

"Indeed it did," he said. "My father, too, told me of a debt. My test has proven to me that this is the one of which he spoke, and that the woman standing before me carries the other half of the link."

"So, what was the engendering?" the sorceress asked.

He turned his palms up. "It seems to have slipped my mind. I'm sorry; I find myself to be more forgetful than usual of late."

Delora sniffed. "And you dare to call sorceresses taciturn?"

Wizard Zorander silently considered her a moment and then turned a squint on the Mother Confessor. "The council wants it done, do they?" He smiled a sly smile. "Then it shall be done."

The Mother Confessor cocked her head. "Zedd . . . are you sure about this?"

"About what?" Abby asked. "Are you going to honor the debt or not?"

The wizard shrugged. "You have declared the debt due." He plucked a small book from the table and slipped it into a pocket in his robe. "Who am I to argue?"

"Dear spirits," the Mother Confessor whispered to herself. "Zedd, just because the council—"

"I am just a wizard," he said, cutting her off, "serving the wants and wishes of the people."

"But if you travel to this place you would be exposing yourself to needless danger."

"I must be near the border—or it will claim parts of the Midlands, too. Coney Crossing is as good a place as any other to ignite the conflagration."

Beside herself with relief, Abby was hardly hearing anything else he said. "Thank you, Wizard Zorander. Thank you."

He strode around the table and gripped her shoulder with sticklike fingers of surprising strength.

"We are bound, you and I, in a debt of bones. Our life paths have intersected." His smile looked at once sad and sincere. His powerful fingers closed around her wrist, around her bracelet, and he put her mother's skull in her hands. "Please, Abby, call me Zedd."

Near tears, she nodded. "Thank you, Zedd."

Outside, in the early light, they were accosted by the waiting crowd. Wizard Thomas, waving his papers, shoved his way through.

"Zorander! I've been studying these elements you've provided. I have to talk to you."

"Talk, then," the First Wizard said as he marched by. The crowd followed in his wake.

"This is madness."

"I never said it wasn't."

Wizard Thomas shook the papers as if for proof. "You can't do this, Zorander!"

"The council has decided that it is to be done. The war must be ended while we have the upper hand and before Panis Rahl comes up with something we won't be able to counter."

"No, I mean I've studied this thing, and you won't be able to do it. We don't understand the power those wizards wielded. I've looked over the elements you've shown me. Even trying to invoke such a thing will create intense heat."

Zedd halted and put his face close to Thomas. He lifted his eyebrows in mock surprise. "Really, Thomas? Do you think? Igniting a light spell that will rip the fabric of the world of life might cause an instability in the elements of the web field?"

Thomas charged after as Zedd stormed off. "Zorander! You won't be able to control it! If you were able to invoke it—and I'm not saying I believe you can—you would breach the Grace. The invocation uses heat. The breach feeds it. You won't be able to control the cascade. No one can do such a thing!"

"I can do it," the First Wizard muttered.

Thomas shook the fists of papers in a fury. "Zorander, your arrogance will be the end of us all! Once parted, the veil will be rent and all life will be consumed. I demand to see the book in which you found this spell. I demand to see it myself. The whole thing, not just parts of it!"

The First Wizard paused and lifted a finger. "Thomas, if you were meant to see the book, then you would be First Wizard and have access to the First Wizard's private enclave. But you are not, and you don't."

Thomas's face glowed scarlet above his white beard. "This is a foolhardy act of desperation!"

Wizard Zorander flicked the finger. The papers flew from the old wizard's hand and swirled up into a whirlwind, there to ignite, flaring into ashes that lifted away on the wind.

"Sometimes, Thomas, all that is left to you is an act of desperation. I am First Wizard, and I will do as I must. That is the end of it. I will hear no more." He turned and snatched the sleeve of an officer. "Alert the lancers. Gather all the cavalry available. We ride for Pendisan Reach at once."

The man thumped a quick salute to his chest before dashing off. Another officer, older and looking to be of much higher rank, cleared his throat.

"Wizard Zorander, may I know of your plan?"

"It is Anargo," the First Wizard said, "who is

the right hand of Panis Rahl, and in conjunction with Rahl conjures death to stalk us. Quite simply put, I intend to send death back at them.''

"By leading the lancers into Pendisan Reach?''

"Yes. Anargo holds at Coney Crossing. We have General Brainard driving north toward Pendisan Reach, General Sanderson sweeping south to join with him, and Mardale charging up from the southwest. We will go in there with the lancers and whoever of the rest of them is able to join with us.''

"Anargo is no fool. We don't know how many other wizards and gifted he has with him, but we know what they're capable of. They've bled us time and time again. At last we have dealt them a blow.'' The officer chose his words carefully. "Why do you think they wait? Why wouldn't they simply slip back into D'Hara?''

Zedd rested a hand on the crenellated wall and gazed out on the dawn, out on the city below.

"Anargo relishes the game. He performs it with high drama; he wants us to think them wounded. Pendisan Reach is the only terrain in all those mountains that an army can get through with any speed. Coney Crossing provides a wide field for battle, but not wide enough to let us maneuver easily, or flank them. He is trying to bait us in.''

The officer didn't seem surprised. "But why?''

Zedd looked back over his shoulder at the officer. "Obviously, he believes that in such terrain he can defeat us. I believe otherwise. He knows that we can't allow the menace to remain there, and he knows our plans. He thinks to draw me in, kill me, and end the threat I alone hold over them."

"So . . ." the officer reasoned aloud, "you are saying that for Anargo, it is worth the risk."

"If Anargo is right, he could win it all at Coney Crossing. When he has finished me, he will turn his gifted loose, slaughter the bulk of our forces all in one place, and then, virtually unopposed, cut out the heart of the Midlands:"—Zedd swept his arm out, indicating the city below the Wizard's Keep— "Aydindril."

"Anargo plans that before the snow flies, he will have killed me, annihilated our joint forces, have the people of the Midlands in chains, and be able to hand the whip to Panis Rahl."

The officer stared, dumbfounded. "And you plan to do as Anargo is hoping and go in there to face him?"

Zedd shrugged. "What choice have I?"

"And do you at least know how Anargo plans to kill you, so that we might take precautions? Take countermeasures?"

"I'm afraid not." Vexed, he waved his hand, dismissing the matter. He turned to Abby. "The lancers have swift horses. We will ride hard. We will be to your home soon—we will be there in time—and then we'll see to our business.''

Abby only nodded. She couldn't put into words the relief of her petition granted, nor could she express the shame she felt to have her prayer answered. But most of all, she couldn't utter a word of her horror at what she was doing, for she knew the D'Harans' plan.

Flies swarmed around dried scraps of viscera, all that was left of Abby's prized bearded pigs. Apparently, even the breeding stock, which Abby's parents had given her as a wedding gift, had been slaughtered and taken.

Abby's parents, too, had chosen Abby's husband. Abby had never met him before: he came from the town of Lynford, where her mother and father bought the pigs. Abby had been beside herself with anxiety over who her parents would choose for her husband. She had hoped for a man who would be of good cheer—a man to bring a smile to the difficulties of life.

When she first saw Philip, she thought he must be the most serious man in all the world. His young face looked to her as if it had never once smiled. That first night after meeting him, she had cried herself to sleep over thoughts of sharing her life with so solemn a man. She thought her life caught up on the sharp tines of grim fate.

Abby came to find that Philip was a hardworking man who looked out at life through a great grin. That first day she had seen him, she only later learned, he had been putting on his most sober face so that his new family would not think him a slacker unworthy of their daughter. In a short time, Abby had come to know that Philip was a man upon whom she could depend. By the time Jana had been born, she had come to love him.

Now Philip, and so many others, depended upon her.

Abby brushed her hands clean after putting her mother's bones to rest once more. The fences Jana had watched Philip so often mend, she saw, were all broken down. Coming back around the house, she noticed that barn doors were missing. Anything an animal or human could eat was gone. Abby could not recall having ever seen her home looking so barren.

It didn't matter, she told herself. It didn't matter, if only Jana would be returned to her. Fences could be mended. Pigs could be replaced, somehow, someday. Jana could never be replaced.

"Abby," Zedd asked as he peered around at the ruins of her home, "how is it that you weren't taken, when your husband and daughter and everyone else were?"

Abby stepped through the broken doorway, thinking that her home had never looked so small. Before she had gone to Aydindril, to the Wizard's Keep, her home had seemed as big as anything she could imagine. Here, Philip had laughed and filled the simple room with his comfort and conversation. With charcoal he had drawn animals on the stone hearth for Jana.

Abby pointed. "Under that door is the root cellar. That's where I was when I heard the things I told you about."

Zedd ran the toe of his boot across the knothole used as a fingerhold to lift the hatch. "They were taking your husband, and your daughter, and you stayed down there? While your daughter was screaming for you, you didn't run up to help her?"

Abby summoned her voice. "I knew that if I came up, they would have me, too. I knew that the only chance my family had was if I waited and then went for help. My mother always told me that even a sorceress was no more than a fool if she acted one. She always told me to think things through, first."

"Wise advice." Zedd set down a ladle that had been bent and holed. He rested a gentle hand on her shoulder. "It would have been hard to leave your daughter crying for you, and do the wise thing."

Abby could only manage a whisper. "You speak the spirits' own truth." She pointed through the window on the side wall. "That way—across the Coney River—lies town. They took Jana and Philip with them as they went on to take all the people from town. They had others, too, that they had already captured. The army set up camp in the hills beyond."

Zedd stood at the window, gazing out at the distant hills. "Soon, I hope, this war will be ended. Dear spirits, let it end."

Remembering the Mother Confessor's admonition not to repeat the story she told, Abby never asked about the wizard's daughter or murdered wife. When on their swift journey back to Coney Crossing she spoke of her love for Jana, it must have broken his heart to think of his own daughter in the brutal hands of the enemy, knowing that he had left her to death lest many more die.

Zedd pushed open the bedroom door. "And back here?" he asked as he put his head into the room beyond.

Abby looked up from her thoughts. "The bedroom. In the rear is a door back to the garden and the barn."

Though he never once mentioned his dead wife or missing daughter, Abby's knowledge of them ate away at her as a swelling spring river ate at a hole in the ice.

Zedd stepped back in from the bedroom as Delora came silently slipping in through the front doorway. "As Abigail said, the town across the river has been sacked," the sorceress reported. "From the looks of it, the people were all taken."

Zedd brushed back his wavy hair. "How close is the river?"

Abby gestured out the window. Night was falling. "Just there. A walk of five minutes."

In the valley, on its way to join the Kern, the Coney River slowed and spread wide, so that it became shallow enough to cross easily. There was no bridge; the road simply led to the river's edge and took up again on the other side. Though the river was near to a quarter mile across in most of the valley, it was in no place much more than knee-deep. Only in the spring melt was it occasionally treacherous to cross. The town of Coney Crossing was two miles beyond, up on the rise of hills, safe from spring floods, as was the knoll where Abby's farmyard stood.

Zedd took Delora by the elbow. "Ride back and tell everyone to hold station. If anything goes wrong . . . well, if anything goes wrong, then they must attack. Anargo's legion must be stopped, even if they have to go into D'Hara after them."

Delora did not look pleased. "Before we left, the Mother Confessor made me promise that I would be sure that you were not left alone. She told me to see to it that gifted were always near if you needed them."

Abby, too, had heard the Mother Confessor issue the orders. Looking back at the Keep as they had crossed the stone bridge, Abby had seen the Mother Confessor up on a high rampart, watching them leave. The Mother Confessor had helped when Abby had feared all was lost. She wondered what would become of the woman.

Then she remembered that she didn't have to wonder. She knew.

The wizard ignored what the sorceress had said. "As soon as I help Abby, I'll send her back, too. I don't want anyone near when I unleash the spell."

Delora gripped his collar and pulled him close. She looked as if she might be about to give him a heated scolding. Instead she drew him into an embrace.

"Please, Zedd," she whispered, "don't leave us without you as First Wizard."

Zedd smoothed back her dark hair. "And abandon you all to Thomas?" He smirked. "Never."

The dust from Delora's horse drifted away into the gathering darkness as Zedd and Abby descended the slope toward the river. Abby led him along the path through the tall grasses and rushes, explaining that the path would offer them better concealment than the road. Abby was thankful that he didn't argue for the road.

Her eyes darted from the deep shadows on one side to the shadows on the other as they were swallowed into the brush. Her pulse raced. She flinched whenever a twig snapped underfoot.

It happened as she feared it would, as she knew it would.

A figure enfolded in a long hooded cloak darted out of nowhere, knocking Abby aside. She saw the flash of a blade as Zedd flipped the attacker into the brush. He squatted, putting a hand back on Abby's shoulder as she lay in the grass panting.

"Stay down," he whispered urgently.

Light gathered at his fingers. He was conjuring magic. That was what they wanted him to do.

Tears welled, burning her eyes. She snatched his sleeve. "Zedd, don't use magic." She could hardly speak past the tightening pain in her chest. "Don't—"

The figure sprang again from the gloom of the bushes. Zedd threw up a hand. The night lit with a flash of hot light that struck the cloaked figure.

Rather than the assailant going down, it was Zedd who cried out and crumpled to the ground. Whatever he had thought to do to the attacker, it had been turned back on him, and he was in the grip of the most terrible anguish, preventing him from rising, or speaking. That was why they had wanted him to conjure magic: so they could capture him.

The figure standing over the wizard glowered at Abby. "Your part here is finished. Go."

Abby scuttled into the grass. The woman pushed the hood back, and cast off her cloak. In the near darkness, Abby could see the woman's long braid and red leather uniform. It was one of the women Abby had been told about, the women used to capture those with magic: the Mord-Sith.

The Mord-Sith watched with satisfaction as the wizard at her feet writhed in choking pain. "Well, well. Looks like the First Wizard himself has just made a very big mistake."

The belts and straps of her red leather uniform creaked as she leaned down toward him, grinning at his agony. "I have been given the whole night to make you regret ever having lifted a finger to resist us. In the morning I'm to allow you to watch as our forces annihilate your people. Afterward, I am to take you to Lord Rahl himself, the man who ordered the death of your wife, so you can beg him to order me to kill you, too." She kicked him. "So you can beg Lord Rahl for your death, as you watch your daughter die before your eyes."

Zedd could only scream in horror and pain.

On her hands and knees, Abby crabbed her way farther back into the weeds and rushes. She wiped at her eyes, trying to see. She was horrified to witness what was being done to the man who had agreed to help her for no more reason than a debt to her mother. By contrast, these people had coerced her service by holding hostage the life of her child.

As she backed away, Abby saw the knife the Mord-Sith had dropped when Zedd had thrown her into the weeds. The knife was a pretext, used to provoke him to act; it was magic that was the true weapon. The Mord-Sith had used his own magic against him—used it to cripple and capture him, and now used it to hurt him.

It was the price demanded. Abby had complied. She had had no choice.

But what toll was she imposing on others?

How could she save her daughter's life at the cost of so many others? Would Jana grow up to be a slave to people who would do this? With a mother who would allow it? Jana would grow up to learn to bow to Panis Rahl and his minions, to submit to evil, or worse, grow up to become a willing part in the scourge, never tasting liberty or knowing the value of honor.

With dreadful finality, everything seemed to fall to ruin in Abby's mind.

She snatched up the knife. Zedd was wailing in pain as the Mord-Sith bent, doing some foul thing to him. Before she had time to lose her resolve, Abby was moving toward the woman's back.

Abby had butchered animals. She told herself that this was no different. These were not people, but animals. She lifted the knife.

A hand clamped over her mouth. Another seized her wrist.

Abby moaned against the hand, against her failure to stop this madness when she had had the chance. A mouth close to her ear urged her to hush.

Struggling against the figure in hooded cloak that held her, Abby turned her head as much as she could, and in the last of the daylight saw violet eyes looking back. For a moment she couldn't make sense of it, couldn't make sense of how the woman could be there when Abby had seen her remain behind. But it truly was her.

Abby stilled. The Mother Confessor released her and, with a quick hand signal, urged her back. Abby didn't question; she scurried back into the rushes as the Mother Confessor reached out toward the woman in red leather. The Mord-Sith was bent over, intent on her grisly business with the screaming wizard.

In the distance, bugs chirped and clicked. Frogs called with insistent croaks. Not far away the river sloshed and burbled as it always did—a familiar, comforting sound of home.

And then there came a sudden, violent concussion to the air. Thunder without sound. It drove the wind from Abby's lungs. The wallop nearly knocked her senseless, making every joint in her body burn in sharp pain.

There was no flash of light—just that pure and flawless jolt to the air. The world seemed to stop in its terrible splendor.

Grass flattened as if in a wind radiating out in a ring from the Mord-Sith and the Mother Confessor. Abby's senses returned as the pain in her joints thankfully melted away.

Abby had never seen it done before, and had never expected to see it in the whole of her life, but she knew without doubt that she had just witnessed a Confessor unleashing her power. From what Abby's mother had told her, it was the destruction of a person's mind so complete that it left only numb devotion to the Confessor. She had but to ask and they would confess any truth, no matter the crime they had previously attempted to conceal or deny.

"Mistress," the Mord-Sith moaned in piteous lamentation.

Abby, first staggered by the shock of the soundless thunder of the Mother Confessor's power, and now stunned by the abject anguish of the woman crumpled on the ground, felt a hand grip her arm. It was the wizard.

With the back of his other hand he wiped blood from his mouth. He labored to get his breath. "Leave her to it."

"Zedd . . . I . . . I'm so sorry. I tried to tell you not to use magic, but I didn't call loud enough for you to hear."

He managed to smile through obvious pain. "I heard you."

"But why then did you use your gift?"

"I thought that in the end, you would not be the kind of person to do such a terrible thing, and that you would show your true heart." He pulled her away from the cries. "We used you. We wanted them to think they had succeeded."

"You knew what I was going to do? You knew I was to bring you to them so that they could capture you?"

"I had a good idea. From the first there seemed more to you than you presented. You are not very talented at being a spy and a traitor. Since we arrived here you've been watching the shadows and jumping at the chirp of every bug."

The Mother Confessor rushed up. "Zedd, are you all right?"

He put a hand on her shoulder. "I'll be fine."

His eyes still held the glaze of terror. "Thank you for not being late. For a moment, I feared . . ."

"I know." The Mother Confessor offered a quick smile. "Let us hope your trick was worth it. You have until dawn. She said they expect her to torture you all night before bringing you to them in the morning. Their scouts alerted Anargo to our troops' arrival."

Back in the rushes the Mord-Sith was screaming as though she were being flayed alive.

Shivers ran through Abby's shoulders. "They'll hear her and know what's happened."

"Even if they could hear at this distance, they will think it is Zedd, being tortured by her." The Mother Confessor took the knife from Abby's hand. "I am glad that you rewarded my faith and in the end chose not to join with them."

Abby wiped her palms on her skirts, shamed by all she had done, by what she had intended to do. She was beginning to shake. "Are you going to kill her?"

The Mother Confessor, despite looking bone-weary after having touched the Mord-Sith, still had iron resolve in her eyes. "A Mord-Sith is different from anyone else. She does not recover from the touch of a Confessor. She would suffer in profound agony until she died, sometime before morning." She glanced back toward the cries. "She has told us what we need to know, and Zedd must have his power back. It is the merciful thing to do."

"It also buys me time to do what I must do." Zedd's fingers turned Abby's face toward him, away from the shrieks. "And time to get Jana back. You will have until morning."

"I will have until morning? What do you mean?"

"I'll explain. But we must hurry if you are to have enough time. Now, take off your clothes."

Abby was running out of time.

She moved through the D'Haran camp, holding herself stiff and tall, trying not to look frantic, even though that was how she felt. All night long she had been doing as the wizard had instructed: acting haughty. To anyone who noticed her, she directed disdain. To anyone who looked her way, thinking to speak to her, she growled.

Not that many, though, so much as dared to catch the attention of what appeared to be a red-leather-clad Mord-Sith. Zedd had told her, too, to keep the Mord-Sith's weapon in her fist. It looked like nothing more than a small red leather rod. How it worked, Abby had no idea—the wizard had said only that it involved magic, and she wouldn't be able to call it to her aid—but it did have an effect on those who saw it in her hand: it made them melt back into the darkness, away from the light of the campfires, away from Abby.

Those who were awake, anyway. Although most people in the camp were sleeping, there was no shortage of alert guards. Zedd had cut the long braid from the Mord-Sith who had attacked him, and tied it into Abby's hair. In the dark, the mismatch of color wasn't obvious. When the guards looked at Abby they saw a Mord-Sith, and quickly turned their attention elsewhere.

By the apprehension on people's faces when they saw her coming, Abby knew she must look fearsome. They didn't know how her heart pounded. She was thankful for the mantle of night so that the D'Harans couldn't see her knees trembling. She had seen only two real Mord-Sith, both sleeping, and she had kept far away from them, as Zedd had warned her. Real Mord-Sith were not likely to be fooled so easily.

Zedd had given her until dawn. Time was running out. He had told her that if she wasn't back in time, she would die.

Abby was thankful she knew the lay of the land, or long since would have become lost among the confusion of tents, campfires, wagons, horses, and mules. Everywhere pikes and lances were stacked upright in circles with their points leaning together. Men—farriers, fletchers, blacksmiths, and craftsmen of all sorts—worked through the night.

The air was thick with woodsmoke and rang with the sound of metal being shaped and sharpened and wood being worked for everything from bows to wagons. Abby didn't know how people could sleep through the noise, but sleep they did.

Shortly the immense camp would wake to a new day—a day of battle, a day the soldiers went to work doing what they did best. They were getting a good night's sleep so they would be rested for the killing of the Midlands army. From what she had heard, D'Haran soldiers were very good at their job.

Abby had searched relentlessly, but she had been unable to find her father, her husband, or her daughter. She had no intention of giving up. She had resigned herself to the knowledge that if she didn't find them, she would die with them.

She had found captives tied together and staked to trees, or the ground, to keep them from running. Many more were chained. Some she recognized, but many more she didn't. Most were kept in groups and under guard.

Abby never once saw a guard asleep at his post. When they looked her way, she acted as if she were looking for someone, and she wasn't going to go easy on them when she found them. Zedd had told her that her safety, and the safety of her family, depended on her playing the part convincingly. Abby thought about these people hurting her daughter, and it wasn't hard to act angry.

But she was running out of time. She couldn't find them, and she knew that Zedd would not wait. Too much was at stake; she understood that, now. She was coming to appreciate that the wizard and the Mother Confessor were trying to stop a war; that they were people resolved to the dreadful task of weighing the lives of a few against the lives of many.

Abby lifted another tent flap, and saw soldiers sleeping. She squatted and looked at the faces of prisoners tied to wagons. They stared back with hollow expressions. She bent to gaze at the faces of children pressed together in nightmares. She couldn't find Jana. The huge camp sprawled across the hilly countryside; there were a thousand places she could be.

As she marched along a crooked line of tents, she scratched at her wrist. Only when she went farther did she notice that it was the bracelet warming that made her wrist itch. It warmed yet more as she proceeded, but then the warmth began fading. Her brow twitched. Out of curiosity, she turned and went back the way she had come.

Where a pathway between tents turned off, her bracelet tingled again with warmth. Abby paused a moment, looking off into the darkness. The sky was just beginning to color with light. She took the path between the tents, following until the bracelet cooled, then backtracked to where it warmed again and took a new direction where it warmed yet more.

Abby's mother had given her the bracelet, telling her to wear it always, and that someday it would be of value. Abby wondered if somehow the bracelet had magic that would help her find her daughter. With dawn nearing, this seemed the only chance she had left. She hurried onward, wending where the warmth from the bracelet directed.

The bracelet led her to an expanse of snoring soldiers. There were no prisoners in sight. Guards patrolled the men in bedrolls and blankets. There was one tent set among the big men—for an officer, she guessed.

Not knowing what else to do, Abby strode among the sleeping men. Near the tent, the bracelet sent tingling heat up her arm.

Abby saw that sentries hung around the small tent like flies around meat. The canvas sides glowed softly, probably from a candle inside. Off to the side, she noticed a sleeping form different from the men. As she got closer, she saw that it was a woman; Mariska.

The old woman breathed with a little raspy

whistle as she slept. Abby stood paralyzed. Guards looked up at her.

Needing to do something before they asked any questions, Abby scowled at them and marched toward the tent. She tried not to make any noise; the guards might think she was a Mord-Sith, but Mariska would not long be fooled. A glare from Abby turned the guards' eyes to the dark countryside.

Her heart pounding nearly out of control, Abby gripped the tent flap. She knew Jana would be inside. She told herself that she must not cry out when she saw her daughter. She reminded herself that she must put a hand over Jana's mouth before she could cry out with joy, lest they be caught before they had a chance to escape.

The bracelet was so hot it felt as if it would blister her skin. Abby ducked into the low tent.

A trembling little girl huddled in a tattered wool cloak sat in blankets on the ground. She stared up with big eyes that blinked with the terror of what might come next. Abby felt a stab of anguish. It was not Jana.

They stared at each other. The child's face was lit clearly by the candle set to the side, as Abby's must be. In those big gray eyes that looked to have beheld unimaginable terrors, the little girl seemed to reach a judgment.

Her arms stretched up in supplication.

Instinctively, Abby fell to her knees and scooped up the little girl, hugging her small trembling body. The girl's spindly arms came out from the tattered cloak and wrapped around Abby's neck, holding on for dear life.

"Help me? Please?" the child whimpered in Abby's ear.

Before she had picked her up she had seen the face in the candlelight. There was no doubt in Abby's mind. It was Zedd's daughter.

"I've come to help you," Abby comforted. "Zedd sent me."

The child moaned expectantly.

Abby held the girl out at arm's length. "I'll take you to your father, but you mustn't let these people know I'm rescuing you. Can you play along with me? Can you pretend that you're my prisoner, so that I can get you away?"

Near tears, the girl nodded. She had the same wavy hair as Zedd, and the same eyes, although they were an arresting gray, not hazel.

"Good," Abby whispered, cupping a chilly cheek, almost lost in those gray eyes. "Trust me, then, and I will get you away."

"I trust you," came the small voice.

Abby snatched up a rope lying nearby and looped it around the girl's neck. "I'll try not to hurt you, but I must make them think you are my prisoner."

The girl cast a worried look at the rope, as if she knew the rope well, and then nodded that she would go along.

Abby stood, once outside the tent, and by the rope pulled the child out after her. The guards looked her way. Abby started out.

One of them scowled as he stepped close. "What's going on?"

Abby stomped to a halt and lifted the red leather rod, pointing it at the guard's nose. "She has been summoned. And who are you to question? Get out of my way or I'll have you gutted and cleaned for my breakfast!"

The man paled and hurriedly stepped aside. Before he had time to reconsider, Abby charged off, the girl in tow at the end of the rope, dragging her heels, making it look real.

No one followed. Abby wanted to run, but she couldn't. She wanted to carry the girl, but she couldn't. It had to look as if a Mord-Sith were taking a prisoner away.

Rather than take the shortest route back to Zedd, Abby followed the hills upriver to a place where the trees offered concealment almost to the water's edge. Zedd had told her where to cross, and warned her not to return by a different way; he had set traps of magic to prevent the D'Harans from charging down from the hills to stop whatever it was he was going to do.

Closer to the river she saw, downstream a ways, a bank of fog hanging close to the ground. Zedd had emphatically warned her not to go near any fog. She suspected that it was a poison cloud of some sort that he had conjured.

The sound of the water told her she was close to the river. The pink sky provided enough light to finally see it when she reached the edge of the trees. Although she could see the massive camp on the hills in the distance behind her, she saw no one following.

Abby took the rope from the child's neck. The girl watched her with those big round eyes. Abby lifted her and held her tight.

"Hold on, and keep quiet."

Pressing the girl's head to her shoulder, Abby ran for the river.

There was light, but it was not the dawn. They had crossed the frigid water and made the other side when she first noticed it. Even as she ran along the river's bank, before she could see the source of the light, Abby knew that magic was being called there that was unlike any magic she had ever seen before. A sound, low and thin, whined up the river toward her. A smell, as if the air itself had been burned, hung along the riverbank.

The little girl clung to Abby, tears running down

her face, afraid to speak—afraid, it seemed, to hope that she had at last been rescued, as if asking a question might somehow make it all vanish like a dream, upon waking. Abby felt tears coursing down her own cheeks.

When she rounded a bend in the river, she spotted the wizard. He stood in the center of the river, on a rock that Abby had never before seen. The rock was just large enough to clear the surface of the water by a few inches, making it almost appear as if the wizard stood on the surface of the water.

Before him as he faced toward distant D'Hara, shapes, dark and wavering, floated in the air. They curled around, as if confiding in him, conversing, warning, tempting him with floating arms and reaching fingers that wreathed like smoke.

Animate light twisted up around the wizard. Colors both dark and wondrous glimmered about him, cavorting with the shadowy forms undulating through the air. It was at once the most enchanting and the most frightening thing Abby had ever seen. No magic her mother conjured had ever seemed . . . aware.

But the most frightening thing by far was what hovered in the air before the wizard. It appeared to be a molten sphere, so hot it glowed from within, its surface a crackling of fluid dross. An arm of water from the river magically turned skyward in a fountain spray and poured down over the rotating silvery mass.

The water hissed and steamed as it hit the sphere, leaving behind clouds of white vapor to drift away in the gentle dawn wind. The molten form blackened at the touch of the water cascading over it, and yet the intense inner heat melted the glassy surface again as fast as the water cooled it, making the whole thing bubble and boil in midair, a pulsing sinister menace.

Transfixed, Abby let the child slip to the silty ground.

The little girl's arms stretched out. "Papa."

He was too far away to hear her, but he heard.

Zedd turned, at once larger than life in the midst of magic Abby could see but not begin to fathom, yet at the same time small with the frailty of human need. Tears filled his eyes as he gazed at his daughter standing beside Abby. This man who seemed to be consulting with spirits looked as if for the first time he were seeing a true apparition.

Zedd leaped off the rock and charged through the water. When he reached her and took her up in the safety of his arms, she began to wail at last with the contained terror released.

"There, there, dear one," Zedd comforted. "Papa is here now."

"Oh, Papa," she cried against his neck, "they

hurt Mama. They were wicked. They hurt her so . . ."

He hushed her tenderly. "I know, dear one. I know."

For the first time, Abby saw the sorceress and the Mother Confessor standing off to the side, watching. They, too, shed tears at what they were seeing. Though Abby was glad for the wizard and his daughter, the sight only intensified the pain in her chest at what she had lost. She was choked with tears.

"There, there, dear one," Zedd was cooing. "You're safe, now. Papa won't let anything happen to you. You're safe now."

Zedd turned to Abby. By the time he had smiled his tearful appreciation, the child was asleep.

"A little spell," he explained when Abby's brow twitched with surprise. "She needs to rest. I need to finish what I am doing."

He put his daughter in Abby's arms. "Abby, would you take her up to your house where she can sleep until I'm finished here? Please, put her in bed and cover her up to keep her warm. She will sleep for now."

Thinking about her own daughter in the hands of the brutes across the river, Abby could only nod before turning to the task. She was happy for Zedd, and even felt pride at having rescued his little girl, but as she ran for her home, she was near to dying with grief over her failure to recover her own family.

Abby settled the dead weight of the sleeping child into her bed. She drew the curtain across the small window in her bedroom and, unable to resist, smoothed back silky hair and pressed a kiss to the soft brow before leaving the girl to her blessed rest.

With the child safe at last and asleep, Abby raced back down the knoll to the river. She thought to ask Zedd to give her just a little more time so she could return to look for her own daughter. Fear for Jana had her heart pounding wildly. He owed her a debt, and had not yet seen it through.

Wringing her hands, Abby came to a panting halt at the water's edge. She watched the wizard up on his rock in the river, light and shadow coursing up around him. She had been around magic enough to have the sense to fear approaching him. She could hear his chanted words; though they were words she had never heard before, she recognized the idiosyncratic cadence of words spoken in a spell, words calling together frightful forces.

On the ground beside her was the strange Grace she had seen him draw before, the one that breached the worlds of life and death. The Grace was drawn with a sparkling, pure white sand that stood out in stark relief against the dark silt. Abby shuddered even to look upon it, much less contemplate its meaning. Around the Grace, carefully drawn with the same sparkling white sand, were geometric forms of magical invocations.

Abby lowered her fists, about to call out to the wizard, when Delora leaned close. Abby flinched in surprise.

"Not now, Abigail," the sorceress murmured. "Don't disturb him in the middle of this part."

Reluctantly, Abby heeded the sorceress's words. The Mother Confessor was there, too. Abby chewed her bottom lip as she watched the wizard throw up his arms. Sparkles of colored light curled up along twisting shafts of shadows. "But I must. I haven't been able to find my family. He must help me. He must save them. It's a debt of bones that must be satisfied."

The other two women shared a look. "Abby," the Mother Confessor said, "he gave you a chance, gave you time. He tried. He did his best, but he has everyone else to think of, now."

The Mother Confessor took up Abby's hand, and the sorceress put an arm around Abby's shoulders as she stood weeping on the riverbank. It wasn't supposed to end this way, not after all she had been through, not after all she had done. Despair crushed her.

The wizard, his arms raised, called forth more

light, more shadows, more magic. The river roiled around him. The hissing thing in the air grew as it slowly slumped closer to the water. Shafts of light shot from the hot, rotating bloom of power.

The sun was rising over the hills behind the D'Harans. This part of the river wasn't as wide as elsewhere, and Abby could see the activity in the trees beyond. Men moved about, but the fog hanging on the far bank kept them wary, kept them in the trees.

Also across the river, at the edge of the tree-covered hills, another wizard had appeared to conjure magic. He too stood atop a rock as his arms launched sparkling light up into the air. Abby thought that the strong morning sun might outshine the conjured illuminations, but it didn't.

Abby could stand it no longer. "Zedd!" she called out across the river. "Zedd! Please, you promised! I found your daughter! What about mine? Please don't do this until she is safe!"

Zedd turned and looked at her as if from a great distance, as if from another world. Arms of dark forms caressed him. Fingers of dark smoke dragged along his jaw, urging his attention back to them, but he gazed instead at Abby.

"I'm so sorry." Despite the distance, Abby could clearly hear his whispered words. "I gave you time to try to find them. I can spare no more, or countless other mothers will weep for their children—mothers still living, and mothers in the spirit world.''

Abby cried out in an anguished wail as he turned back to the ensorcellment. The two women tried to comfort her, but Abby was not to be comforted in her grief.

Thunder rolled through the hills. A clacking clamor from the spell around Zedd rose to echo up and down the valley. Shafts of intense light shot upward. It was a disorienting sight, light shining up into sunlight.

Across the river, the counter to Zedd's magic seemed to spring forth. Arms of light twisted like smoke, lowering to tangle with the light radiating up around Zedd. The fog along the riverbank diffused suddenly.

In answer, Zedd spread his arms wide. The glowing tumbling furnace of molten light thundered. The water sluicing over it roared as it boiled and steamed. The air wailed as if in protest.

Behind the wizard, across the river, the D'Haran soldiers were pouring out of the trees, driving their prisoners before them. People cried out in terror. They quailed at the wizard's magic, only to be driven onward by the spears and swords at their backs.

Abby saw several who refused to move fall to

the blades. At the mortal cries, the rest rushed on-ward, like sheep before wolves.

If whatever Zedd was doing failed, the army of the Midlands would then charge into this valley to confront the enemy. The prisoners would be caught in the middle.

A figure worked its way up along the opposite bank, dragging a child behind. Abby's flesh flashed icy cold with sudden frigid sweat. It was Mariska. Abby shot a quick glance back over her shoulder. It was impossible. She squinted across the river.

"Nooo!" Zedd called out.

It was Zedd's little girl that Mariska had by the hair.

Somehow, Mariska had followed and found the child sleeping in Abby's home. With no one there to watch over her as she slept, Mariska had stolen the child back.

Mariska held the child out before herself, for Zedd to see. "Cease and surrender, Zorander, or she dies!"

Abby tore away from the arms holding her and charged into the water. She struggled to run against the current, to reach the wizard. Part way there, he turned to stare into her eyes.

Abby froze. "I'm sorry." Her own voice sounded to her like a plea before death. "I thought she was safe."

Zedd nodded in resignation. It was out of his hands. He turned back to the enemy. His arms lifted to his sides. His fingers spread, as if commanding all to stop—magic and men alike.

"Let the prisoners go!" Zedd called across the water to the enemy wizard. "Let them go, Anargo, and I'll give you all your lives!"

Anargo's laugh rang out over the water.

"Surrender," Mariska hissed, "or she dies."

The old woman pulled the knife she kept in the wrap around her waist. She pressed the blade to the child's throat. The girl was screaming in terror, her arms reaching to her father, her little fingers clawing the air.

Abby struggled ahead into the water. She called out, begging Mariska to let Zedd's daughter go free. The woman paid no more heed to Abby than to Zedd.

"Last chance!" Mariska called.

"You heard her," Anargo growled out across the water. "Surrender now or she will die."

"You know I can't put myself above my people!" Zedd called back. "This is between us, Anargo! Let them all go!"

Anargo's laugh echoed up and down the river. "You are a fool, Zorander! You had your chance!" His expression twisted to rage. "Kill her!" he screamed to Mariska.

Fists at his side, Zedd shrieked. The sound seemed to split the morning with its fury.

Mariska lifted the squealing child by her hair. Abby gasped in disbelief as the woman sliced the little girl's throat.

The child flailed. Blood spurted across Mariska's gnarly fingers as she viciously sawed the blade back and forth. She gave a final, mighty yank of the knife. The blood-soaked body dropped in a limp heap. Abby felt vomit welling up in the back of her throat. The silty dirt of the riverbank turned a wet red.

Mariska held the severed head high with a howl of victory. Strings of flesh and blood swung beneath it. The mouth hung in a slack, silent cry.

Abby threw her arms around Zedd's legs. "Dear spirits, I'm sorry! Oh, Zedd, forgive me!"

She wailed in anguish, unable to gather her senses at witnessing a sight so grisly.

"And now, child," Zedd asked in a hoarse voice from above, "what would you have me do? Would you have me let them win, to save your daughter from what they have done to mine? Tell me, child, what should I do?"

Abby couldn't beg for the life of her family at a cost of such people rampaging unchecked across the land. Her sickened heart wouldn't allow it. How could she sacrifice the lives and peace of everyone else just so her loved ones would live?

She would be no better than Mariska, killing innocent children.

"Kill them all!" Abby screamed up at the wizard. She threw her arm out, pointing at Mariska and the hateful wizard Anargo. "Kill the bastards! Kill them all!"

Zedd's arms flung upward. The morning cracked with a peal of thunder. As if he had loosed it, the molten mass before him plunged into the water. The ground shook with a jolt. A huge geyser of water exploded forth. The air itself quaked. All around the most dreadful rumbling whipped the water into froth.

Abby, squatted down with the water to her waist, felt numb not only from the cold, but also from the cold knowledge that she'd been forsaken by the good spirits she had always thought would watch over her. Zedd turned and snatched her arm, dragging her up on the rock with him.

It was another world.

The shapes around them called to her, too. They reached out, bridging the distance between life and death. Searing pain, frightful joy, profound peace, spread through her at their touch. Light moved up through her body, filling her like air filled her lungs, and exploded in showers of sparks in her mind's eye. The thick howl of the magic was deafening.

Green light ripped through the water. Across the river, Anargo had been thrown to the ground. The rock atop which he had stood had shattered into needle-like shards. The soldiers called out in fright as the air all about danced with swirling smoke and sparks of light.

"Run!" Mariska screamed. "While you have the chance! Run for your lives!" Already she was racing toward the hills. "Leave the prisoners to die! Save yourselves! Run!"

The mood across the river suddenly galvanized with a single determination. The D'Harans dropped their weapons. They cast aside the ropes and chains holding the prisoners. They kicked up dirt as they turned and ran. In a single instant, the whole of an army that had a moment before stood grimly facing them were all, as if of a single fright, running for their lives.

From the corner of her eye, Abby saw the Mother Confessor and the sorceress struggling to run into the water. Although the water was hardly above their knees, it bogged them down in their rush nearly as much as would mud.

Abby watched it all as if in a dream. She floated in the light surrounding her. Pain and rapture were one within her. Light and dark, sound and silence, joy and sorrow, all were one, everything and nothing together in a caldron of raging magic.

Across the river, the D'Haran army had vanished into the woods. Dust rose above the trees, marking their horses, wagons, and footfalls racing away, while at the riverbank the Mother Confessor and the sorceress were shoving people into the water, screaming at them, though Abby didn't hear the words, so absorbed was she by the strange harmonious trills twisting her thoughts into visions of dancing color overlaying what her eyes were trying to tell her.

She thought briefly that surely she was dying. She thought briefly that it didn't matter. And then her mind was swimming again in the cold color and hot light, the drumming music of magic and worlds meshing. The wizard's embrace made her feel as if she were being held in her mother's arms again. Maybe she was.

Abby was aware of the people reaching the Midlands side of the river and running ahead of the Mother Confessor and sorceress. They vanished into the rushes and then Abby saw them far away, beyond the tall grass, running uphill, away from the sublime sorcery erupting from the river.

The world thundered around her. A subterranean thump brought sharp pain deep in her chest. A whine, like steel being shredded, tore through the morning air. All around the water danced and quaked.

Hot steam felt as if it would scald Abby's legs. The air went white with it. The noise hurt her ears so much that she squeezed her eyes shut. She saw the same thing with her eyes closed as she saw with them open—shadowy shapes swirling through the green air. Everything was going crazy in her mind, making no sense. Green fury tore at her body and soul.

Abby felt pain, as if something inside her tore asunder. She gasped and opened her eyes. A horrific wall of green fire was receding away from them, toward the far side of the river. Founts of water lashed upward, like a thunderstorm in reverse. Lightning laced together above the surface of the river.

As the conflagration reached the far bank, the ground beneath it rent apart. Shafts of violet light shot up from the ripping wounds in the earth, like the blood of another realm.

Worse, though, than any of it were the howls. Howls of the dead, Abby was sure. It felt as if her own soul moaned in sympathy with the agony of cries filling the air. From the receding green wall of glimmering fire, the shapes twisted and turned, calling, begging, trying to escape the world of the dead.

She understood now that that was what the wall of green fire was—death, come to life.

The wizard had breached the boundary between worlds.

Abby had no idea how much time passed; in the grip of the strange light in which she swam there seemed to be no time, any more than there was anything solid. There was nothing familiar about any of the sensations upon which to hang understanding.

It seemed to Abby that the wall of green fire had halted its advance in the trees on the far hillside. The trees over which it had passed, and those she could see embraced by the shimmering curtain, had been blackened and shriveled by the profound touch of death itself. Even the grass over which the grim presence had passed looked to have been baked black and crisp by a high summer sun.

As Abby watched the wall, it dulled. As she stared, it seemed to waver in and out of her vision, sometimes a glimmering green gloss, like molten glass, and sometimes no more than a pale hint, like a fog just now passed from the air.

To each side, it was spreading, a wall of death raging across the world of life.

Abby realized she heard the river again, the comfortable, common, sloshing, lapping, burbling sounds that she lived her life hearing but most of the time didn't notice.

Zedd hopped down from the rock. He took her

hand and helped her down. Abby gripped his hand tightly to brace against the dizzying sensations swimming through her head.

Zedd snapped his fingers, and the rock upon which they had just stood leaped into the air, causing her to gasp in fright. In an instant so brief that she doubted she had seen it, Zedd caught the rock. It had become a small stone, smaller than an egg. He winked at her as he slipped it into a pocket. She thought the wink the oddest thing she could imagine, odder even than the boulder now a stone in his pocket.

On the bank, the Mother Confessor and the sorceress waited. They took her arms, helping her out of the water.

The sorceress looked grim. "Zedd, why isn't it moving?"

It sounded to Abby more like an accusation than a question. Either way, Zedd ignored it.

"Zedd," Abby mumbled, "I'm so sorry. It's my fault. I shouldn't have left her alone. I should have stayed. I'm so sorry."

The wizard, hardly hearing her words, was looking off to the wall of death on the other side of the river. He brought his clawed fingers up past his chest, calling something forth from within himself.

With a sudden thump to the air, fire erupted between his hands. He held it out as he would hold an offering. Abby threw an arm up in front of her face at the heat.

Zedd lifted the roiling ball of liquid fire. It grew between his hands, tumbling and turning, roaring and hissing with rage.

The three women backed away. Abby had heard of such fire. She had once heard her mother name it in a hushed tone: wizard's fire. Even then, not seeing or knowing its like, those whispered words forming a picture in Abby's mind as her mother recounted it, had sent a chill through Abby. Wizard's fire was the bane of life, called forth to scourge an enemy. This could be nothing else.

"For killing my love, my Erilyn, the mother of our daughter, and all the other innocent loved ones of innocent people," Zedd whispered, "I send you, Panis Rahl, the gift of death."

The wizard opened his arms outward. The liquid blue and yellow fire, bidden by its master, tumbled forward, gathering speed, roaring away toward D'Hara. As it crossed the river, it grew like angry lightning blooming forth, wailing with wrathful fury, reflecting in glimmering points from the water in thousands of bright sparkles.

The wizard's fire shot across the growing wall of green, just catching the upper edge. At the contact, green flame flared forth, some of it tearing away, caught up behind the wizard's fire, trailing after like smoke behind flame. The deadly mix howled toward the horizon. Everyone stood transfixed, watching, until all trace of it had vanished in the distance.

When Zedd, pale and drawn, turned back to them, Abby clutched his robes. "Zedd, I'm so sorry. I shouldn't—"

He put his fingers to her lips to silence her. "There is someone waiting for you."

He tilted his head. She turned. Back by the rushes, Philip stood holding Jana's hand. Abby gasped with a jolt of giddy joy. Philip grinned his familiar grin. At his other side, her father smiled and nodded his approval to her.

Arms reaching, Abby ran to them. Jana's face wrinkled. She backed against Philip. Abby fell to her knees before her.

"It's Mama," Philip said to Jana. "She just has herself some new clothes."

Abby realized Jana was frightened by the red leather outfit she was wearing. Abby grinned through her tears.

"Mama!" Jana cried at seeing the smile.

Abby threw her arms around her daughter. She laughed and hugged Jana so hard the child squeaked in protest. Abby felt Philip's hand on her shoulder in loving greeting. Abby stood and threw an arm around him, tears choking her voice. Her father put a comforting hand to her back while she squeezed Jana's hand.

Zedd, Delora, and the Mother Confessor gathered them and herded them up the hill toward the people waiting at the top. Soldiers, mostly officers, some that Abby recognized, a few other people from Aydindril, and the wizard Thomas waited with the freed prisoners. Among the people liberated were those of Coney Crossing; people who held Abby, the daughter of a sorceress, in no favor. But they were her people, the people from her home, the people she had wanted saved.

Zedd rested a hand on Abby's shoulder. Abby was shocked to see that his wavy brown hair was now partly snow white. She knew without a looking glass that hers had undergone the same transformation in the place beyond the world of life, where, for a time, they had been.

"This is Abigail, born of Helsa," the wizard called out to the people gathered. "She is the one who went to Aydindril to seek my help. Though she does not have magic, it is because of her that you people are all free. She cared enough to beg for your lives."

Abby, with Philip's arm around her waist and Jana's hand in hers, looked from the wizard to the sorceress, and then to the Mother Confessor. The Mother Confessor smiled. Abby thought it a cold-hearted thing to do in view of the fact that Zedd's daughter had been murdered before their eyes not long before. She whispered as much.

The Mother Confessor's smile widened. "Don't you remember?" she asked as she leaned close. "Don't you remember what I told you we call him?"

Abby, confused by everything that had happened, couldn't imagine what the Mother Confessor was talking about. When she admitted she didn't, the Mother Confessor and the sorceress shepherded her onward, past the grave where Abby had reburied her mother's skull upon her return, and into the house.

With a hand, the Mother Confessor eased back the door to Abby's bedroom. There, on the bed where Abby had placed her, was Zedd's daughter, still sleeping. Abby stared in disbelief.

"The trickster," the Mother Confessor said. "I told you that was our name for him."

"And not a very flattering one," Zedd grumbled as he stepped up behind them.

"But . . . how?" Abby pressed her fingers to her temples. "I don't understand."

Zedd gestured. Abby saw, for the first time, the body lying just beyond the door out the back. It was Mariska.

"When you showed me the room when we first

came here," Zedd told her, "I laid a few traps for those intent on harm. That woman was killed by those traps because she came here intent on taking my daughter from where she slept."

"You mean it was all an illusion?" Abby was dumbfounded. "Why would you do such a cruel thing? How could you?"

"I am the object of vengeance," the wizard explained. "I didn't want my daughter to pay the price her mother has already paid. Since my spell killed the woman as she tried to harm my daughter, I was able to use a vision of her to accomplish the deception. The enemy knew the woman, and that she acted for Anargo. I used what they expected to see to convince them and to frighten them into running and leaving the prisoners.

"I cast the death spell so that everyone would think they saw my daughter being killed. This way, the enemy thinks my daughter dead, and will have no reason to hunt her or ever again try to harm her. I did it to protect her from the unforeseen."

The sorceress scowled at him. "If it were any but you, Zeddicus, and for any reason but the reason you had, I'd see you brought up on charges for casting such a web as a death spell." She broke into a grin. "Well done, First Wizard."

Outside, the officers all wanted to know what was happening.

"No battle today," Zedd told them. "I've just ended the war."

They cheered with genuine joy. Had Zedd not been the First Wizard, Abby suspected they would have hoisted him on their shoulders. It seemed that there was no one more glad for peace than those whose job it was to fight for it.

Wizard Thomas, looking more humble than Abby had ever seen him, cleared his throat. "Zorander, I . . . I . . . I simply can't believe what my own eyes have seen." His face finally took on its familiar scowl. "But we have people already in near revolt over magic. When news of this spreads, it is only going to make it worse. The demands for relief from magic grow every day and you have fed the fury. With this, we're liable to have revolt on our hands."

"I still want to know why it isn't moving," Delora growled from behind. "I want to know why it's just sitting there, all green and still."

Zedd ignored her and directed his attention to the old wizard. "Thomas, I have a job for you."

He motioned several officers and officials from Aydindril forward, and passed a finger before all their faces, his own turning grim and determined. "I have a job for all of you. The people have reason to fear magic. Today we have seen magic deadly and dangerous. I can understand those fears.

"In appreciation of these fears, I shall grant their wish."

"What!" Thomas scoffed. "You can't end magic, Zorander! Not even you can accomplish such a paradox."

"Not end it," Zedd said. "But give them a place without it. I want you to organize an official delegation large enough to travel all the Midlands with the offer. All those who would quit a world with magic are to move to the lands to the west. There they shall set up new lives free of any magic. I shall insure that magic cannot intrude on their peace."

Thomas threw up his hands. "How can you make such a promise!"

Zedd's arm lifted to point off behind him, to the wall of green fire growing toward the sky. "I shall call up a second wall of death, through which none can pass. On the other side of it shall be a place free of magic. There, people will be able to live their lives without magic.

"I want you all to see that the word is passed through the land. People have until spring to emigrate to the lands west. Thomas, you will warrant that none with magic make the journey. We have books we can use to insure that we purge a place of any with a trace of magic. We can assure that there will be no magic there.

"In the spring, when all who wish have gone to their new homeland, I will seal them off from magic. In one fell swoop, I will satisfy the large majority of the petitions come to us; they will have lives without magic. May the good spirits watch over them, and may they not come to regret their wish granted."

Thomas pointed heatedly at the thing Zedd had brought into the world. "But what about that? What if people go wandering into it in the dark? They will be walking into death."

"Not only in the dark," Zedd said. "Once it has stabilized, it will be hard to see at all. We will have to set up guards to keep people away. We will have to set aside land near the boundary and have men guard the area to keep people out."

"Men?" Abby asked. "You mean you will have to start a corps of boundary wardens?"

"Yes," Zedd said, his eyebrows lifting, "that's a good name for them. Boundary wardens."

Silence settled over those leaning in to hear the wizard's words. The mood had changed and was now serious with the grim matter at hand. Abby couldn't imagine a place without magic, but she knew how vehemently some wished it.

Thomas finally nodded. "Zedd, this time I think you've gotten it right. Sometimes, we must serve the people by not serving them." The others mumbled their agreement, though, like Abby, they thought it a bleak solution.

Zedd straightened. "Then it is decided."

He turned and announced to the crowd the end of the war, and the division to come in which those who had petitioned for years would finally have their petition granted; for those who wished it, a land outside the Midlands, without magic, would be created.

While everyone was chattering about such a mysterious and exotic thing as a land without magic, or cheering and celebrating the end of the war, Abby whispered to Jana to wait with her father a moment. She kissed her daughter and then took the opportunity to pull Zedd aside.

"Zedd, may I speak with you? I have a question."

Zedd smiled and took her by the elbow, urging Abby into her small home. "I'd like to check on my daughter. Come along."

Abby cast caution to the winds and took the Mother Confessor's hand in one of hers, Delora's in the other, and pulled them in with her. They had a right to hear this, too.

"Zedd," Abby asked once they were away from the crowd in her yard, "may I please know the debt your father owed my mother?"

Zedd lifted an eyebrow. "My father owed your mother no debt."

Abby frowned. "But it was a debt of bones, passed down from your father to you, and from my mother to me."

"Oh, it was a debt all right, but not owed to your mother, but by your mother."

"What?" Abby asked in stunned confusion. "What do you mean?"

Zedd smiled. "When your mother was giving birth to you, she was in trouble. You both were dying in the labor. My father used magic to save her. Helsa begged him to save you, too. In order to keep you in the world of the living and out of the Keeper's grasp, without thought to his own safety, he worked far beyond the endurance anyone would expect of a wizard.

"Your mother was a sorceress, and understood the extent of what was involved in saving your life. In appreciation of what my father had done, she swore a debt to him. When she died, the debt passed to you."

Abby, eyes wide, tried to reconcile the whole thing in her mind. Her mother had never told her the nature of the debt.

"But . . . but you mean that it is I who owe the debt to you? You mean that the debt of bones is my burden?"

Zedd pushed open the door to the room where his daughter slept, smiling as he looked in. "The debt is paid, Abby. The bracelet your mother gave you had magic, linking you to the debt. Thank you for my daughter's life.''

Abby glanced to the Mother Confessor. Trickster indeed. ''But why would you help me, if it was really not a debt of bones you owed me? If it was really a debt I owed you?''

Zedd shrugged. ''We reap a reward merely in the act of helping others. We never know how, or if, that reward will come back to us. Helping is the reward; none other is needed nor better.''

Abby watched the beautiful little girl sleeping in the room beyond. ''I am thankful to the good spirits that I could help keep such a life in this world. I may not have the gift, but I can foresee that she will go on to be a person of import, not only for you, but for others.''

Zedd smiled idly as he watched his daughter sleeping. ''I think you may have the gift of prophecy, my dear, for she is already a person who has played a part in bringing a war to an end, and in so doing, saved the lives of countless people.''

The sorceress pointed out the window. ''I still want to know why that thing isn't moving. It was supposed to pass over D'Hara and purge it of all life, to kill them all for what they have done.'' Her scowl deepened. ''Why is it just sitting there?''

Zedd folded his hands. ''It ended the war. That

is enough. The wall is a part of the underworld itself, the world of the dead. Their army will not be able to cross it and make war on us for as long as such a boundary stands.''

''And how long will that be?''

Zedd shrugged. ''Nothing remains forever. For now, there will be peace. The killing is ended.''

The sorceress did not look to be satisfied. ''But they were trying to kill us all!''

''Well, now they can't. Delora, there are those in D'Hara who are innocent, too. Just because Panis Rahl wished to conquer and subjugate us, that does not mean that all the D'Haran people are evil. Many good people in D'Hara have suffered under harsh rule. How could I kill everyone there, including all the people who have caused no harm, and themselves wish only to live their lives in peace?''

Delora wiped a hand across her face. ''Zeddicus, sometimes I don't know about you. Sometimes, you make a lousy wind of death.''

The Mother Confessor stood staring out the window, toward D'Hara. Her violet eyes turned back to the wizard.

''There will be those over there who will be your foes for life because of this, Zedd. You have made bitter enemies with this. You have left them alive.''

''Enemies,'' the wizard said, ''are the price of honor.''

A Song of Ice and Fire

❦

George R. R. Martin

The South

A GAME OF THRONES (1996)
A CLASH OF KINGS (1998)
A DANCE WITH DRAGONS (forthcoming)
THE WINDS OF WINTER (forthcoming)

One of the most recent of the great multivolume fantasy epics is George R. R. Martin's *A Song of Ice and Fire*, which when complete will span four volumes. This immense saga is set in the world of the Seven Kingdoms, a land where seasons have been thrown out of balance, with summer and winter both lasting for years.

As the first book opens, the reader learns that three noble families had conspired to depose their insane king and take control of the kingdom. The Lannisters, the Baratheons, and the Starks all exist in an uneasy truce that is soon broken when the current king, Robert Baratheon, asks Ned Stark to come down from the northern city of Winterfell and help him to rule, giving him the coveted title of Hand of the King, which makes him the second most powerful man of the Seven Kingdoms. Ned's efforts to solve the murder of his predecessor in that post soon embroil him in conflict with the queen and her brothers. The balance of power among the great families is thus unsettled. As the game of thrones grows deadly, even more sinister forces are stirring in the north, behind the great ice wall that protects the Seven Kingdoms and all the realms of men.

A civil war threatens to sweep the land when the Lannisters kill Robert and attempt to seize power, opposed only by the Starks and Baratheons. Meanwhile, the head of the Targaryen family, Viserys, sells his sister into marriage in return for armies that will help him reconquer the Seven Kingdoms.

The forthcoming volumes of the series will depict the gradual unfolding and resolution of the terrible many-sided conflict that will rack' this troubled world.

The story offered here, "The Hedge Knight," takes place about a hundred years prior to the events described in *A Game of Thrones*.

THE HEDGE KNIGHT

❦

A Tale of the Seven Kingdoms
George R. R. Martin

The spring rains had softened the ground, so Dunk had no trouble digging the grave. He chose a spot on the western slope of a low hill, for the old man had always loved to watch the sunset. "Another day done," he would sigh, "and who knows what the morrow will bring us, eh, Dunk?"

Well, one morrow had brought rains that soaked them to the bones, and the one after had brought wet gusty winds, and the next a chill. By the fourth day the old man was too weak to ride. And now he was gone. Only a few days past, he had been singing as they rode, the old song about going to Gulltown to see a fair maid, but instead of Gulltown he'd sung of Ashford. *Off to Ashford to see the fair maid, heigh-ho, heigh-ho,* Dunk thought miserably as he dug.

When the hole was deep enough, he lifted the old man's body in his arms and carried him there. He had been a small man, and slim; stripped of hauberk, helm, and sword belt, he seemed to weigh no more than a bag of leaves. Dunk was hugely tall for his age, a shambling, shaggy, big-boned boy of sixteen or seventeen years (no one was quite certain which) who stood closer to seven feet than to six, and had only just begun to fill out his frame. The old man had often praised his strength. He had always been generous in his praise. It was all he had to give.

He laid him out in the bottom of the grave and stood over him for a time. The smell of rain was in the air again, and he knew he ought to fill the hole before the rain broke, but it was hard to throw dirt down on that tired old face. *There ought to be a septon here, to say some prayers over him, but he only has me.* The old man had taught Dunk all he knew of swords and shields and lances, but had never been much good at teaching him words.

"I'd leave your sword, but it would rust in the ground," he said at last, apologetic. "The gods will give you a new one, I guess. I wish you didn't die, ser." He paused, uncertain what else needed to be said. He didn't know any prayers, not all the way through; the old man had never been much for praying. "You were a true knight, and you never beat me when I didn't deserve it," he finally managed, "except that one time in Maidenpool. It was the inn boy who ate the widow woman's pie, not me, I told you. It don't matter now. The gods keep you, ser." He kicked dirt in the hole, then began to fill it methodically, never looking at the thing at the bottom. *He had a long life*, Dunk thought. *He must have been closer to sixty than to fifty, and how many men can say that?* At least he had lived to see another spring.

The sun was westering as he fed the horses. There were three; his swaybacked stot, the old man's palfrey, and Thunder, his warhorse, who was ridden only in tourney and battle. The big brown stallion was not as swift or strong as he had once been, but he still had his bright eye and fierce spirit, and he was more valuable than everything else Dunk owned. *If I sold Thunder and old Chestnut, and the saddles and bridles too, I'd come away with enough silver to . . .* Dunk frowned. The only life he knew was the life of a hedge knight, riding from keep to keep, taking service with this lord and that lord, fighting in their battles and eating in their halls until the war was done, then moving on. There were tourneys from time to time as well, though less often, and he knew that some hedge knights turned robber during lean winters, though the old man never had.

I could find another hedge knight in need of a squire to tend his animals and clean his mail, he thought, *or might be I could go to some city, to Lannisport or King's Landing, and join the City Watch. Or else . . .*

He had piled the old man's things under an oak. The cloth purse contained three silver stags, nineteen copper pennies, and a chipped garnet; as with most hedge knights, the greatest part of his worldly wealth had been tied up in his horses and weapons. Dunk now owned a chain-mail hauberk that he had scoured the rust off a thousand times. An iron half-helm with a broad nasal and a dent on the left temple. A sword belt of cracked brown leather, and a longsword in a wood-and-leather scabbard. A dagger, a razor, a whetstone. Greaves and gorget, an eight-foot war lance of turned ash topped by a cruel iron point, and an oaken shield with a scarred metal rim, bearing the sigil of Ser Arlan of Pennytree: a winged chalice, silver on brown.

Dunk looked at the shield, scooped up the sword belt, and looked at the shield again. The belt was made for the old man's skinny hips. It would never do for him, no more than the hauberk would. He tied the scabbard to a length of hempen rope, knotted it around his waist, and drew the longsword.

The blade was straight and heavy, good castle-forged steel, the grip soft leather wrapped over wood, the pommel a smooth polished black stone. Plain as it was, the sword felt good in his hand, and Dunk knew how sharp it was, having worked it with whetstone and oilcloth many a night before they went to sleep. *It fits my grip as well as it ever fit his,* he thought to himself, *and there is a tourney at Ashford Meadow.*

Sweetfoot had an easier gait than old Chestnut, but Dunk was still sore and tired when he spied the inn ahead, a tall daub-and-timber building beside a stream. The warm yellow light spilling from its windows looked so inviting that he could not pass it by. *I have three silvers,* he told himself, *enough for a good meal and as much ale as I care to drink.*

As he dismounted, a naked boy emerged dripping from the stream and began to dry himself on a roughspun brown cloak. "Are you the stable-boy?" Dunk asked him. The lad looked to be no more than eight or nine, a pasty-faced skinny thing, his bare feet caked in mud up to the ankle. His hair was the queerest thing about him. He had none. "I'll want my palfrey rubbed down. And oats for all three. Can you tend to them?"

The boy looked at him brazenly. "I could. If I wanted."

Dunk frowned. "I'll have none of that. I am a knight, I'll have you know."

"You don't look to be a knight."

"Do all knights look the same?"

"No, but they don't look like you, either. Your sword belt's made of rope."

"So long as it holds my scabbard, it serves. Now see to my horses. You'll get a copper if you do well, and a clout in the ear if you don't." He did not wait to see how the stableboy took that, but turned away and shouldered through the door.

At this hour, he would have expected the inn to be crowded, but the common room was almost empty. A young lordling in a fine damask mantle was passed out at one table, snoring softly into a pool of spilled wine. Otherwise there was no one. Dunk looked around uncertainly until a stout, short, whey-faced woman emerged from the kitchens and said, "Sit where you like. Is it ale you want, or food?"

"Both." Dunk took a chair by the window, well away from the sleeping man.

"There's good lamb, roasted with a crust of herbs, and some ducks my son shot down. Which will you have?"

He had not eaten at an inn in half a year or more. "Both."

The woman laughed. "Well, you're big enough

for it.'' She drew a tankard of ale and brought it to his table. ''Will you be wanting a room for the night as well?''

''No.'' Dunk would have liked nothing better than a soft straw mattress and a roof above his head, but he needed to be careful with his coin. The ground would serve. ''Some food, some ale, and it's on to Ashford for me. How much farther is it?''

''A day's ride. Bear north when the road forks at the burned mill. Is my boy seeing to your horses, or has he run off again?''

''No, he's there,'' said Dunk. ''You seem to have no custom.''

''Half the town's gone to see the tourney. My own would as well, if I allowed it. They'll have this inn when I go, but the boy would sooner swagger about with soldiers, and the girl turns to sighs and giggles every time a knight rides by. I swear I couldn't tell you why. Knights are built the same as other men, and I never knew a joust to change the price of eggs.'' She eyed Dunk curiously; his sword and shield told her one thing, his rope belt and roughspun tunic quite another. ''You're bound for the tourney yourself?''

He took a sip of the ale before he answered. A nut brown color it was, and thick on the tongue, the way he liked it. ''Aye,'' he said. ''I mean to be a champion.''

"Do you, now?" the innkeep answered, polite enough.

Across the room, the lordling raised his head from the wine puddle. His face had a sallow, unhealthy cast to it beneath a rat's nest of sandy brown hair, and blond stubble crusted his chin. He rubbed his mouth, blinked at Dunk, and said, "I dreamed of you." His hand trembled as he pointed a finger. "You stay away from me, do you hear? You stay *well* away."

Dunk stared at him uncertainly. "My lord?"

The innkeep leaned close. "Never you mind that one, ser. All he does is drink and talk about his dreams. I'll see about that food." She bustled off.

"Food?" The lordling made the word an obscenity. He staggered to his feet, one hand on the table to keep himself from falling. "I'm going to be sick," he announced. The front of his tunic was crusty red with old wine stains. "I wanted a whore, but there's none to be found here. All gone to Ashford Meadow. Gods be good, I need some wine." He lurched unsteadily from the common room, and Dunk heard him climbing steps, singing under his breath.

A sad creature, thought Dunk. *But why did he think he knew me?* He pondered that a moment over his ale.

The lamb was as good as any he had ever eaten,

and the duck was even better, cooked with cherries and lemons and not near as greasy as most. The innkeep brought buttered pease as well, and oaten bread still hot from her oven. *This is what it means to be a knight*, he told himself as he sucked the last bit of meat off the bone. *Good food, and ale whenever I want it, and no one to clout me in the head.* He had a second tankard of ale with the meal, a third to wash it down, and a fourth because there was no one to tell him he couldn't, and when he was done he paid the woman with a silver stag and still got back a fistful of coppers.

It was full dark by the time Dunk emerged. His stomach was full and his purse was a little lighter, but he felt good as he walked to the stables. Ahead, he heard a horse whicker. "Easy, lad," a boy's voice said. Dunk quickened his step, frowning.

He found the stableboy mounted on Thunder and wearing the old man's armor. The hauberk was longer than he was, and he'd had to tilt the helm back on his bald head or else it would have covered his eyes. He looked utterly intent, and utterly absurd. Dunk stopped in the stable door and laughed.

The boy looked up, flushed, vaulted to the ground. "My lord, I did not mean—"

"Thief," Dunk said, trying to sound stern. "Take off that armor, and be glad that Thunder didn't kick you in that fool head. He's a warhorse, not a boy's pony."

The boy took off the helm and flung it to the straw. "I could ride him as well as you," he said, bold as you please.

"Close your mouth, I want none of your insolence. The hauberk too, take it off. What did you think you were doing?"

"How can I tell you, with my mouth closed?" The boy squirmed out of the chain mail and let it fall.

"You can open your mouth to answer," said Dunk. "Now pick up that mail, shake off the dirt, and put it back where you found it. And the half-helm too. Did you feed the horses, as I told you? And rub down Sweetfoot?"

"Yes," the boy said, as he shook straw from the mail. "You're going to Ashford, aren't you? Take me with you, ser."

The innkeep had warned him of this. "And what might your mother say to that?"

"My mother?" The boy wrinkled up his face. "My mother's dead, she wouldn't say anything."

He was surprised. Wasn't the innkeep his mother? Perhaps he was only 'prenticed to her. Dunk's head was a little fuzzy from the ale. "Are you an orphan boy?" he asked uncertainly.

"Are you?" the boy threw back.

"I was once," Dunk admitted. *Till the old man took me in.*

"If you took me, I could squire for you."

"I have no need of a squire," he said.

"Every knight needs a squire," the boy said. "You look as though you need one more than most."

Dunk raised a hand threateningly. "And you look as though you need a clout in the ear, it seems to me. Fill me a sack of oats. I'm off for Ashford . . . alone."

If the boy was frightened, he hid it well. For a moment he stood there defiant, his arms crossed, but just as Dunk was about to give up on him the lad turned and went for the oats.

Dunk was relieved. *A pity I couldn't . . . but he has a good life here at the inn, a better one than he'd have squiring for a hedge knight. Taking him would be no kindness.*

He could still feel the lad's disappointment, though. As he mounted Sweetfoot and took up Thunder's lead, Dunk decided that a copper penny might cheer him. "Here, lad, for your help." He flipped the coin down at him with a smile, but the stableboy made no attempt to catch it. It fell in the dirt between his bare feet, and there he let it lie.

He'll scoop it up as soon as I am gone, Dunk told himself. He turned the palfrey and rode from the inn, leading the other two horses. The trees were bright with moonlight, and the sky was cloudless and speckled with stars. Yet as he headed down the road he could feel the stableboy watching his back, sullen and silent.

The shadows of the afternoon were growing long when Dunk reined up on the edge of broad Ashford Meadow. Three score pavilions had already risen on the grassy field. Some were small, some large; some square, some round; some of sailcloth, some of linen, some of silk; but all were brightly colored, with long banners streaming from their center poles, brighter than a field of wildflowers with rich reds and sunny yellows, countless shades of green and blue, deep blacks and greys and purples.

The old man had ridden with some of these knights; others Dunk knew from tales told in common rooms and round campfires. Though he had never learned the magic of reading or writing, the old man had been relentless when it came to teaching him heraldry, often drilling him as they rode. The nightingales belonged to Lord Caron of the Marches, as skilled with the high harp as he was with a lance. The crowned stag was for Ser Lyonel Baratheon, the Laughing Storm. Dunk picked out the Tarly huntsman, House Dondarrion's purple lightning, the red apple of the Fossoways. There roared the lion of Lannister gold on crimson, and there the dark green sea turtle of the Estermonts swam across a pale green field. The brown tent beneath red stallion could only belong to Ser Otho Bracken, who was called the Brute of Bracken since slaying Lord Quentyn Blackwood three years past during a tourney at King's Landing. Dunk heard that Ser Otho struck so hard with the blunted longaxe that he stove in the visor of Lord Blackwood's helm and the face beneath it. He saw some Blackwood banners as well, on the west edge of the meadow, as distant from Ser Otho as they could be. Marbrand, Mallister, Cargyll, Westerling, Swann, Mullendore, Hightower, Florent, Frey, Penrose, Stokeworth, Darry, Parren, Wylde; it seemed as though every lordly house of the west and south had sent a knight or three to Ashford to see the fair maid and brave the lists in her honor.

Yet however fine their pavilions were to look upon, he knew there was no place there for him. A threadbare wool cloak would be all the shelter he had tonight. While the lords and great knights dined on capons and suckling pigs, Dunk's supper would be a hard, stringy piece of salt beef. He knew full well that if he made his camp upon that gaudy field, he would need to suffer both silent scorn and open mockery. A few perhaps would treat him kindly, yet in a way that was almost worse.

A hedge knight must hold tight to his pride.

Without it, he was no more than a sellsword. *I must earn my place in that company. If I fight well, some lord may take me into his household. I will ride in noble company then, and eat fresh meat every night in a castle hall, and raise my own pavilion at tourneys. But first I must do well.* Reluctantly, he turned his back on the tourney grounds and led his horses into the trees.

On the outskirts of the great meadow a good half mile from town and castle he found a place where a bend in a brook had formed a deep pool. Reeds grew thick along its edge, and a tall leafy elm presided over all. The spring grass there was as green as any knight's banner and soft to the touch. It was a pretty spot, and no one had yet laid claim to it. *This will be my pavilion*, Dunk told himself, *a pavilion roofed with leaves, greener even than the banners of the Tyrells and the Estermonts.*

His horses came first. After they had been tended, he stripped and waded into the pool to wash away the dust of travel. "A true knight is cleanly as well as godly," the old man always said, insisting that they wash themselves head to heels every time the moon turned, whether they smelled sour or not. Now that he was a knight, Dunk vowed he would do the same.

He sat naked under the elm while he dried, enjoying the warmth of the spring air on his skin as he watched a dragonfly move lazily among the reeds. *Why would they name it a dragonfly?* he wondered. *It looks nothing like a dragon.* Not that Dunk had ever seen a dragon. The old man had, though. Dunk had heard the story half a hundred times, how Ser Arlan had been just a little boy when his grandfather had taken him to King's Landing, and how they'd seen the last dragon there the year before it died. She'd been a green female, small and stunted, her wings withered. None of her eggs had ever hatched. "Some say King Aegon poisoned her," the old man would tell. "The third Aegon that would be, not King Daeron's father, but the one they named Dragonbane, or Aegon the Unlucky. He was afraid of dragons, for he'd seen his uncle's beast devour his own mother. The summers have been shorter since the last dragon died, and the winters longer and crueler."

The air began to cool as the sun dipped below the tops of the trees. When Dunk felt gooseflesh prickling his arms, he beat his tunic and breeches against the trunk of the elm to knock off the worst of the dirt, and donned them once again. On the morrow he could seek out the master of the games and enroll his name, but he had other matters he ought to look into tonight if he hoped to challenge.

He did not need to study his reflection in the water to know that he did not look much a knight, so he slung Ser Arlan's shield across his back to display the sigil. Hobbling the horses, Dunk left them to crop the thick green grass beneath the elm as he set out on foot for the tourney grounds.

In normal times the meadow served as a commons for the folk of Ashford town across the river, but now it was transformed. A second town had sprung up overnight, a town of silk instead of stone, larger and fairer than its elder sister. Dozens of merchants had erected their stalls along the edge of the field, selling felts and fruits, belts and boots, hides and hawks, earthenware, gemstones, pewterwork, spices, feathers, and all manner of other goods. Jugglers, puppeteers, and magicians wandered among the crowds plying their trades . . . as did the whores and cutpurses. Dunk kept a wary hand on his coin.

When he caught the smell of sausages sizzling over a smoky fire, his mouth began to water. He bought one with a copper from his pouch, and a horn of ale to wash it down. As he ate he watched a painted wooden knight battle a painted wooden dragon. The puppeteer who worked the dragon was good to watch too; a tall drink of water, with the olive skin and black hair of Dorne. She was slim as a lance with no breasts to speak of, but Dunk liked her face and the way her fingers made the dragon snap and slither at the end of its strings. He would have tossed the girl a copper if he'd had one to spare, but just now he needed every coin.

There were armorers among the merchants, as he had hoped. A Tyroshi with a forked blue beard was selling ornate helms, gorgeous fantastical things wrought in the shapes of birds and beasts and chased with gold and silver. Elsewhere he found a swordmaker hawking cheap steel blades, and another whose work was much finer, but it was not a sword he lacked.

The man he needed was all the way down at the end of the row, a shirt of fine chain mail and a pair of lobstered steel gauntlets displayed on the table before him. Dunk inspected them closely. "You do good work," he said.

"None better." A stumpy man, the smith was no more than five feet tall, yet wide as Dunk about the chest and arms. He had a black beard, huge hands, and no trace of humility.

"I need armor for the tourney," Dunk told him. "A suit of good mail, with gorget, greaves, and greathelm." The old man's halfhelm would fit his head, but he wanted more protection for his face than a nasal bar alone could provide.

The armorer looked him up and down. "You're a big one, but I've armored bigger." He came out from behind the table. "Kneel, I want to measure those shoulders. Aye, and that thick neck o' yours." Dunk knelt, The armorer laid a length of knotted rawhide along his shoulders, grunted, slipped it about his throat, grunted again. "Lift your arm. No, the right." He grunted a third time. "Now you can stand." The inside of a leg, the thickness of his calf, and the size of his waist elicited further grunts. "I have some pieces in me wagon that might do for you," the man said when he was done. "Nothing prettied up with gold nor silver, mind you, just good steel, strong and plain. I make helms that look like helms, not winged pigs and queer foreign fruits, but mine will serve you better if you take a lance in the face."

"That's all I want," said Dunk. "How much?"

"Eight hundred stags, for I'm feeling kindly."

"*Eight hundred?*" It was more than he had expected. "I . . . I could trade you some old armor, made for a smaller man . . . a halfhelm, a mail hauberk . . ."

"Steely Pate sells only his own work," the man declared, "but it might be I could make use of the metal. If it's not too rusted, I'll take it and armor you for six hundred."

Dunk could beseech Pate to give him the armor on trust, but he knew what sort of answer that request would likely get. He had traveled with the old man long enough to learn that merchants were notoriously mistrustful of hedge knights, some of whom were little better than robbers. "I'll give you two silvers now, and the armor and the rest of the coin on the morrow."

The armorer studied him a moment. "Two silvers buys you a day. After that, I sell me work to the next man."

Dunk scooped the stags out of his pouch and placed them in the armorer's callused hand. "You'll get it all. I mean to be a champion here."

"Do you?" Pate bit one of the coins. "And these others, I suppose they all came just to cheer you on?"

The moon was well up by the time he turned his steps back toward his elm. Behind him, Ashford Meadow was ablaze with torchlight. The sounds of song and laughter drifted across the grass, but his own mood was somber. He could think of only one way to raise the coin for his armor. And if he should be defeated . . . "One victory is all I need," he muttered aloud. "That's not so much to hope for."

Even so, the old man would never have hoped for it. Ser Arlan had not ridden a tilt since the day he had been unhorsed by the Prince of Dragonstone in a tourney at Storm's End, many years before. "It is not every man who can boast that he broke seven lances against the finest knight in the Seven Kingdoms,'' he would say. ''I could never hope to do better, so why should I try?''

Dunk had suspected that Ser Arlan's age had more to do with it than the Prince of Dragonstone did, but he never dared say as much. The old man had his pride, even at the last. *I am quick and strong, he always said so, what was true for him need not be true for me,* he told himself stubbornly.

He was moving through a patch of weed, chewing over his chances in his head, when he saw the flicker of firelight through the bushes. *What is this?* Dunk did not stop to think. Suddenly his sword was in his hand and he was crashing through the grass.

He burst out roaring and cursing, only to jerk to a sudden halt at the sight of the boy beside the campfire. ''You!'' He lowered the sword. ''What are you doing here?''

''Cooking a fish,'' said the bald boy. ''Do you want some?''

''I meant, how did you *get* here? Did you steal a horse?''

''I rode in the back of a cart, with a man who was bringing some lambs to the castle for my lord of Ashford's table.''

''Well, you'd best see if he's gone yet, or find another cart. I won't have you here.''

''You can't make me go,'' the boy said, impertinent. ''I'd had enough of that inn.''

"I'll have no more insolence from you," Dunk warned. "I should throw you over my horse right now and take you home."

"You'd need to ride all the way to King's Landing," said the boy. "You'd miss the tourney."

King's Landing. For a moment Dunk wondered if he was being mocked, but the boy had no way of knowing that he had been born in King's Landing as well. *Another wretch from Flea Bottom, like as not, and who can blame him for wanting out of that place?*

He felt foolish standing there with sword in hand over an eight-year-old orphan. He sheathed it, glowering so the boy would see that he would suffer no nonsense. *I ought to give him a good beating at the least*, he thought, but the child looked so pitiful he could not bring himself to hit him. He glanced around the camp. The fire was burning merrily within a neat circle of rocks. The horses had been brushed, and clothes were hanging from the elm, drying above the flames. "What are those doing there?"

"I washed them," the boy said. "And I groomed the horses, made the fire, and caught this fish. I would have raised your pavilion, but I couldn't find one."

"There's my pavilion." Dunk swept a hand above his head, at the branches of the tall elm that loomed above them.

"That's a tree," the boy said, unimpressed.

"It's all the pavilion a true knight needs. I would sooner sleep under the stars than in some smoky tent."

"What if it rains?"

"The tree will shelter me."

"Trees leak."

Dunk laughed. "So they do. Well, if truth be told, I lack the coin for a pavilion. And you'd best turn that fish, or it will be burned on the bottom and raw on the top. You'd never make a kitchen boy."

"I would if I wanted," the boy said, but he turned the fish.

"What happened to your hair?" Dunk asked of him.

"The maesters shaved it off." Suddenly self-conscious, the boy pulled up the hood of his dark brown cloak, covering his head.

Dunk had heard that they did that sometimes, to treat lice or rootworms or certain sicknesses. "Are you ill?"

"No," said the boy. "What's your name?"

"Dunk," he said.

The wretched boy laughed aloud, as if that was the funniest thing he'd ever heard. "*Dunk?*" he said. "Ser Dunk? That's no name for a knight. Is it short for Duncan?"

Was it? The old man had called him just *Dunk* for as long as he could recall, and he did not remember much of his life before. "Duncan, yes," he said. "Ser Duncan of . . ." Dunk had no other name, nor any house; Ser Arlan had found him living wild in the stews and alleys of Flea Bottom. He had never known his father or mother. What was he to say? "Ser Duncan of Flea Bottom" did not sound very knightly. He could take Pennytree, but what if they asked him where it was? Dunk had never been to Pennytree, nor had the old man talked much about it. He frowned for a moment, and then blurted out, "Ser Duncan the Tall." He *was* tall, no one could dispute that, and it sounded puissant.

Though the little sneak did not seem to think so. "I have never heard of any Ser Duncan the Tall."

"Do you know every knight in the Seven Kingdoms, then?"

The boy looked at him boldly. "The good ones."

"I'm as good as any. After the tourney, they'll all know that. Do *you* have a name, thief?"

The boy hesitated. "Egg," he said.

Dunk did not laugh. *His head does look like an egg. Small boys can be cruel, and grown men as well.* "Egg," he said, "I should beat you bloody and send you on your way, but the truth is, I have no pavilion and I have no squire either. If you'll swear to do as you're told, I'll let you serve me for the tourney. After that, well, we'll see. If I decide you're worth your keep, you'll have clothes on your back and food in your belly. The clothes might be roughspun and the food salt beef and salt fish, and maybe some venison from time to time where there are no foresters about, but you won't go hungry. And I promise not to beat you except when you deserve it."

Egg smiled. "Yes, my lord."

"*Ser*," Dunk corrected. "I am only a hedge knight." He wondered if the old man was looking down on him. *I will teach him the arts of battle, the same as you taught me, ser. He seems a likely lad, might be one day he'll make a knight.*

The fish was still a little raw on the inside when they ate it, and the boy had not removed all the bones, but it still tasted a world better than hard salt beef.

Egg soon fell asleep beside the dying fire. Dunk lay on his back nearby, his big hands behind his head, gazing up at the night sky. He could hear distant music from the tourney grounds, half a mile away. The stars were everywhere, thousands and thousands of them. One fell as he was watching, a bright green streak that flashed across the black and then was gone.

A falling star brings luck to him who sees it, Dunk thought. *But the rest of them are all in their pavilions by now, staring up at silk instead of sky. So the luck is mine alone.*

In the morning, he woke to the sound of a cock crowing. Egg was still there, curled up beneath the old man's second-best cloak. *Well, the boy did not run off during the night, that's a start.* He prodded him awake with his foot. "Up. There's work to do." The boy rose quick enough, rubbing his eyes. "Help me saddle Sweetfoot," Dunk told him.

"What about breakfast?"

"There's salt beef. *After* we're done."

"I'd sooner eat the horse," Egg said. "Ser."

"You'll eat my fist if you don't do as you're told. Get the brushes. They're in the saddle sack. Yes, that one."

Together they brushed out the palfrey's sorrel coat, hefted Ser Arlan's best saddle over her back, and cinched it tight. Egg was a good worker once he put his mind to it, Dunk saw.

"I expect I'll be gone most of the day," he told the boy as he mounted. "You're to stay here and put the camp in order. Make sure no *other* thieves come nosing about."

"Can I have a sword to run them off with?" Egg asked. He had blue eyes, Dunk saw, very dark, almost purple. His bald head made them seem huge, somehow.

"No," said Dunk. "A knife's enough. And you had best be here when I come back, do you hear me? Rob me and run off and I'll hunt you down, I swear I will. With dogs."

"You don't have any dogs," Egg pointed out.

"I'll get some," said Dunk. "Just for you." He turned Sweetfoot's head toward the meadow and moved off at a brisk trot, hoping the threat would be enough to keep the boy honest. Save for the clothes on his back, the armor in his sack, and the horse beneath him, everything Dunk owned in the world was back at that camp. *I am a great fool to trust the boy so far, but it is no more than the old man did for me*, he reflected. *The Mother must have sent him to me so that I could pay my debt.*

As he crossed the field, he heard the ring of hammers from the riverside, where carpenters were nailing together jousting barriers and raising a lofty viewing stand. A few new pavilions were going up as well, while the knights who had come earlier slept off last night's revels or sat to break their fasts. Dunk could smell woodsmoke, and bacon as well.

To the north of the meadow flowed the river Cockleswent, a vassal stream to the mighty Mander. Beyond the shallow ford lay town and castle.

Dunk had seen many a market town during his journeys with the old man. This was prettier than most; the whitewashed houses with their thatched roofs had an inviting aspect to them. When he was smaller, he used to wonder what it would be like to live in such a place; to sleep every night with a roof over your head, and wake every morning with the same walls wrapped around you. *It may be that soon I'll know. Aye, and Egg too.* It could happen. Stranger things happened every day.

Ashford Castle was a stone structure built in the shape of a triangle, with round towers rising thirty feet tall at each point and thick crenellated walls running between. Orange banners flew from its battlements, displaying the white sun-and-chevron sigil of its lord. Men-at-arms in orange-and-white livery stood outside the gates with halberds, watching people come and go, seemingly more intent on joking with a pretty milkmaid than in keeping anyone out. Dunk reined up in front of the short, bearded man he took for their captain and asked for the master of the games.

"It's Plummer you want, he's steward here. I'll show you."

Inside the yard, a stableboy took Sweetfoot for him. Dunk slung Ser Arlan's battered shield over a shoulder and followed the guards captain back of the stables to a turret built into an angle of the curtain wall. Steep stone steps led up to the wall-walk. "Come to enter your master's name for the lists?" the captain asked as they climbed.

"It's my own name I'll be putting in."

"Is it now?" Was the man smirking? Dunk was not certain. "That door there. I'll leave you to it and get back to my post."

When Dunk pushed open the door, the steward was sitting at a trestle table, scratching on a piece of parchment with a quill. He had thinning grey hair and a narrow pinched face. "Yes?" he said, looking up. "What do you want, man?"

Dunk pulled shut the door. "Are you Plummer the steward? I came for the tourney. To enter the lists."

Plummer pursed his lips. "My lord's tourney is a contest for knights. Are you a knight?"

He nodded, wondering if his ears were red.

"A knight with a name, mayhaps?"

"Dunk." Why had he said *that*? "Ser Duncan. The Tall."

"And where might you be from, Ser Duncan the Tall?"

"Everyplace. I was squire to Ser Arlan of Pennytree since I was five or six. This is his shield." He showed it to the steward. "He was coming to the tourney, but he caught a chill and died, so I came in his stead. He knighted me before he passed, with his own sword." Dunk drew the longsword and laid it on the scarred wooden table between them.

The master of the lists gave the blade no more than a glance. "A sword it is, for a certainty. I have never heard of this Arlan of Pennytree, however. You were his squire, you say?"

"He always said he meant for me to be a knight, as he was. When he was dying he called for his longsword and bade me kneel. He touched me once on my right shoulder and once on my left, and said some words, and when I got up he said I was a knight."

"Hmpf." The man Plummer rubbed his nose. "Any knight can make a knight, it is true, though it is more customary to stand a vigil and be anointed by a septon before taking your vows. Were there any witnesses to your dubbing?"

"Only a robin, up in a thorn tree. I heard it as the old man was saying the words. He charged me to be a good knight and true, to obey the seven gods, defend the weak and innocent, serve my lord faithfully and defend the realm with all my might, and I swore that I would."

"No doubt." Plummer did not deign to call him *ser*, Dunk could not help but notice. "I shall need to consult with Lord Ashford. Will you or your late master be known to any of the good knights here assembled?"

Dunk thought a moment. "There was a pavilion flying the banner of House Dondarrion? The black, with purple lightning?"

"That would be Ser Manfred, of that House."

"Ser Arlan served his lord father in Dorne, three years past. Ser Manfred might remember me."

"I would advise you to speak to him. If he will vouch for you, bring him here with you on the morrow, at this same time."

"As you say, m'lord." He started for the door.

"Ser Duncan," the steward called after him.

Dunk turned back.

"You are aware," the man said, "that those vanquished in tourney forfeit their arms, armor, and horse to the victors, and must needs ransom them back?"

"I know."

"And do you have the coin to pay such ransom?"

Now he *knew* his ears were red. "I won't have need of coin," he said, praying it was true. *All I need is one victory. If I win my first tilt, I'll have the loser's armor and horse, or his gold, and I can stand a loss myself.*

He walked slowly down the steps, reluctant to get on with what he must do next. In the yard, he collared one of the stableboys. "I must speak with Lord Ashford's master of horse."

"I'll find him for you."

It was cool and dim in the stables. An unruly grey stallion snapped at him as he passed, but Sweetfoot only whickered softly and nuzzled his hand when he raised it to her nose. "You're a good girl, aren't you?" he murmured. The old man always said that a knight should never love a horse, since more than a few were like to die under him, but he never heeded his own counsel either. Dunk had often seen him spend his last copper on an apple for old Chestnut or some oats for Sweetfoot and Thunder. The palfrey had been Ser Arlan's riding horse, and she had borne him tirelessly over thousands of miles, all up and down the Seven Kingdoms. Dunk felt as though he were betraying an old friend, but what choice did he have? Chestnut was too old to be worth much of anything, and Thunder must carry him in the lists.

Some time passed before the master of horse deigned to appear. As he waited, Dunk heard a blare of trumpets from the walls, and a voice in the yard. Curious, he led Sweetfoot to the stable door to see what was happening. A large party of knights and mounted archers poured through the gates, a hundred men at least, riding some of the most splendid horses that Dunk had ever seen. *Some great lord has come.* He grabbed the arm of a stableboy as he ran past. "Who are they?"

The boy looked at him queerly. "Can't you see the banners?" He wrenched free and hurried off.

The banners . . . As Dunk turned his head, a gust of wind lifted the black silk pennon atop the tall staff, and the fierce three-headed dragon of House Targaryen seemed to spread its wings, breathing scarlet fire. The banner-bearer was a tall knight in white scale armor chased with gold, a pure white cloak streaming from his shoulders. Two of the other riders were armored in white from head to heel as well. *Kingsguard knights with the royal banner.* Small wonder Lord Ashford and his sons came hurrying out the doors of the keep, and the fair maid too, a short girl with yellow hair and a round pink face. *She does not seem so fair to me,* Dunk thought. The puppet girl was prettier.

"Boy, let go of that nag and see to my horse."

A rider had dismounted in front of the stables. *He is talking to me,* Dunk realized. "I am not a stableboy, m'lord."

"Not clever enough?" The speaker wore a black cloak bordered in scarlet satin, but underneath was raiment bright as flame, all reds and yellows and golds. Slim and straight as a dirk, though only of middling height, he was near Dunk's own age. Curls of silver-gold hair framed a face sculpted and imperious; high brow and sharp cheekbones, straight nose, pale smooth skin without blemish.

His eyes were a deep violet color. "If you cannot manage a horse, fetch me some wine and a pretty wench."

"I . . . m'lord, pardons, I'm no serving man either. I have the honor to be a knight."

"Knighthood has fallen on sad days," said the princeling, but then one of the stableboys came rushing up, and he turned away to hand him the reins of his palfrey, a splendid blood bay. Dunk was forgotten in an instant. Relieved, he slunk back inside the stables to wait for the master of horse. He felt ill-at-ease enough around the lords in their pavilions, he had no business speaking to princes.

That the beautiful stripling was a prince he had no doubt. The Targaryens were the blood of lost Valyria across the seas, and their silver-gold hair and violet eyes set them apart from common men. Dunk knew Prince Baelor was older, but the youth might well have been one of his sons: Valarr, who was often called "the Young Prince" to set him apart from his father, or Matarys, "the Even Younger Prince," as old Lord Swann's fool had named him once. There were other princelings as well, cousins to Valarr and Matarys. Good King Daeron had four grown sons, three with sons of their own. The line of the dragonkings had almost died out during his father's day, but it was commonly said that Daeron II and his sons had left it secure for all time.

"You. Man. You asked for me." Lord Ashford's master of horse had a red face made redder by his orange livery, and a brusque manner of speaking. "What is it? I have no time for—"

"I want to sell this palfrey," Dunk broke in quickly, before the man could dismiss him. "She's a good horse, sure of foot—"

"I have no time, I tell you." The man gave Sweetfoot no more than a glance. "My lord of Ashford has no need of such. Take her to the town, perhaps Henly will give you a silver or three." That quick, he was turning away.

"Thank you, m'lord," Dunk said before he could go. "M'lord, has the king come?"

The master of horse laughed at him. "No, thank the gods. This infestation of princes is trial enough. Where am I going to find the stalls for all these animals? And fodder?" He strode off shouting at his stableboys.

By the time Dunk left the stable, Lord Ashford had escorted his princely guests into the hall, but two of the Kingsguard knights in their white armor and snowy cloaks still lingered in the yard, talking with the captain of the guard. Dunk halted before them. "M'lords, I am Ser Duncan the Tall."

"Well met, Ser Duncan," answered the bigger of the white knights. "I am Ser Roland Crakehall, and this is my Sworn Brother, Ser Donnel of Dus-kendale."

The seven champions of the Kingsguard were the most puissant warriors in all the Seven Kingdoms, saving only perhaps the crown prince, Baelor Breakspear himself. "Have you come to enter the lists?" Dunk asked anxiously.

"It would not be fitting for us to ride against those we are sworn to protect," answered Ser Donnel, red of hair and beard.

"Prince Valarr has the honor to be one of Lady Ashford's champions," explained Ser Roland, "and two of his cousins mean to challenge. The rest of us have come only to watch."

Relieved, Dunk thanked the white knights for their kindness, and rode out through the castle gates before another prince should think to accost him. *Three princelings*, he pondered as he turned the palfrey toward the streets of Ashford town. Valarr was the eldest son of Prince Baelor, second in line to the Iron Throne, but Dunk did not know how much of his father's fabled prowess with lance and sword he might have inherited. About the other Targaryen princes he knew even less. *What will I do if I have to ride against a prince? Will I even be allowed to challenge one so highborn?* He did not know the answer. The old man had often said he was thick as a castle wall, and just now he felt it.

*   *   *

Henly liked the look of Sweetfoot well enough until he heard Dunk wanted to sell her. Then all the stableman could see in her were faults. He offered three hundred silvers. Dunk said he must have three thousand. After much arguing and cursing, they settled at seven hundred fifty silver stags. That was a deal closer to Henly's starting price than to Dunk's, which made him feel the loser in the tilt, but the stableman would go no higher, so in the end he had no choice but to yield. A second argument began when Dunk declared that the price did not include the saddle, and Henly insisted that it had.

Finally it was all settled. As Henly left to fetch his coin, Dunk stroked Sweetfoot's mane and told her to be brave. "If I win, I'll come back and buy you again, I promise." He had no doubt that all the palfrey's flaws would vanish in the intervening days, and she would be worth twice what she was today.

The stableman gave him three gold pieces and the rest in silver. Dunk bit one of the gold coins and smiled. He had never tasted gold before, nor handled it. "Dragons," men called the coins, since they were stamped with the three-headed dragon of House Targaryen on one side. The other bore the likeness of the king. Two of the coins Henly gave him had King Daeron's face; the third was older,

well worn, and showed a different man. His name
was there under his head, but Dunk could not read
the letters. Gold had been shaved off its edges too,
he saw. He pointed this out to Henly, and loudly.
The stableman grumbled, but handed over another
few silvers and a fistful of coppers to make up the
weight. Dunk handed a few of the coppers right
back, and nodded at Sweetfoot. ''That's for her,''
he said. ''See that she has some oats tonight. Aye,
and an apple too.''

With the shield on his arm and the sack of old
armor slung over his shoulder, Dunk set out on foot
through the sunny streets of Ashford town. The heft
of all that coin in his pouch made him feel queer;
almost giddy on one hand, and anxious on the
other. The old man had never trusted him with
more than a coin or two at a time. He could live a
year on this much money. *And what will I do when
it's gone, sell Thunder?* That road ended in beggary
or outlawry. *This chance will never come again, I
must risk all.*

By the time he splashed back across the ford to
the south bank of the Cockleswent, the morning
was almost done and the tourney grounds had come
to life once more. The winesellers and sausage
makers were doing a brisk trade, a dancing bear
was shuffling along to his master's playing as a
singer sang ''The Bear, the Bear, and the Maiden

Fair,'' jugglers were juggling, and the puppeteers were just finishing another fight.

Dunk stopped to watch the wooden dragon slain. When the puppet knight cut its head off and the red sawdust spilled out onto the grass, he laughed aloud and threw the girl two coppers. ''One for last night,'' he called. She caught the coins in the air and threw him back a smile as sweet as any he had ever seen.

Is it me she smiles at, or the coins? Dunk had never been with a girl, and they made him nervous. Once, three years past, when the old man's purse was full after half a year in the service of blind Lord Florent, he'd told Dunk the time had come to take him to a brothel and make him a man. He'd been drunk, though, and when he was sober he did not remember. Dunk had been too embarrassed to remind him. He was not certain he wanted a whore anyway. If he could not have a highborn maiden like a proper knight, he wanted one who at least liked him more than his silver.

''Will you drink a horn of ale?'' he asked the puppet girl as she was scooping the sawdust blood back into her dragon. ''With me, I mean? Or a sausage? I had a sausage last night, and it was good. They're made with pork, I think.''

''I thank you, m'lord, but we have another show.'' The girl rose, and ran off to the fierce fat

Dornishwoman who worked the puppet knight while Dunk stood there feeling stupid. He liked the way she ran, though. *A pretty girl, and tall. I would not have to kneel to kiss that one.* He knew how to kiss. A tavern girl had showed him one night in Lannisport, a year ago, but she'd been so short she had to sit on the table to reach his lips. The memory made his ears burn. What a great fool he was. It was jousting he should be thinking about, not kissing.

Lord Ashford's carpenters were whitewashing the waist-high wooden barriers that would separate the jousters. Dunk watched them work awhile. There were five lanes, arrayed north to south so none of the competitors would ride with the sun in his eyes. A three-tiered viewing stand had been raised on the eastern side of the lists, with an orange canopy to shield the lords and ladies from rain and sun. Most would sit on benches, but four high-backed chairs had been erected in the center of the platform, for Lord Ashford, the fair maid, and the visiting princes.

On the eastern verge of the meadow, a quintain had been set up and a dozen knights were tilting at it, sending the pole arm spinning every time they struck the splintered shield suspended from one end. Dunk watched the Brute of Bracken take his turn, and then Lord Caron of the Marches. *I do not have as good a seat as any of them,* he thought uneasily.

Elsewhere, men were training afoot, going at each other with wooden swords while their squires stood shouting ribald advice. Dunk watched a stocky youth try to hold off a muscular knight who seemed lithe and quick as a mountain cat. Both had the red apple of the Fossoways painted on their shields, but the younger man's was soon hacked and chipped to pieces. "Here's an apple that's not ripe yet," the older said as he slammed the other's helm. The younger Fossoway was bruised and bloody by the time he yielded, but his foe was hardly winded. He raised his visor, looked about, saw Dunk, and said, "You there. Yes, you, the big one. Knight of the winged chalice. Is that a long-sword you wear?"

"It is mine by rights," Dunk said defensively. "I am Ser Duncan the Tall."

"And I Ser Steffon Fossoway. Would you care to try me, Ser Duncan the Tall? It would be good to have someone new to cross swords with. My cousin's not ripe yet, as you've seen."

"Do it, Ser Duncan," urged the beaten Fossoway as he removed his helm. "I may not be ripe, but my good cousin is rotten to the core. Knock the seeds out of him."

Dunk shook his head. Why were these lordlings

involving him in their quarrel? He wanted no part of it. "I thank you, ser, but I have matters to attend." He was uncomfortable carrying so much coin. The sooner he paid Steely Pate and got his armor, the happier he would be.

Ser Steffon looked at him scornfully. "The hedge knight has matters." He glanced about and found another likely opponent loitering nearby. "Ser Grance, well met. Come try me. I know every feeble trick my cousin Raymun has mastered, and it seems that Ser Duncan needs to return to the hedges. Come, come."

Dunk stalked away red-faced. He did not have many tricks himself, feeble or otherwise, and he did not want anyone to see him fight until the tourney. The old man always said that the better you knew your foe, the easier it was to best him. Knights like Ser Steffon had sharp eyes to find a man's weakness at a glance. Dunk was strong and quick, and his weight and reach were in his favor, but he did not believe for a moment that his skills were the equal of these others. Ser Arlan had taught him as best he could, but the old man had never been the greatest of knights even when young. Great knights did not live their lives in the hedges, or die by the side of a muddy road. *That will not happen to me,* Dunk vowed. *I will show them that I can be more than a hedge knight.*

"Ser Duncan." The younger Fossoway hurried to catch him. "I should not have urged you to try my cousin. I was angry with his arrogance, and you are so large, I thought . . . well, it was wrong of me. You wear no armor. He would have broken your hand if he could, or a knee. He likes to batter men in the training yard, so they will be bruised and vulnerable later, should he meet them in the lists."

"He did not break you."

"No, but I am his own blood, though his is the senior branch of the apple tree, as he never ceases to remind me. I am Raymun Fossoway."

"Well met. Will you and your cousin ride in the tourney?"

"He will, for a certainty. As to me, would that I could. I am only a squire as yet. My cousin has promised to knight me, but insists that I am not ripe yet." Raymun had a square face, a pug nose, and short woolly hair, but his smile was engaging. "You have the look of a challenger, it seems to me. Whose shield do you mean to strike?"

"It makes no difference," said Dunk. That was what you were supposed to say, though it made all the difference in the world. "I will not enter the lists until the third day."

"And by then some of the champions will have fallen, yes," Raymun said. "Well, may the Warrior smile on you, ser."

"And you." *If he is only a squire, what business do I have being a knight? One of us is a fool.* The silver in Dunk's pouch clinked with every step, but he could lose it all in a heartbeat, he knew. Even the rules of this tourney worked against him, making it very unlikely that he would face a green or feeble foe.

There were a dozen different forms a tourney might follow, according to the whim of the lord who hosted it. Some were mock battles between teams of knights, others wild melees where the glory went to the last fighter left standing. Where individual combats were the rule, pairings were sometimes determined by lot, and sometimes by the master of the games.

Lord Ashford was staging this tourney to celebrate his daughter's thirteenth nameday. The fair maid would sit by her father's side as the reigning Queen of Love and Beauty. Five champions wearing her favors would defend her. All others must perforce be challengers, but any man who could defeat one of the champions would take his place and stand as a champion himself, until such time as another challenger unseated him. At the end of three days of jousting, the five who remained would determine whether the fair maid would retain the crown of Love and Beauty, or whether another would wear it in her place.

Dunk stared at the grassy lists and the empty chairs on the viewing stand and pondered his chances. One victory was all he needed; then he could name himself one of the champions of Ashford Meadow, if only for an hour. The old man had lived nigh on sixty years and had never been a champion. *It is not too much to hope for, if the gods are good.* He thought back on all the songs he had heard, songs of blind Symeon Star-Eyes and noble Serwyn of the Mirror Shield, of Prince Aemon the Dragonknight, Ser Ryam Redwyne, and Florian the Fool. They had all won victories against foes far more terrible than any he would face. *But they were great heroes, brave men of noble birth, except for Florian. And what am I? Dunk of Flea Bottom? Or Ser Duncan the Tall?*

He supposed he would learn the truth of that soon enough. He hefted the sack of armor and turned his feet toward the merchants' stalls, in search of Steely Pate.

Egg had worked manfully at the campsite. Dunk was pleased; he had been half afraid his squire would run off again. "Did you get a good price for your palfrey?" the boy asked.

"How did you know I'd sold her?"

"You rode off and walked back, and if robbers had stolen her you'd be more angry than you are."

"I got enough for this." Dunk took out his new armor to show the boy. "If you're ever to be a knight, you'll need to know good steel from bad. Look here, this is fine work. This mail is double-chain, each link bound to two others, see? It gives more protection than single-chain. And the helm, Pate's rounded the top, see how it curves? A sword or an axe will slide off, where they might bite through a flat-topped helm." Dunk lowered the greathelm over his head. "How does it look?"

"There's no visor," Egg pointed out.

"There's air holes. Visors are points of weakness." Steely Pate had said as much. "If you knew how many knights have taken an arrow in the eye as they lifted their visor for a suck o' cool air, you'd never want one," he'd told Dunk.

"There's no crest either," said Egg. "It's just plain."

Dunk lifted off the helm. "Plain is fine for the likes of me. See how bright the steel is? It will be your task to keep it that way. You know how to scour mail?"

"In a barrel of sand," said the boy, "but you don't have a barrel. Did you buy a pavilion too, ser?"

"I didn't get *that* good a price." *The boy is too bold for his own good, I ought to beat that out of him.* He knew he would not, though. He liked the boldness. He needed to be bolder himself. *My squire is braver than I am, and more clever.* "You did well here, Egg," Dunk told him. "On the morrow, you'll come with me. Have a look at the tourney grounds. We'll buy oats for the horses and fresh bread for ourselves. Maybe a bit of cheese as well, they were selling good cheese at one of the stalls."

"I won't need to go into the castle, will I?"

"Why not? One day, I mean to live in a castle. I hope to win a place above the salt before I'm done."

The boy said nothing. *Perhaps he fears to enter a lord's hall,* Dunk reflected. *That's no more than might be expected. He will grow out of it in time.* He went back to admiring his armor, and wondering how long he would wear it.

Ser Manfred was a thin man with a sour look on his face. He wore a black surcoat slashed with the purple lightning of House Dondarrion, but Dunk would have remembered him anyway by his unruly mane of red-gold hair. "Ser Arlan served your lord father when he and Lord Caron burned the Vulture King out of the Red Mountains, ser," he said from one knee. "I was only a boy then, but I squired for him. Ser Arlan of Pennytree."

Ser Manfred scowled. "No. I know him not. Nor you, boy."

Dunk showed him the old man's shield. "This was his sigil, the winged chalice."

"My lord father took eight hundred knights and near four thousand foot into the mountains. I cannot be expected to remember every one of them, nor what shields they carried. It may be that you were with us, but . . ." Ser Manfred shrugged.

Dunk was struck speechless for an instant. *The old man took a wound in your father's service, how can you have forgotten him?* "They will not allow me to challenge unless some knight or lord will vouch for me."

"And what is that to me?" said Ser Manfred. "I have given you enough of my time, ser."

If he went back to the castle without Ser Manfred, he was lost. Dunk eyed the purple lightning embroided across the black wool of Ser Manfred's surcoat and said, "I remember your father telling the camp how your house got its sigil. One stormy night, as the first of your line bore a message across the Dornish Marches, an arrow killed his horse beneath him and spilled him on the ground. Two Dornishmen came out of the darkness in ring mail and crested helms. His sword had broken beneath him when he fell. When he saw that, he thought he was doomed. But as the Dornishmen closed to cut him down, lightning cracked from the sky. It was a bright burning purple, and it split, striking the Dornishmen in their steel and killing them both where they stood. The message gave the Storm King victory over the Dornish, and in thanks he raised the messenger to lordship. He was the first Lord Dondarrion, so he took for his arms a forked purple lightning bolt, on a black field powdered with stars."

If Dunk thought the tale would impress Ser Manfred, he could not have been more wrong. "Every pot boy and groom who has ever served my father hears that story soon or late. Knowing it does not make you a knight. Begone with you, ser."

It was with a leaden heart that Dunk returned to Ashford Castle, wondering what he might say so that Plummer would grant him the right of challenge. The steward was not in his turret chamber, however. A guard told him he might be found in the Great Hall. "Shall I wait here?" Dunk asked. "How long will he be?"

"How should I know? Do what you please."

The Great Hall was not so great, as halls went, but Ashford was a small castle. Dunk entered through a side door, and spied the steward at once. He was standing with Lord Ashford and a dozen other men at the top of the hall. He walked toward them, beneath a wall hung with wool tapestries of fruits and flowers.

"—more concerned if they were *your* sons, I'll wager," an angry man was saying as Dunk approached. His straight hair and square-cut beard were so fair they seemed white in the dimness of the hall, but as he got closer he saw that they were in truth a pale silvery color touched with gold.

"Daeron has done this before," another replied. Plummer was standing so as to block Dunk's view of the speaker. "You should never have commanded him to enter the lists. He belongs on a tourney field no more than Aerys does, or Rhaegel."

"By which you mean he'd sooner ride a whore than a horse," the first man said. Thickly built and powerful, the prince—he was surely a prince— wore a leather brigandine covered with silver studs beneath a heavy black cloak trimmed with ermine. Pox scars marked his cheeks, only partly concealed by his silvery beard. "I do not need to be reminded of my son's failings, brother. He has only eighteen years. He can change. He *will* change, gods be damned, or I swear I'll see him dead."

"Don't be an utter fool. Daeron is what he is, but he is still your blood and mine. I have no doubt Ser Roland will turn him up, and Aegon with him."

"When the tourney is over, perhaps."

"Aerion is here. He is a better lance than Daeron

in any case, if it is the tourney that concerns you.''
Dunk could see the speaker now. He was seated in
the high seat, a sheaf of parchments in one hand,
Lord Ashford hovering at his shoulder. Even
seated, he looked to be a head taller than the other,
to judge from the long straight legs stretched out
before him. His short-cropped hair was dark and
peppered with grey, his strong jaw clean-shaven.
His nose looked as though it had been broken more
than once. Though he was dressed very plainly, in
green doublet, brown mantle, and scuffed boots,
there was a weight to him, a sense of power and
certainty.

It came to Dunk that he had walked in on something that he ought never have heard. *I had best go
and come back later, when they are done,* he decided. But it was already too late. The prince with
the silvery beard suddenly took note of him. ''Who
are you, and what do you mean by bursting in on
us?'' he demanded harshly.

''He is the knight that our good steward was expecting,'' the seated man said, smiling at Dunk in
a way that suggested he had been aware of him all
the time. ''You and I are the intruders here, brother.
Come closer, ser.''

Dunk edged forward, uncertain what was expected of him. He looked at Plummer, but got no
help there. The pinch-faced steward who had been

so forceful yesterday now stood silent, studying the stones of the floor. "My lords," he said, "I asked Ser Manfred Dondarrion to vouch for me so I might enter the lists, but he refuses. He says he knows me not. Ser Arlan served him, though, I swear it. I have his sword and shield, I—"

"A shield and a sword do not make a knight," declared Lord Ashford, a big bald man with a round red face. "Plummer has spoken to me of you. Even if we accept that these arms belonged to this Ser Arlan of Pennytree, it may well be that you found him dead and stole them. Unless you have some better proof of what you say, some writing or—"

"I remember Ser Arlan of Pennytree," the man in the high seat said quietly. "He never won a tourney that I know, but he never shamed himself either. At King's Landing sixteen years ago, he overthrew Lord Stokeworth and the Bastard of Harrenhal in the melee, and many years before at Lannisport he unhorsed the Grey Lion himself. The lion was not so grey then, to be sure."

"He told me about that, many a time," said Dunk.

The tall man studied him. "Then you will remember the Grey Lion's true name, I have no doubt."

For a moment there was nothing in Dunk's head

at all. *A thousand times the old man had told that tale, a thousand times, the lion, the lion, his name, his name, his name* ... He was near despair when suddenly it came. "Ser Damon Lannister!" he shouted. "The Grey Lion! He's Lord of Casterly Rock now."

"So he is," said the tall man pleasantly, "and he enters the lists on the morrow." He rattled the sheaf of papers in his hand.

"How can you possibly remember some insignificant hedge knight who chanced to unhorse Damon Lannister sixteen years ago?" said the prince with the silver beard, frowning.

"I make it a practice to learn all I can of my foes."

"Why would you deign to joust with a hedge knight?"

"It was nine years past, at Storm's End. Lord Baratheon held a hastilude to celebrate the birth of a grandson. The lots made Ser Arlan my opponent in the first tilt. We broke four lances before I finally unhorsed him."

"*Seven*," insisted Dunk, "and that was against the Prince of Dragonstone!" No sooner were the words out than he wanted them back. *Dunk the lunk, thick as a castle wall,* he could hear the old man chiding.

"So it was." The prince with the broken nose

smiled gently. "Tales grow in the telling, I know. Do not think ill of your old master, but it was four lances only, I fear."

Dunk was grateful that the hall was dim; he knew his ears were red. "My lord." *No, that's wrong too.* "Your Grace." He fell to his knees and lowered his head. "As you say, four, I meant no . . . I never . . . The old man, Ser Arlan, he used to say I was thick as a castle wall and slow as an aurochs."

"And strong as an aurochs, by the look of you," said Baelor Breakspear. "No harm was done, ser. Rise."

Dunk got to his feet, wondering if he should keep his head down or if he was allowed to look a prince in the face. *I am speaking with Baelor Targaryen, Prince of Dragonstone, Hand of the King, and heir apparent to the Iron Throne of Aegon the Conqueror.* What could a hedge knight dare say to such a person? "Y-you gave him back his horse and armor and took no ransom, I remember," he stammered. "The old—Ser Arlan, he told me you were the soul of chivalry, and that one day the Seven Kingdoms would be safe in your hands."

"Not for many a year still, I pray," Prince Baelor said.

"No," said Dunk, horrified. He almost said, *I didn't mean that the king should die,* but stopped himself in time. "I am sorry, m'lord. Your Grace, I mean."

Belatedly he recalled that the stocky man with the silver beard had addressed Prince Baelor as brother. *He is blood of the dragon as well, damn me for a fool.* He could only be Prince Maekar, the youngest of King Daeron's four sons. Prince Aerys was bookish and Prince Rhaegel mad, meek, and sickly. Neither was like to cross half the realm to attend a tourney, but Maekar was said to be a redoubtable warrior in his own right, though ever in the shadow of his eldest brother.

"You wish to enter the lists, is that it?" asked Prince Baelor. "That decision rests with the master of the games, but I see no reason to deny you."

The steward inclined his head. "As you say, my lord."

Dunk tried to stammer out thanks, but Prince Maekar cut him off. "Very well, ser, you are grateful. Now be off with you."

"You must forgive my noble brother, ser," said Prince Baelor. "Two of his sons have gone astray on their way here, and he fears for them."

"The spring rains have swollen many of the streams," said Dunk. "Perhaps the princes are only delayed."

"I did not come here to take counsel from a hedge knight," Prince Maekar declared to his brother.

"You may go, ser," Prince Baelor told Dunk, not unkindly.

"Yes, my lord." He bowed and turned.

But before he could get away, the prince called after him. "Ser. One thing more. You are not of Ser Arlan's blood?"

"Yes, m'lord. I mean, no. I'm not."

The prince nodded at the battered shield Dunk carried, and the winged chalice upon its face. "By law, only a trueborn son is entitled to inherit a knight's arms. You must needs find a new device, ser, a sigil of your own."

"I will," said Dunk. "Thank you again, Your Grace. I will fight bravely, you'll see." *As brave as Baelor Breakspear,* the old man would often say.

The winesellers and sausage makers were doing a brisk trade, and whores walked brazenly among the stalls and pavilions. Some were pretty enough, one red-haired girl in particular. He could not help staring at her breasts, the way they moved under her loose shift as she sauntered past. He thought of the silver in his pouch. *I could have her, if I liked. She'd like the clink of my coin well enough, I could take her back to my camp and have her, all night if I wanted.* He had never lain with a woman, and for all he knew he might die in his first tilt. Tourneys could be dangerous . . . but whores could be dangerous too, the old man had warned him of that. *She might rob me while I slept, and what would I do then?* When the red-haired girl glanced back over her shoulder at him, Dunk shook his head and walked away.

He found Egg at the puppet show, sitting cross-legged on the ground with the hood of his cloak pulled all the way forward to hide his baldness. The boy had been afraid to enter the castle, which Dunk put down to equal parts shyness and shame. *He does not think himself worthy to mingle with lords and ladies, let alone great princes.* It had been the same with him when he was little. The world beyond Flea Bottom had seemed as frightening as it was exciting. *Egg needs time, that's all.* For the present, it seemed kinder to give the lad a few coppers and let him enjoy himself among the stalls than to drag him along unwilling into the castle.

This morning the puppeteers were doing the tale of Florian and Jonquil. The fat Dornishwoman was working Florian in his armor made of motley, while the tall girl held Jonquil's strings. "You are no knight," she was saying as the puppet's mouth moved up and down. "I know you. You are Florian the Fool."

"I am, my lady," the other puppet answered, kneeling. "As great a fool as ever lived, and as great a knight as well."

"A fool *and* a knight?" said Jonquil. "I have never heard of such a thing."

"Sweet lady," said Florian, "all men are fools, and all men are knights, where women are concerned."

It was a good show, sad and sweet both, with a sprightly swordfight at the end, and a nicely painted giant. When it was over, the fat woman went among the crowd to collect coins while the girl packed away the puppets.

Dunk collected Egg and went up to her.

"M'lord?" she said, with a sideways glance and a half-smile. She was a head shorter than he was, but still taller than any other girl he had ever seen.

"That was good," Egg enthused. "I like how you make them move, Jonquil and the dragon and all. I saw a puppet show last year, but they moved all jerky. Yours are more smooth."

"Thank you," she told the boy politely.

Dunk said, "Your figures are well carved too. The dragon, especially. A fearsome beast. You make them yourself?"

She nodded. "My uncle does the carving. I paint them."

"Could you paint something for me? I have the coin to pay." He slipped the shield off his shoulder and turned it to show her. "I need to paint something over the chalice."

The girl glanced at the shield, and then at him. "What would you want painted?"

Dunk had not considered that. If not the old man's winged chalice, what? His head was empty. *Dunk the lunk, thick as a castle wall.* "I don't . . . I'm not certain." His ears were turning red, he realized miserably. "You must think me an utter fool."

She smiled. "All men are fools, and all men are knights."

"What color paint do you have?" he asked, hoping that might give him an idea.

"I can mix paints to make any color you want."

The old man's brown had always seemed drab to Dunk. "The field should be the color of sunset," he said suddenly. "The old man liked sunsets. And the device . . ."

"An elm tree," said Egg. "A big elm tree, like the one by the pool, with a brown trunk and green branches."

"Yes," Dunk said. "That would serve. An elm tree . . . but with a shooting star above. Could you do that?"

The girl nodded. "Give me the shield. I'll paint it this very night, and have it back to you on the morrow."

Dunk handed it over. "I am called Ser Duncan the Tall."

"I'm Tanselle," she laughed. "Tanselle Too-Tall, the boys used to call me."

"You're not too tall," Dunk blurted out. "You're just right for . . ." He realized what he had been about to say, and blushed furiously.

"For?" said Tanselle, cocking her head inquisitively.

"Puppets," he finished lamely.

The first day of the tourney dawned bright and clear. Dunk bought a sackful of foodstuffs, so they were able to break their fast on goose eggs, fried bread, and bacon, but when the food was cooked he found he had no appetite. His belly felt hard as a rock, even though he knew he would not ride today. The right of first challenge would go to knights of higher birth and greater renown, to lords and their sons and champions from other tourneys.

Egg chattered all through their breakfast, talking of this man and that man and how they might fare. *He was not japing me when he said he knew every good knight in the Seven Kingdoms,* Dunk thought ruefully. He found it humbling to listen so intently to the words of a scrawny orphan boy, but Egg's knowledge might serve him should he face one of these men in a tilt.

The meadow was a churning mass of people, all trying to elbow their way closer for a better view.

Dunk was as good an elbower as any, and bigger than most. He squirmed forward to a rise six yards from the fence. When Egg complained that all he could see were arses, Dunk sat the boy on his shoulders. Across the field, the viewing stand was filling up with highborn lords and ladies, a few rich townfolk, and a score of knights who had decided not to compete today. Of Prince Maekar he saw no sign, but he recognized Prince Baelor at Lord Ashford's side. Sunlight flashed golden off the shoulder clasp that held his cloak and the slim coronet about his temples, but otherwise he dressed far more simply than most of the other lords. *He does not look a Targaryen in truth, with that dark hair.* Dunk said as much to Egg.

"It's said he favors his mother," the boy reminded him. "She was a Dornish princess."

The five champions had raised their pavilions at the north end of the lists with the river behind them. The smallest two were orange, and the shields hung outside their doors displayed the white sun-and-chevron. Those would be Lord Ashford's sons Androw and Robert, brothers to the fair maid. Dunk had never heard other knights speak of their prowess, which meant they would likely be the first to fall.

Beside the orange pavilions stood one of deep-dyed green, much larger. The golden rose of Highgarden flapped above it, and the same device was emblazoned on the great green shield outside the door. "That's Leo Tyrell, Lord of Highgarden," said Egg.

"I knew that," said Dunk, irritated. "The old man and I served at Highgarden before you were ever born." He hardly remembered that year himself, but Ser Arlan had often spoken of Leo Longthorn, as he was sometimes called; a peerless jouster, for all the silver in his hair. "That must be Lord Leo beside the tent, the slender greybeard in green and gold."

"Yes," said Egg. "I saw him at King's Landing once. He's not one you'll want to challenge, ser."

"Boy, I do not require your counsel on who to challenge."

The fourth pavilion was sewn together from diamond-shaped pieces of cloth, alternating red and white. Dunk did not know the colors, but Egg said they belonged to a knight from the Vale of Arryn named Ser Humfrey Hardyng. "He won a great melee at Maidenpool last year, ser, and overthrew Ser Donnel of Duskendale and the Lords Arryn and Royce in the lists."

The last pavilion was Prince Valarr's. Of black silk it was, with a line of pointed scarlet pennons hanging from its roof like long red flames. The shield on its stand was glossy black, emblazoned with the three-headed dragon of House Targaryen. One of the Kingsguard knights stood beside it, his shining white armor stark against the black of the tentcloth. Seeing him there, Dunk wondered whether any of the challengers would dare to touch the dragon shield. Valarr was the king's grandson, after all, and son to Baelor Breakspear.

He need not have worried. When the horns blew to summon the challengers, all five of the maid's champions were called forth to defend her. Dunk could hear the murmur of excitement in the crowd as the challengers appeared one by one at the south end of the lists. Heralds boomed out the name of each knight in turn. They paused before the viewing stand to dip their lances in salute to Lord Ashford, Prince Baelor, and the fair maid, then circled to the north end of the field to select their opponents. The Grey Lion of Casterly Rock struck the shield of Lord Tyrell, while his golden-haired heir Ser Tybolt Lannister challenged Lord Ashford's eldest son. Lord Tully of Riverrun tapped the diamond-patterned shield of Ser Humfrey Hardyng, Ser Abelar Hightower knocked upon Valarr's, and the younger Ashford was called out by Ser Lyonel Baratheon, the knight they called the Laughing Storm.

The challengers trotted back to the south end of the lists to await their foes: Ser Abelar in silver and smoke colors, a stone watchtower on his shield, crowned with fire; the two Lannisters all crimson, bearing the golden lion of Casterly Rock; the Laughing Storm shining in cloth-of-gold, with a black stag on breast and shield and a rack of iron antlers on his helm; Lord Tully wearing a striped blue-and-red cloak clasped with a silver trout at each shoulder. They pointed their twelve-foot lances skyward, the gusty winds snapping and tugging at the pennons.

At the north end of the field, squires held brightly barded destriers for the champions to mount. They donned their helms and took up lance and shield, in splendor the equal of their foes: the Ashfords' billowing orange silks, Ser Humfrey's red-and-white diamonds, Lord Leo on his white charger with green satin trappings patterned with golden roses, and of course Valarr Targaryen. The Young Prince's horse was black as night, to match the color of his armor, lance, shield, and trappings. Atop his helm was a gleaming three-headed dragon, wings spread, enameled in a rich red; its twin was painted upon the glossy black surface of his shield. Each of the defenders had a wisp of orange silk knotted about an arm, a favor bestowed by the fair maid.

As the champions trotted into position, Ashford Meadow grew almost still. Then a horn sounded, and stillness turned to tumult in half a heartbeat. Ten pairs of gilded spurs drove into the flanks of ten great warhorses, a thousand voices began to scream and shout, forty iron-shod hooves pounded and tore the grass, ten lances dipped and steadied, the field seemed almost to shake, and champions and challengers came together in a rending crash of wood and steel. In an instant, the riders were beyond each other, wheeling about for another pass. Lord Tully reeled in his saddle but managed to keep his seat. When the commons realized that all ten of the lances had broken, a great roar of approval went up. It was a splendid omen for the success of the tourney, and a testament to the skill of the competitors.

Squires handed fresh lances to the jousters to replace the broken ones they cast aside, and once more the spurs dug deep. Dunk could feel the earth trembling beneath the soles of his feet. Atop his shoulders, Egg shouted happily and waved his pipestem arms. The Young Prince passed nearest to them. Dunk saw the point of his black lance kiss the watchtower on his foe's shield and slide off to slam into his chest, even as Ser Abelar's own lance burst into splinters against Valarr's breastplate. The grey stallion in the silver-and-smoke trappings reared with the force of the impact, and Ser Abelar Hightower was lifted from his stirrups and dashed violently to the ground.

Lord Tully was down as well, unhorsed by Ser Humfrey Hardyng, but he sprang up at once and drew his longsword, and Ser Humfrey cast aside his lance—unbroken—and dismounted to continue their fight afoot. Ser Abelar was not so sprightly. His squire ran out, loosened his helm, and called for help, and two servingmen lifted the dazed knight by the arms to help him back to his pavilion. Elsewhere on the field, the six knights who had remained ahorse were riding their third course. More lances shattered, and this time Lord Leo Tyrell aimed his point so expertly he ripped the Grey Lion's helm cleanly off his head. Barefaced, the Lord of Casterly Rock raised his hand in salute and dismounted, yielding the match. By then Ser Humfrey had beaten Lord Tully into surrender, showing himself as skilled with a sword as he was with a lance.

Tybolt Lannister and Androw Ashford rode against each other thrice more before Ser Androw finally lost shield, seat, and match all at once. The younger Ashford lasted even longer, breaking no less than nine lances against Ser Lyonel Baratheon, the Laughing Storm. Champion and challenger both lost their saddles on their tenth course, only to rise together to fight on, sword against mace. Finally a battered Ser Robert Ashford admitted defeat, but on the viewing stand his father looked anything but dejected. Both Lord Ashford's sons had been ushered from the ranks of the champions, it was true, but they had acquitted themselves nobly against two of the finest knights in the Seven Kingdoms.

I must do even better, though, Dunk thought as he watched victor and vanquished embrace and walk together from the field. *It is not enough for me to fight well and lose. I must win at least the first challenge, or I lose all.*

Ser Tybolt Lannister and the Laughing Storm would now take their places among the champions, replacing the men they had defeated. Already the orange pavilions were coming down. A few feet away, the Young Prince sat at his ease in a raised camp chair before his great black tent. His helm was off. He had dark hair like his father, but a bright streak ran through it. A servingman brought him a silver goblet and he took a sip. *Water, if he is wise,* Dunk thought, *wine if not.* He found himself wondering if Valarr had indeed inherited a measure of his father's prowess, or whether it had only been that he had drawn the weakest opponent.

A fanfare of trumpets announced that three new challengers had entered the lists. The heralds shouted their names. *"Ser Pearse of House Caron, Lord of the Marches."* He had a silver harp emblazoned on his shield, though his surcoat was patterned with nightingales. "*Ser Joseth of House Mallister, from Seagard.*" Ser Joseth sported a winged helm; on his shield, a silver eagle flew across an indigo sky. "*Ser Gawen of House Swann, Lord of Stonehelm on the Cape of Wrath.*" A pair of swans, one black and one white, fought furiously on his arms. Lord Gawen's armor, cloak, and horse bardings were a riot of black and white as well, down to the stripes on his scabbard and lance.

Lord Caron, harper and singer and knight of renown, touched the point of his lance to Lord Tyrell's rose. Ser Joseth thumped on Ser Humfrey Hardyng's diamonds. And the black-and-white knight, Lord Gawen Swann, challenged the black prince with the white guardian. Dunk rubbed his chin. Lord Gawen was even older than the old man, and the old man was dead. "Egg, who is the least dangerous of these challengers?" he asked the boy on his shoulders, who seemed to know so much of these knights.

"Lord Gawen," the boy said at once. "Valarr's foe."

"*Prince* Valarr," he corrected. "A squire must keep a courteous tongue, boy."

The three challengers took their places as the three champions mounted up. Men were making wagers all around them and calling out encouragement to their choices, but Dunk had eyes only for the prince. On the first pass he struck Lord Gawen's shield a glancing blow, the blunted point of the lance sliding aside just as it had with Ser Abelar Hightower, only this time it was deflected the other way, into empty air. Lord Gawen's own lance broke clean against the prince's chest, and Valarr seemed about to fall for an instant before he recovered his seat.

The second time through the lists, Valarr swung his lance left, aiming for his foe's breast, but struck his shoulder instead. Even so, the blow was enough to make the older knight lose his lance. One arm flailed for balance and Lord Gawen fell. The Young Prince swung from the saddle and drew his sword, but the fallen man waved him off and raised his visor. "I yield, Your Grace," he called. "Well fought." The lords in the viewing stand echoed him, shouting, "*Well fought! Well fought!*" as Valarr knelt to help the grey-haired lord to his feet.

"It was not either," Egg complained.

"Be quiet, or you can go back to camp."

Farther away, Ser Joseth Mallister was being carried off the field unconscious, while the harp lord and the rose lord were going at each other lustily with blunted longaxes, to the delight of the roaring crowd. Dunk was so intent on Valarr Targaryen that he scarcely saw them. *He is a fair knight, but no more than that,* he found himself thinking. *I*

would have a chance against him. If the gods were
good, I might even unhorse him, and once afoot my
weight and strength would tell.

"Get him!" Egg shouted merrily, shifting his
seat on Dunk's back in his excitement. "Get him!
Hit him! Yes! He's right there, he's *right there*!"
It seemed to be Lord Caron he was cheering on.
The harper was playing a different sort of music
now, driving Lord Leo back and back as steel sang
on steel. The crowd seemed almost equally divided
between them, so cheers and curses mingled freely
in the morning air. Chips of wood and paint were
flying from Lord Leo's shield as Lord Pearse's axe
knocked the petals off his golden rose, one by one,
until the shield finally shattered and split. But as it
did, the axehead hung up for an instant in the wood
. . . and Lord Leo's own axe crashed down on the
haft of his foe's weapon, breaking it off not a foot
from his hand. He cast aside his broken shield, and
suddenly he was the one on the attack. Within moments, the harper knight was on one knee, singing
his surrender.

For the rest of the morning and well into the
afternoon, it was more of the same, as challengers
took the field in twos and threes, and sometimes
five together. Trumpets blew, the heralds called out
names, warhorses charged, the crowd cheered,
lances snapped like twigs, and swords rang against

helms and mail. It was, smallfolk and high lord alike agreed, a splendid day of jousting. Ser Humfrey Hardyng and Ser Humfrey Beesbury, a bold young knight in yellow and black stripes with three beehives on his shield, splintered no less than a dozen lances apiece in an epic struggle the smallfolk soon began calling "the Battle of Humfrey." Ser Tybolt Lannister was unhorsed by Ser Jon Penrose and broke his sword in his fall, but fought back with shield alone to win the bout and remain a champion. One-eyed Ser Robyn Rhysling, a grizzled old knight with a salt-and-pepper beard, lost his helm to Lord Leo's lance in their first course, yet refused to yield. Three times more they rode at each other, the wind whipping Ser Robyn's hair while the shards of broken lances flew round his bare face like wooden knives, which Dunk thought all the more wondrous when Egg told him that Ser Robyn had lost his eye to a splinter from a broken lance not five years earlier. Leo Tyrell was too chivalrous to aim another lance at Ser Robyn's unprotected head, but even so Rhysling's stubborn courage (or was it folly?) left Dunk astounded. Finally the Lord of Highgarden struck Ser Robyn's breastplate a solid thump right over the heart and sent him cartwheeling to the earth.

Ser Lyonel Baratheon also fought several notable matches. Against lesser foes, he would often break into booming laughter the moment they touched his shield, and laugh all the time he was mounting and charging and knocking them from their stirrups. If his challengers wore any sort of crest on their helm, Ser Lyonel would strike it off and fling it into the crowd. The crests were ornate things, made of carved wood or shaped leather, and sometimes gilded and enameled or even wrought in pure silver, so the men he beat did not appreciate this habit, though it made him a great favorite of the commons. Before long, only crestless men were choosing him. As loud and often as Ser Lyonel laughed down a challenger, though, Dunk thought the day's honors should go to Ser Humfrey Hardyng, who humbled fourteen knights, each one of them formidable.

Meanwhile the Young Prince sat outside his black pavilion, drinking from his silver goblet and rising from time to time to mount his horse and vanquish yet another undistinguished foe. He had won nine victories, but it seemed to Dunk that every one was hollow. *He is beating old men and upjumped squires, and a few lords of high birth and low skill. The truly dangerous men are riding past his shield as if they do not see it.*

Late in the day, a brazen fanfare announced the entry of a new challenger to the lists. He rode in on a great red charger whose black bardings were slashed to reveal glimpses of yellow, crimson, and orange beneath. As he approached the viewing stand to make his salute, Dunk saw the face beneath the raised visor, and recognized the prince he'd met in Lord Ashford's stables.

Egg's legs tightened around his neck. "Stop that," Dunk snapped, yanking them apart. "Do you mean to choke me?"

"*Prince Aerion Brightflame*," a herald called, "*of the Red Keep of King's Landing, son of Maekar Prince of Summerhall of House Targaryen, grandson to Daeron the Good, the Second of His Name, King of the Andals, the Rhoynar, and the First Men, and Lord of the Seven Kingdoms.*"

Aerion bore a three-headed dragon on his shield, but it was rendered in colors much more vivid than Valarr's; one head was orange, one yellow, one red, and the flames they breathed had the sheen of gold leaf. His surcoat was a swirl of smoke and fire woven together, and his blackened helm was surmounted by a crest of red enamel flames.

After a pause to dip his lance to Prince Baelor, a pause so brief that was almost perfunctory, he galloped to the north end of the field, past Lord Leo's pavilion and the Laughing Storm's, slowing only when he approached Prince Valarr's tent. The Young Prince rose and stood stiffly beside his shield, and for a moment Dunk was certain that

Aerion meant to strike it . . . but then he laughed and trotted past, and banged his point hard against Ser Humfrey Hardyng's diamonds. "Come out, come out, little knight," he sang in a loud clear voice, "it's time you faced the dragon."

Ser Humfrey inclined his head stiffly to his foe as his destrier was brought out, and then ignored him while he mounted, fastened his helm, and took up lance and shield. The spectators grew quiet as the two knights took their places. Dunk heard the *clang* of Prince Aerion dropping his visor. The horn blew.

Ser Humfrey broke slowly, building speed, but his foe raked the red charger hard with both spurs, coming hard. Egg's legs tightened again. "*Kill him!*" he shouted suddenly. "*Kill him, he's right there, kill him, kill him, kill him!*" Dunk was not certain which of the knights he was shouting to.

Prince Aerion's lance, gold-tipped and painted in stripes of red, orange, and yellow, swung down across the barrier. *Low, too low,* thought Dunk the moment he saw it. *He'll miss the rider and strike Ser Humfrey's horse, he needs to bring it up.* Then, with dawning horror, he began to suspect that Aerion intended no such thing. *He cannot mean to . . .*

At the last possible instant, Ser Humfrey's stallion reared away from the oncoming point, eyes rolling in terror, but too late. Aerion's lance took the animal just above the armor that protected his breastbone, and exploded out of the back of his neck in a gout of bright blood. Screaming, the horse crashed sideways, knocking the wooden barrier to pieces as he fell. Ser Humfrey tried to leap free, but a foot caught in a stirrup and they heard his shriek as his leg was crushed between the splintered fence and falling horse.

All of Ashford Meadow was shouting. Men ran onto the field to extricate Ser Humfrey, but the stallion, dying in agony, kicked at them as they approached. Aerion, having raced blithely around the carnage to the end of the lists, wheeled his horse and came galloping back. He was shouting too, though Dunk could not make out the words over the almost human screams of the dying horse. Vaulting from the saddle, Aerion drew his sword and advanced on his fallen foe. His own squires and one of Ser Humfrey's had to pull him back. Egg squirmed on Dunk's shoulders. "Let me down," the boy said. "The poor horse, *let me down.*"

Dunk felt sick himself. *What would I do if such a fate befell Thunder?* A man-at-arms with a pole-axe dispatched Ser Humfrey's stallion, ending the hideous screams. Dunk turned and forced his way through the press. When he came to open ground, he lifted Egg off his shoulders. The boy's hood had fallen back and his eyes were red. "A terrible sight, aye," he told the lad, "but a squire must needs be strong. You'll see worse mishaps at other tourneys, I fear."

"It was no mishap," Egg said, mouth trembling. "Aerion meant to do it. You saw."

Dunk frowned. It had looked that way to him as well, but it was hard to accept that any knight could be so unchivalrous, least of all one who was blood of the dragon. "I saw a knight green as summer grass lose control of his lance," he said stubbornly, "and I'll hear no more of it. The jousting is done for the day, I think. Come, lad."

He was right about the end of the day's contests. By the time the chaos had been set to rights, the sun was low in the west, and Lord Ashford had called a halt.

As the shadows of evening crept across the meadow, a hundred torches were lit along the merchant's row. Dunk bought a horn of ale for himself and half a horn for the boy, to cheer him. They wandered for a time, listening to a sprightly air on pipes and drums and watching a puppet show about Nymeria, the warrior queen with the ten thousand ships. The puppeteers had only two ships, but managed a rousing sea battle all the same. Dunk wanted to ask the girl Tanselle if she had finished painting his shield, but he could see that she was busy. *I'll wait until she is done for the night*, he resolved. *Perhaps she'll have a thirst then.*

"Ser Duncan," a voice called behind him. And then again, "Ser Duncan." Suddenly Dunk remembered that was him. "I saw you among the small-folk today, with this boy on your shoulders," said Raymun Fossoway as he came up, smiling. "Indeed, the two of you were hard to miss."

"The boy is my squire. Egg, this is Raymun Fossoway." Dunk had to pull the boy forward, and even then Egg lowered his head and stared at Raymun's boots as he mumbled a greeting.

"Well met, lad," Raymun said easily. "Ser Duncan, why not watch from the viewing gallery? All knights are welcome there."

Dunk was at ease among smallfolk and servants; the idea of claiming a place among the lords, ladies, and landed knights made him uncomfortable. "I would not have wanted any closer view of that last tilt."

Raymun grimaced. "Nor I. Lord Ashford declared Ser Humfrey the victor and awarded him Prince Aerion's courser, but even so, he will not be able to continue. His leg was broken in two places. Prince Baelor sent his own maester to tend him."

"Will there be another champion in Ser Humfrey's place?"

"Lord Ashford had a mind to grant the place to Lord Caron, or perhaps the other Ser Humfrey, the one who gave Hardyng such a splendid match, but Prince Baelor told him that it would not be seemly to remove Ser Humfrey's shield and pavilion under the circumstances. I believe they will continue with four champions in place of five."

Four champions, Dunk thought. *Leo Tyrell, Lyonel Baratheon, Tybolt Lannister, and Prince Valarr*. He had seen enough this first day to know how little chance he would stand against the first three. Which left only . . .

A hedge knight cannot challenge a prince. Valarr is second in line to the Iron Throne. He is Baelor Breakspear's son, and his blood is the blood of Aegon the Conqueror and the Young Dragon and Prince Aemon the Dragonknight, and I am some boy the old man found behind a pot shop in Flea Bottom.

His head hurt just thinking about it. "Who does your cousin mean to challenge?" he asked Raymun.

"Ser Tybolt, all things being equal. They are well matched. My cousin keeps a sharp watch on every tilt, though. Should any man be wounded on the morrow, or show signs of exhaustion or weakness, Steffon will be quick to knock on his shield, you may count on it. No one has ever accused him of an excess of chivalry.'' He laughed, as if to take the sting from his words. ''Ser Duncan, will you join me for a cup of wine?''

''I have a matter I must attend to,'' said Dunk, uncomfortable with the notion of accepting hospitality he could not return.

''I could wait here and bring your shield when the puppet show is over, ser,'' said Egg. ''They're going to do Symeon Star-Eyes later, and make the dragon fight again as well.''

''There, you see, your matter is attended to, and the wine awaits,'' said Raymun. ''It's an Arbor vintage, too. How can you refuse me?''

Bereft of excuses, Dunk had no choice but to follow, leaving Egg at the puppet show. The apple of House Fossoway flew above gold-colored pavilion where Raymun attended his cousin. Behind it, two servants were basting a goat with honey and herbs over a small cookfire. ''There's food as well, if you're hungry,'' Raymun said negligently as he held the flap for Dunk. A brazier of coals lit the interior and made the air pleasantly warm. Raymun filled two cups with wine. ''They say Aerion is in a rage at Lord Ashford for awarding his charger to Ser Humfrey,'' he commented as he poured, ''but I'll wager it was his uncle who counseled it.'' He handed Dunk a wine cup.

"Prince Baelor is an honorable man."

"As the Bright Prince is not?" Raymun laughed. "Don't look so anxious, Ser Duncan, there's none here but us. It is no secret that Aerion is a bad piece of work. Thank the gods that he is well down in the order of succession."

"You truly believe he meant to kill the horse?"

"Is there any doubt of it? If Prince Maekar had been here, it would have gone differently, I promise you. Aerion is all smiles and chivalry so long as his father is watching, if the tales be true, but when he's not . . ."

"I saw that Prince Maekar's chair was empty."

"He's left Ashford to search for his sons, along with Roland Crakehall of the Kingsguard. There's a wild tale of robber knights going about, but I'll wager the prince is just off drunk again."

The wine was fine and fruity, as good a cup as he had ever tasted. He rolled it in his mouth, swallowed, and said, "Which prince is this now?"

"Maekar's heir. Daeron, he's named, after the king. They call him Daeron the Drunken, though not in his father's hearing. The youngest boy was with him as well. They left Summerhall together but never reached Ashford." Raymun drained his cup and set it aside. "Poor Maekar."

"Poor?" said Dunk, startled. "The king's son?"

"The king's *fourth* son," said Raymun, "not

quite as bold as Prince Baelor, nor as clever as Prince Aerys, nor as gentle as Prince Rhaegel. And now he must suffer seeing his own sons overshadowed by his brother's. Daeron is a sot, Aerion is vain and cruel, the third son was so unpromising they gave him to the Citadel to make a maester of him, and the youngest—"

"*Ser! Ser Duncan!*" Egg burst in panting. His hood had fallen back, and the light from the brazier shone in his big dark eyes. "You have to run, he's hurting her!"

Dunk lurched to his feet, confused. "Hurting? Who?"

"*Aerion!*" the boy shouting. "He's *hurting* her. The puppet girl. *Hurry.*" Whirling, he darted back out into the night.

Dunk made to follow, but Raymun caught his arm. "Ser Duncan. Aerion, he said. A prince of the blood. Be careful."

It was good counsel, he knew. The old man would have said the same. But he could not listen. He wrenched free of Raymun's hand and shouldered his way out of the pavilion. He could hear shouting off in the direction of the merchants' row. Egg was almost out of sight. Dunk ran after him. His legs were long and the boy's short; he quickly closed the distance.

A wall of watchers had gathered around the puppeteers. Dunk shouldered through them, ignoring their curses. A man-at-arms in the royal livery stepped up to block him. Dunk put a big hand on his chest and shoved, sending the man flailing backward to sprawl on his arse in the dirt.

The puppeteer's stall had been knocked on its side. The fat Dornishwoman was on the ground weeping. One man-at-arms was dangling the puppets of Florian and Jonquil from his hands as another set them afire with a torch. Three more men were opening chests, spilling more puppets on the ground and stamping on them. The dragon puppet was scattered all about them, a broken wing here, its head there, its tail in three pieces. And in the midst of it all stood Prince Aerion, resplendent in a red velvet doublet with long dagged sleeves, twisting Tanselle's arm in both hands. She was on her knees, pleading with him. Aerion ignored her. He forced open her hand and seized one of her fingers. Dunk stood there stupidly, not quite believing what he saw. Then he heard a *crack*, and Tanselle screamed.

One of Aerion's men tried to grab him, and went flying. Three long strides, then Dunk grabbed the prince's shoulder and wrenched him around hard. His sword and dagger were forgotten, along with everything the old man had ever taught him. His fist knocked Aerion off his feet, and the toe of his boot slammed into the prince's belly. When Aerion went for his knife, Dunk stepped on his wrist and then kicked him again, right in the mouth. He might have kicked him to death right then and there, but the princeling's men swarmed over him. He had a man on each arm and another pounding him across the back. No sooner had he wrestled free of one than two more were on him.

Finally they shoved him down and pinned his arms and legs. Aerion was on his feet again. The prince's mouth was bloody. He pushed inside it with a finger. "You've loosened one of my teeth," he complained, "so we'll start by breaking all of yours." He pushed his hair from his eyes. "You look familiar."

"You took me for a stableboy."

Aerion smiled redly. "I recall. You refused to take my horse. Why did you throw your life away? For this whore?" Tanselle was curled up on the ground, cradling her maimed hand. He gave her a shove with the toe of his boot. "She's scarcely worth it. A traitor. The dragon ought never lose."

He is mad, thought Dunk, *but he is still a prince's son, and he means to kill me.* He might have prayed then, if he had known a prayer all the way through, but there was no time. There was hardly even time to be afraid.

"Nothing more to say?" said Aerion. "You bore

me, ser.'' He poked at his bloody mouth again.
''Get a hammer and break all his teeth out, Wate,''
he commanded, ''and then let's cut him open and
show him the color of his entrails.''

''*No!*'' a boy's voice said. ''Don't hurt him!''

Gods be good, the boy, the brave foolish boy,
Dunk thought. He fought against the arms restraining him, but it was no good. ''Hold your tongue,
you stupid boy. Run away. They'll hurt you!''

''No they won't.'' Egg moved closer. ''If they
do, they'll answer to my father. And my uncle as
well. Let go of him, I said. Wate, Yorkel, you know
me. Do as I say.''

The hands holding his left arm were gone, and
then the others. Dunk did not understand what was
happening. The men-at-arms were backing away.
One even knelt. Then the crowd parted for Raymun
Fossoway. He had donned mail and helm, and his
hand was on his sword. His cousin Ser Steffon, just
behind him, had already bared his blade, and with
them were a half-dozen men-at-arms with the red
apple badge sewn on their breasts.

Prince Aerion paid them no mind. ''Impudent
little wretch,'' he said to Egg, spitting a mouthful
of blood at the boy's feet. ''What happened to your
hair?''

''I cut it off, brother,'' said Egg. ''I didn't want
to look like you.''

* * *

The second day of the tourney was overcast, with a gusty wind blowing from the west. *The crowds should be less on a day like this,* Dunk thought. It would have been easier for them to find a spot near the fence to see the jousting up close. *Egg might have sat on the rail, while I stood behind him.*

Instead Egg would have a seat in the viewing box, dressed in silks and furs, while Dunk's view would be limited to the four walls of the tower cell where Lord Ashford's men had confined him. The chamber had a window, but it faced in the wrong direction. Even so, Dunk crammed himself into the window seat as the sun came up, and stared gloomily off across town and field and forest. They had taken his hempen sword belt, and his sword and dagger with it, and they had taken his silver as well. He hoped Egg or Raymun would remember Chestnut and Thunder.

"Egg," he muttered low under his breath. His squire, a poor lad plucked from the streets of King's Landing. Had ever a knight been made such a fool? *Dunk the lunk, thick as a castle wall and slow as an aurochs.*

He had not been permitted to speak to Egg since Lord Ashford's soldiers had scooped them all up at the puppet show. Nor Raymun, nor Tanselle, nor anyone, not even Lord Ashford himself. He wondered if he would ever see any of them again. For all he knew, they meant to keep him in this small room until he died. *What did I think would happen?* he asked himself bitterly. *I knocked down a prince's son and kicked him in the face.*

Beneath these grey skies, the flowing finery of the highborn lords and great champions would not seem quite so splendid as it had the day before. The sun, walled behind the clouds, would not brush their steel helms with brilliance, nor make their gold and silver chasings glitter and flash, but even so, Dunk wished he were in the crowd to watch the jousting. It would be a good day for hedge knights, for men in plain mail on unbarded horses.

He could *hear* them, at least. The horns of the heralds carried well, and from time to time a roar from the crowd told him that someone had fallen, or risen, or done something especially bold. He heard faint hoofbeats too, and once in a great while the clash of swords or the *snap* of a lance. Dunk winced whenever he heard that last; it reminded him of the noise Tanselle's finger had made when Aerion broke it. There were other sounds too, closer at hand: footfalls in the hall outside his door, the stamp of hooves in the yard below, shouts and voices from the castle walls. Sometimes they drowned out the tourney. Dunk supposed that was just as well.

"A hedge knight is the truest kind of knight, Dunk," the old man had told him, a long long time ago. "Other knights serve the lords who keep them, or from whom they hold their lands, but we serve where we will, for men whose causes we believe in. Every knight swears to protect the weak and innocent, but we keep the vow best, I think." Queer how strong that memory seemed. Dunk had quite forgotten those words. And perhaps the old man had as well, toward the end.

The morning turned to afternoon. The distant sounds of the tourney began to dwindle and die. Dusk began to seep into the cell, but Dunk still sat in the window seat, looking out on the gathering dark and trying to ignore his empty belly.

And then he heard footsteps and a jangling of iron keys. He uncoiled and rose to his feet as the door opened. Two guards pushed in, one bearing an oil lamp. A servingman followed with a tray of food. Behind came Egg. "Leave the lamp and the food and go," the boy told them.

They did as he commanded, though Dunk noticed that they left the heavy wooden door ajar. The smell of the food made him realize how ravenous he was. There was hot bread and honey, a bowl of pease porridge, a skewer of roast onions and well-charred meat. He sat by the tray, pulled apart the bread with his hands, and stuffed some into his mouth. "There's no knife," he observed. "Did they think I'd stab you, boy?"

"They didn't tell me what they thought." Egg wore a close-fitting black wool doublet with a tucked waist and long sleeves lined with red satin. Across his chest was sewn the three-headed dragon of House Targaryen. "My uncle says I must humbly beg your forgiveness for deceiving you."

"Your uncle," said Dunk. "That would be Prince Baelor."

The boy looked miserable. "I never meant to lie."

"But you did. About everything. Starting with your name. I never heard of a Prince Egg."

"It's short for Aegon. My brother Aemon named me Egg. He's off at the Citadel now, learning to be a maester. And Daeron sometimes calls me Egg as well, and so do my sisters."

Dunk lifted the skewer and bit into a chunk of meat. Goat, flavored with some lordly spice he'd never tasted before. Grease ran down his chin. "Aegon," he repeated. "Of course it would be Aegon. Like Aegon the Dragon. How many Aegons have been king?"

"Four," the boy said. "Four Aegons."

Dunk chewed, swallowed, and tore off some more bread. "Why did you do it? Was it some jape, to make a fool of the stupid hedge knight?"

"No." The boy's eyes filled with tears, but he stood there manfully. "I was supposed to squire for Daeron. He's my oldest brother. I learned everything I had to learn to be a good squire, but Daeron isn't a very good knight. He didn't want to ride in the tourney, so after we left Summerhall he stole away from our escort, only instead of doubling back he went straight on toward Ashford, thinking they'd never look for us that way. It was him shaved my head. He knew my father would send men hunting us. Daeron has common hair, sort of a pale brown, nothing special, but mine is like Aerion's and my father's."

"The blood of the dragon," Dunk said. "Silver-gold hair and purple eyes, everyone knows that." *Thick as a castle wall, Dunk.*

"Yes. So Daeron shaved it off. He meant for us to hide until the tourney was over. Only then you took me for a stableboy, and . . ." He lowered his eyes. "I didn't care if Daeron fought or not, but I wanted to be *somebody's* squire. I'm sorry, ser. I truly am."

Dunk looked at him thoughtfully. He knew what it was like to want something so badly that you would tell a monstrous lie just to get near it. "I thought you were like me," he said. "Might be you are. Only not the way I thought."

"We're both from King's Landing still," the boy said hopefully.

Dunk had to laugh. "Yes, you from the top of Aegon's Hill and me from the bottom."

"That's not so far, ser."

Dunk took a bite from an onion. "Do I need to call you *m'lord* or *Your Grace* or something?"

"At court," the boy admitted, "but other times you can keep on calling me Egg if you like. Ser."

"What will they do with me, Egg?"

"My uncle wants to see you. After you're done eating, ser."

Dunk shoved the platter aside, and stood. "I'm done now, then. I've already kicked one prince in the mouth, I don't mean to keep another waiting."

Lord Ashford had turned his own chambers over to Prince Baelor for the duration of his stay, so it was to the lord's solar that Egg—no, *Aegon,* he would have to get used to that—conducted him. Baelor sat reading by the light of beeswax candle. Dunk knelt before him. "Rise," the prince said. "Would you care for wine?"

"As it please you, Your Grace."

"Pour Ser Duncan a cup of the sweet Dornish red, Aegon," the prince commanded. "Try not to spill it on him, you've done him sufficient ill already."

"The boy won't spill, Your Grace," said Dunk. "He's a good boy. A good squire. And he meant no harm to me, I know."

"One need not intend harm to do it. Aegon should have come to me when he saw what his brother was doing to those puppeteers. Instead he ran to you. That was no kindness. What you did, ser . . . well, I might have done the same in your place, but I am a prince of the realm, not a hedge knight. It is never wise to strike a king's grandson in anger, no matter the cause."

Dunk nodded grimly. Egg offered him a silver goblet, brimming with wine. He accepted it and took a long swallow.

"I *hate* Aerion," Egg said with vehemence. "And I had to run for Ser Duncan, uncle, the castle was too far."

"Aerion is your brother," the prince said firmly, "and the septons say we must love our brothers. Aegon, leave us now, I would speak with Ser Duncan privately."

The boy put down the flagon of wine and bowed stiffly. "As you will, Your Grace." He went to the door of the solar and closed it softly behind him.

Baelor Breakspear studied Dunk's eyes for a long moment. "Ser Duncan, let me ask you this— how good a knight are you, truly? How skilled at arms?"

Dunk did not know what to say. "Ser Arlan taught me sword and shield, and how to tilt at rings and quintains."

Prince Baelor seemed troubled by that answer. "My brother Maekar returned to the castle a few hours ago. He found his heir drunk in an inn a day's ride to the south. Maekar would never admit as much, but I believe it was his secret hope that his sons might outshine mine in this tourney. Instead they have both shamed him, but what is he to do? They are blood of his blood. Maekar is angry, and must needs have a target for his wrath. He has chosen you."

"Me?" Dunk said miserably.

"Aerion has already filled his father's ear. And Daeron has not helped you either. To excuse his own cowardice, he told my brother that a huge robber knight, chance met on the road, made off with Aegon. I fear you have been cast as this robber knight, ser. In Daeron's tale, he has spent all these days pursuing you hither and yon, to win back his brother."

"But Egg will tell him the truth. Aegon, I mean."

"Egg *will* tell him, I have no doubt," said Prince Baelor, "but the boy has been known to lie too, as you have good reason to recall. Which son will my brother believe? As for the matter of these puppeteers, by the time Aerion is done twisting the tale it will be high treason. The dragon is the sigil of the royal House. To portray one being slain, sawdust blood spilling from its neck . . . well, it was doubtless innocent, but it was far from wise. Aerion calls it a veiled attack on House Targaryen, an incitement to revolt. Maekar will likely agree. My brother has a prickly nature, and he has placed all his best hopes on Aerion, since Daeron has been such a grave disappointment to him.'' The prince took a sip of wine, then set the goblet aside. ''Whatever my brother believes or fails to believe, one truth is beyond dispute. You laid hands upon the blood of the dragon. For that offense, you must be tried, and judged, and punished.''

''Punished?'' Dunk did not like the sound of that.

''Aerion would like your head, with or without teeth. He will not have it, I promise you, but I cannot deny him a trial. As my royal father is hundreds of leagues away, my brother and I must sit in judgment of you, along with Lord Ashford, whose domains these are, and Lord Tyrell of Highgarden, his liege lord. The last time a man was found guilty of striking one of royal blood, it was decreed that he should lose the offending hand.''

''My *hand*?'' said Dunk, aghast.

''And your foot. You kicked him too, did you not?''

Dunk could not speak.

''To be sure, I will urge my fellow judges to be

merciful. I am the King's Hand and the heir to the throne, my word carries some weight. But so does my brother's. The risk is there.''

"I," said Dunk, "I . . . Your Grace, I . . ." *They meant no treason, it was only a wooden dragon, it was never meant to be a royal prince,* he wanted to say, but his words had deserted him once and all. He had never been any good with words.

"You have another choice, though," Prince Baelor said quietly. "Whether it is a better choice or a worse one, I cannot say, but I remind you that any knight accused of a crime has the right to demand trial by combat. So I ask you once again, Ser Duncan the Tall—how good a knight are you? Truly?''

A trial of seven," said Prince Aerion, smiling. "That is *my* right, I do believe.''

Prince Baelor drummed his fingers on the table, frowning. To his left, Lord Ashford nodded slowly. "Why?" Prince Maekar demanded, leaning forward toward his son. "Are you afraid to face this hedge knight alone, and let the gods decide the truth of your accusations?''

"Afraid?" said Aerion. "Of such as this? Don't be absurd, Father. My thought is for my beloved brother. Daeron has been wronged by this Ser Duncan as well, and has first claim to his blood. A trial of seven allows both of us to face him.''

''Do me no favors, brother,'' muttered Daeron Targaryen. The eldest son of Prince Maekar looked even worse than he had when Dunk had encountered him in the inn. He seemed to be sober this time, his red-and-black doublet unstained by wine, but his eyes were bloodshot, and a fine sheen of sweat covered his brow. ''I am content to cheer you on as you slay the rogue.''

''You are too kind, sweet brother,'' said Prince Aerion, all smiles, ''but it would be selfish of me to deny you the right to prove the truth of your words at the hazard of your body. I must insist upon a trial of seven.''

Dunk was lost. ''Your Grace, my lords,'' he said to the dais. ''I do not understand. What is this *trial of seven*?''

Prince Baelor shifted uncomfortably in his seat. ''It is another form of trial by combat. Ancient, seldom invoked. It came across the narrow sea with the Andals and their seven gods. In any trial by combat, the accuser and accused are asking the gods to decide the issue between them. The Andals believed that if the seven champions fought on each side, the gods, being thus honored, would be more like to take a hand and see that a just result was achieved.''

''Or mayhap they simply had a taste for swordplay," said Lord Leo Tyrell, a cynical smile touching his lips. "Regardless, Ser Aerion is within his rights. A trial of seven it must be."

"I must fight *seven men,* then?" Dunk asked hopelessly.

"Not alone, ser," Prince Maekar said impatiently. "Don't play the fool, it will not serve. It must be seven against seven. You must needs find six other knights to fight beside you."

Six knights, Dunk thought. They might as well have told him to find six thousand. He had no brothers, no cousins, no old comrades who had stood beside him in battle. Why would six strangers risk their own lives to defend a hedge knight against two royal princelings? "Your Graces, my lords," he said, "what if no one will take my part?"

Maekar Targaryen looked down on him coldly. "If a cause is just, good men will fight for it. If you can find no champions, ser, it will be because you are guilty. Could anything be more plain?"

Dunk had never felt so alone as he did when he walked out the gates of Ashford Castle and heard the portcullis rattle down behind him. A soft rain was falling, light as dew on his skin, and yet he shivered at the touch of it. Across the river, colored rings haloed the scant few pavilions where fires still burned. The night was half gone, he guessed. Dawn would be on him in few hours. *And with dawn comes death.*

They had given him back his sword and silver, yet as he waded across the ford, his thoughts were bleak. He wondered if they expected him to saddle a horse and flee. He could, if he wished. That would be the end of his knighthood, to be sure; he would be no more than an outlaw henceforth, until the day some lord took him and struck off his head. *Better to die a knight than live like that*, he told himself stubbornly. Wet to the knee, he trudged past the empty lists. Most of the pavilions were dark, their owners long asleep, but here and there a few candles still burned. Dunk heard soft moans and cries of pleasure coming from within one tent. It made him wonder whether he would die without ever having known a maid.

Then he heard the snort of a horse, a snort he somehow knew for Thunder's. He turned his steps and ran, and there he was, tied up with Chestnut outside a round pavilion lit from within by a vague golden glow. On its center pole the banner hung sodden, but Dunk could still make out the dark curve of the Fossoway apple. It looked like hope.

A trial by combat,'' Raymun said heavily. "Gods be good, Duncan, that means lances of war, morningstars, battle-axes . . . the swords won't be blunted, do you understand that?''

"Raymun the Reluctant," mocked his cousin Ser Steffon. An apple made of gold and garnets fastened his cloak of yellow wool. "You need not fear, cousin, this is a knightly combat. As you are no knight, your skin is not at risk. Ser Duncan, you have one Fossoway at least. The ripe one. I saw what Aerion did to those puppeteers. I am for you."

"And I," snapped Raymun angrily. "I only meant—"

His cousin cut him off. "Who else fights with us, Ser Duncan?"

Dunk spread his hands hopelessly. "I know no one else. Well, except for Ser Manfred Dondarrion. He wouldn't even vouch that I was a knight, he'll never risk his life for me."

Ser Steffon seemed little perturbed. "Then we need five more good men. Fortunately, I have more than five friends. Leo Longthorn, the Laughing Storm, Lord Caron, the Lannisters, Ser Otho Bracken . . . aye, and the Blackwoods as well, though you will never get Blackwood and Bracken on the same side of a melee. I shall go and speak with some of them."

"They won't be happy at being woken," his cousin objected.

"Excellent," declared Ser Steffon. "If they are angry, they'll fight all the more fiercely. You may rely on me, Ser Duncan. Cousin, if I do not return before dawn, bring my armor and see that Wrath is saddled and barded for me. I shall meet you both in the challengers' paddock." He laughed. "This will be a day long remembered, I think." When he strode from the tent, he looked almost happy.

Not so Raymun. "Five knights," he said glumly after his cousin had gone. "Duncan, I am loath to dash your hopes, but . . ."

"If your cousin can bring the men he speaks of . . ."

"Leo Longthorn? The Brute of Bracken? The Laughing Storm?" Raymun stood. "He knows all of them, I have no doubt, but I would be less certain that any of them know *him*. Steffon sees this as a chance for glory, but it means your life. You should find your own men. I'll help. Better you have too many champions than too few." A noise outside made Raymun turn his head. "Who goes there?" he demanded, as a boy ducked through the flap, followed by a thin man in a rain-sodden black cloak.

"Egg?" Dunk got to his feet. "What are you doing here?"

"I'm your squire," the boy said. "You'll need someone to arm you, ser."

"Does your lord father know you've left the castle?"

"Gods be good, I hope not." Daeron Targaryen undid the clasp of his cloak and let it slide from his thin shoulders.

"*You?* Are you mad, coming here?" Dunk pulled his knife from his sheath. "I ought to shove this through your belly."

"Probably," Prince Daeron admitted. "Though I'd sooner you poured me a cup of wine. Look at my hands." He held one out and let them all see how it shook.

Dunk stepped toward him, glowering. "I don't care about your hands. You lied about me."

"I had to say *something* when my father demanded to know where my little brother had gotten to," the prince replied. He seated himself, ignoring Dunk and his knife. "If truth be told, I hadn't even realized Egg was gone. He wasn't at the bottom of my wine cup, and I hadn't looked anywhere else, so . . ." He sighed.

"Ser, my father is going to join the seven accusers," Egg broke in. "I begged him not to, but he won't listen. He says it is the only way to redeem Aerion's honor, and Daeron's."

"Not that I ever asked to have my honor redeemed," said Prince Daeron sourly. "Whoever has it can keep it, so far as I'm concerned. Still, here we are. For what it's worth, Ser Duncan, you have little to fear from me. The only thing I like less than horses are swords. Heavy things, and beastly sharp. I'll do my best to look gallant in the first charge, but after that . . . well, perhaps you could strike me a nice blow to the side of the helm. Make it ring, but not *too* loud, if you take my meaning. My brothers have my measure when it comes to fighting and dancing and thinking and reading books, but none of them is half my equal at lying insensible in the mud."

Dunk could only stare at him, and wonder whether the princeling was trying to play him for a fool. "Why did you come?"

"To warn you of what you face," Daeron said. "My father has commanded the Kingsguard to fight with him."

"The Kingsguard?" said Dunk, appalled.

"Well, the three who are here. Thank the gods Uncle Baelor left the other four at King's Landing with our royal grandfather."

Egg supplied the names. "Ser Roland Crakehall, Ser Donnel of Duskendale, and Ser Willem Wylde."

"They have small choice in the matter," said Daeron. "They are sworn to protect the lives of the king and royal family, and my brothers and I are blood of the dragon, gods help us."

Dunk counted on his fingers. "That makes six. Who is the seventh man?"

Prince Daeron shrugged. "Aerion will find someone. If need be, he will buy a champion. He has no lack of gold."

"Who do you have?" Egg asked.

"Raymun's cousin Ser Steffon."

Daeron winced. "Only one?"

"Ser Steffon has gone to some of his friends."

"I can bring people," said Egg. "Knights. I can."

"Egg," said Dunk, "I will be fighting your own brothers."

"You won't hurt Daeron, though," the boy said. "He *told* you he'd fall down. And Aerion . . . I remember, when I was little, he used to come into my bedchamber at night and put his knife between my legs. He had too many brothers, he'd say, maybe one night he'd make me his sister, then he could marry me. He threw my cat in the well too. He says he didn't, but he always lies."

Prince Daeron gave a weary shrug. "Egg has the truth of it. Aerion's quite the monster. He thinks he's a dragon in human form, you know. That's why he was so wroth at that puppet show. A pity he wasn't born a Fossoway, then he'd think himself an apple and we'd all be a deal safer, but there you are." Bending, he scooped up his fallen cloak and shook the rain from it. "I must steal back to the castle before my father wonders why I'm taking so long to sharpen my sword, but before I go, I would like a private word, Ser Duncan. Will you walk with me?"

Dunk looked at the princeling suspiciously a moment. "As you wish. Your Grace." He sheathed his dagger. "I need to get my shield too."

"Egg and I will look for knights," promised Raymun.

Prince Daeron knotted his cloak around his neck and pulled up the hood. Dunk followed him back out into the soft rain. They walked toward the merchants' wagons.

"I dreamed of you," said the prince.

"You said that at the inn."

"Did I? Well, it's so. My dreams are not like yours, Ser Duncan. Mine are true. They frighten me. *You* frighten me. I dreamed of you and a dead dragon, you see. A great beast, huge, with wings so large they could cover this meadow. It had fallen on top of you, but you were alive and the dragon was dead."

"Did I kill it?"

"That I could not say, but you were there, and so was the dragon. We were the masters of dragons once, we Targaryens. Now they are all gone, but we remain. I don't care to die today. The gods alone know why, but I don't. So do me a kindness if you would, and make certain it is my brother Aerion you slay."

"I don't care to die either," said Dunk.

"Well, I shan't kill you, ser. I'll withdraw my accusation as well, but it won't serve unless Aerion withdraws his." He sighed. "It may be that I've killed you with my lie. If so, I am sorry. I'm doomed to some hell, I know. Likely one without wine." He shuddered, and on that they parted, there in the cool soft rain.

The merchants had drawn up their wagons on the western verge of the meadow, beneath a stand of birch and ash. Dunk stood under the trees and looked helplessly at the empty place where the puppeteers' wagon had been. *Gone.* He had feared they might be. *I would flee as well, if I were not thick as a castle wall.* He wondered what he would do for a shield now. He had the silver to buy one, he supposed, *if* he could find one for sale. . . .

"Ser Duncan," a voice called out of the dark. Dunk turned to find Steely Pate standing behind him, holding an iron lantern. Under a short leather cloak, the armorer was bare from the waist up, his broad chest and thick arms covered with coarse black hair. "If you are come for your shield, she left it with me." He looked Dunk up and down.

"Two hands and two feet, I count. So it's to be trial by combat, is it?"

"A trial of seven. How did you know?"

"Well, they might have kissed you and made you a lord, but it didn't seem likely, and if it went t'other way, you'd be short some parts. Now follow me."

His wagon was easy to distinguish by the sword and anvil painted on its side. Dunk followed Pate inside. The armorer hung the lantern on a hook, shrugged out of his wet cloak, and pulled a rough-spun tunic down over his head. A hinged board dropped down from one wall to make a table. "Sit," he said, shoving a low stool toward him.

Dunk sat. "Where did she go?"

"They make for Dorne. The girl's uncle, there's a wise man. Well gone is well forgot. Stay and be seen, and belike the dragon remembers. Besides, he did not think she ought see you die." Pate went to the far end of the wagon, rummaged about in the shadows a moment, and returned with the shield. "Your rim was old cheap steel, brittle and rusted," he said. "I've made you a new one, twice as thick, and put some bands across the back. It will be heavier now, but stronger too. The girl did the paint."

She had made a better job of it than he could ever have hoped for. Even by lantern light, the sunset colors were rich and bright, the tree tall and strong and noble. The falling star was a bright slash of paint across the oaken sky. Yet now that Dunk held it in his hands, it seemed all wrong. The star was *falling*, what sort of sigil was that? Would he fall just as fast? And sunset heralds night. "I should have stayed with the chalice," he said miserably. "It had wings, at least, to fly away, and Ser Arlan said the cup was full of faith and fellowship and good things to drink. This shield is all painted up like death."

"The elm's alive," Pate pointed out. "See how green the leaves are? Summer leaves, for certain. And I've seen shields blazoned with skulls and wolves and ravens, even hanged men and bloody heads. They served well enough, and so will this. You know the old shield rhyme? *Oak and iron, guard me well . . .*"

"*. . . or else I'm dead, and doomed to hell,*" Dunk finished. He had not thought of that rhyme in years. The old man had taught it to him, a long time ago. "How much do you want for the new rim and all?" he asked Pate.

"From you?" Pate scratched his beard. "A copper."

The rain had all but stopped as the first wan light suffused the eastern sky, but it had done its work.

Lord Ashford's men had removed the barriers, and the tourney field was one great morass of grey-brown mud and torn grass. Tendrils of fog were writhing along the ground like pale white snakes as Dunk made his way back toward the lists. Steely Pate walked with him.

The viewing stand had already begun to fill, the lords and ladies clutching their cloaks tight about them against the morning chill. Smallfolk were drifting toward the field as well, and hundreds of them already stood along the fence. *So many come to see me die,* thought Dunk bitterly, but he wronged them. A few steps farther on, a woman called out, "Good fortune to you." An old man stepped up to take his hand and said, "May the gods give you strength, ser." Then a begging brother in a tattered brown robe said a blessing on his sword, and a maid kissed his cheek. *They are for me.* "Why?" he asked Pate. "What am I to them?"

"A knight who remembered his vows," the smith said.

They found Raymun outside the challengers' paddock at the south end of the lists, waiting with his cousin's horse and Dunk's. Thunder tossed restlessly beneath the weight of chinet, chamfron, and blanket of heavy mail. Pate inspected the armor and pronounced it good work, even though someone else had forged it. Wherever the armor had come from, Dunk was grateful.

Then he saw the others: the one-eyed man with the salt-and-pepper beard, the young knight in the striped yellow-and-black surcoat with the beehives on the shield. *Robyn Rhysling and Humfrey Beesbury,* he thought in astonishment. *And Ser Humfrey Hardyng as well.* Hardyng was mounted on Aerion's red charger, now barded in his red-and-white diamonds.

He went to them. "Sers, I am in your debt."

"The debt is Aerion's," Ser Humfrey Hardyng replied, "and we mean to collect it."

"I had heard your leg was broken."

"You heard the truth," Hardyng said. "I cannot walk. But so long as I can sit a horse, I can fight."

Raymun took Dunk aside. "I hoped Hardyng would want another chance at Aerion, and he did. As it happens, the other Humfrey is his brother by marriage. Egg is responsible for Ser Robyn, whom he knew from other tourneys. So you are five."

"Six," said Dunk in wonder, pointing. A knight was entering the paddock, his squire leading his charger behind him. "The Laughing Storm." A head taller than Ser Raymun and almost of a height with Dunk, Ser Lyonel wore a cloth-of-gold surcoat bearing the crowned stag of House Baratheon, and carried his antlered helm under his arm. Dunk reached for his hand. "Ser Lyonel, I cannot thank you enough for coming, nor Ser Steffon for bringing you."

"Ser Steffon?" Ser Lyonel gave him a puzzled look. "It was your squire who came to me. The boy, Aegon. My own lad tried to chase him off, but he slipped between his legs and turned a flagon of wine over my head." He laughed. "There has not been a trial of seven for more than a hundred years, do you know that? I was not about to miss a chance to fight the Kingsguard knights, and tweak Prince Maekar's nose in the bargain."

"Six," Dunk said hopefully to Raymun Fossoway as Ser Lyonel joined the others. "Your cousin will bring the last, surely."

A roar went up from the crowd. At the north end of the meadow, a column of knights came trotting out of the river mist. The three Kingsguard came first, like ghosts in their gleaming white enamel armor, long white cloaks trailing behind them. Even their shields were white, blank and clean as a field of new-fallen snow. Behind rode Prince Maekar and his sons. Aerion was mounted on a dapple grey, orange and red flickering through the slashes in the horse's caparison at each stride. His brother's destrier was a smaller bay, armored in overlapping black and gold scales. A green silk plume trailed from Daeron's helm. It was their father who made the most fearsome appearance, however. Black curved dragon teeth ran across his shoulders, along the crest of his helm, and down his back, and the huge spiked mace strapped to his saddle was as deadly-looking a weapon as any Dunk had ever seen.

"Six," Raymun exclaimed suddenly. "They are only six."

It was true, Dunk saw. *Three black knights and three white. They are a man short as well.* Was it possible that Aerion had not been able to find a seventh man? What would that mean? Would they fight six against six if neither found a seventh?

Egg slipped up beside him as he was trying to puzzle it out. "Ser, it's time you donned your armor."

"Thank you, squire. If you would be so good?"

Steely Pate lent the lad a hand. Hauberk and gorget, greaves and gauntlet, coif and codpiece, they turned him into steel, checking each buckle and each clasp thrice. Ser Lyonel sat sharpening his sword on a whetstone while the Humfreys talked quietly, Ser Robyn prayed, and Raymun Fossoway paced back and forth, wondering where his cousin had got to.

Dunk was fully armored by the time Ser Steffon finally appeared. "Raymun," he called, "my mail, if you please." He had changed into a padded doublet to wear beneath his steel.

"Ser Steffon," said Dunk, "what of your friends? We need another knight to make our seven."

"You need two, I fear," Ser Steffon said. Raymun laced up the back of the hauberk.

"M'lord?" Dunk did not understand. "Two?"

Ser Steffon picked up a gauntlet of fine lobstered steel and slid his left hand into it, flexing his fingers. "I see five here," he said while Raymun fastened his sword belt. "Beesbury, Rhysling, Hardyng, Baratheon, and yourself."

"And you," said Dunk. "You're the sixth."

"I am the seventh," said Ser Steffon, smiling, "but for the other side. I fight with Prince Aerion and the accusers."

Raymun had been about to hand his cousin his helm. He stopped as if struck. "No."

"Yes." Ser Steffon shrugged. "Ser Duncan understands, I am sure. I have a duty to my prince."

"You told him to rely on you." Raymun had gone pale.

"Did I?" He took the helm from his cousin's hands. "No doubt I was sincere at the time. Bring me my horse."

"Get him yourself," said Raymun angrily. "If you think I wish any part of this, you're as thick as you are vile."

"Vile?" Ser Steffon *tsk*ed. "Guard your tongue,

Raymun. We're both apples from the same tree. And you are my squire. Or have you forgotten your vows?"

"No. Have you forgotten yours? You swore to be a knight."

"I shall be more than a knight before this day is done. *Lord* Fossoway. I like the sound of that." Smiling, he pulled on his other gauntlet, turned away, and crossed the paddock to his horse. Though the other defenders stared at him with contemptuous eyes, no one made a move to stop him.

Dunk watched Ser Steffon lead his destrier back across the field. His hands coiled into fists, but his throat felt too raw for speech. *No words would move the likes of him anyway.*

"Knight me." Raymun put a hand on Dunk's shoulder and turned him. "I will take my cousin's place. Ser Duncan, knight me." He went to one knee.

Frowning, Dunk moved a hand to the hilt of his longsword, then hesitated. "Raymun, I . . . I should not."

"You must. Without me, you are only five."

"The lad has the truth of it," said Ser Lyonel Baratheon. "Do it, Ser Duncan. Any knight can make a knight."

"Do you doubt my courage?" Raymun asked.

"No," said Dunk. "Not that, but . . ." Still he hesitated.

A fanfare of trumpets cut the misty morning air. Egg came running up to them. "Ser, Lord Ashford summons you."

The Laughing Storm gave an impatient shake of the head. "Go to him, Ser Duncan. I'll give squire Raymun his knighthood." He slid his sword out of his sheath and shouldered Dunk aside. "Raymun of House Fossoway," he began solemnly, touching the blade to the squire's right shoulder, "in the name of the Warrior I charge you to be brave." The sword moved from his right shoulder to his left. "In the name of the Father I charge you to be just." Back to the right. "In the name of the Mother I charge you to defend the young and innocent." The left. "In the name of the Maid I charge you to protect all women. . . ."

Dunk left them there, feeling as relieved as he was guilty. *We are still one short,* he thought as Egg held Thunder for him. *Where will I find another man?* He turned the horse and rode slowly toward the viewing stand, where Lord Ashford stood waiting. From the north end of the lists, Prince Aerion advanced to meet him. "Ser Duncan," he said cheerfully, "it would seem you have only five champions."

"Six," said Dunk. "Ser Lyonel is knighting Raymun Fossoway. We will fight you six against seven." Men had won at far worse odds, he knew.

But Lord Ashford shook his head. "That is not permitted, ser. If you cannot find another knight to take your side, you must be declared guilty of the crimes of which you stand accused."

Guilty, thought Dunk. *Guilty of loosening a tooth, and for that I must die.* "M'lord, I beg a moment."

"You have it."

Dunk rode slowly along the fence. The viewing stand was crowded with knights. "*M'lords,*" he called to them, "*do none of you remember Ser Arlan of Pennytree? I was his squire. We served many of you. Ate at your tables and slept in your halls.*" He saw Manfred Dondarrion seated in the highest tier. "*Ser Arlan took a wound in your lord father's service.*" The knight said something to the lady beside him, paying no heed. Dunk was forced to move on. "*Lord Lannister, Ser Arlan unhorsed you once in tourney.*" The Grey Lion examined his gloved hands, studiedly refusing to raise his eyes. "*He was a good man, and he taught me how to be a knight. Not only sword and lance, but honor. A knight defends the innocent, he said. That's all I did. I need one more knight to fight beside me. One, that's all. Lord Caron? Lord Swann?*" Lord Swann laughed softly as Lord Caron whispered in his ear.

Dunk reined up before Ser Otho Bracken, lowering his voice. "Ser Otho, all know you for a great champion. Join us, I beg you. In the names of the old gods and the new. My cause is just."

"That may be," said the Brute of Bracken, who had at least the grace to reply, "but it is your cause, not mine. I know you not, boy."

Heartsick, Dunk wheeled Thunder and raced back and forth before the tiers of pale cold men. Despair made him shout. *"ARE THERE NO TRUE KNIGHTS AMONG YOU?"*

Only silence answered.

Across the field, Prince Aerion laughed. "The dragon is not mocked," he called out.

Then came a voice. "I will take Ser Duncan's side."

A black stallion emerged from out of the river mists, a black knight on his back. Dunk saw the dragon shield, and the red enamel crest upon his helm with its three roaring heads. *The Young Prince. Gods be good, it is truly him?*

Lord Ashford made the same mistake. "Prince Valarr?"

"No." The black knight lifted the visor of his helm. "I did not think to enter the lists at Ashford, my lord, so I brought no armor. My son was good enough to lend me his." Prince Baelor smiled almost sadly.

The accusers were thrown into confusion, Dunk

could see. Prince Maekar spurred his mount forward. "Brother, have you taken leave of your senses?" He pointed a mailed finger at Dunk. "This man attacked my son."

"This man protected the weak, as every true knight must," replied Prince Baelor. "Let the gods determine if he was right or wrong." He gave a tug on his reins, turned Valarr's huge black destrier, and trotted to the south end of the field.

Dunk brought Thunder up beside him, and the other defenders gathered round them; Robyn Rhysling and Ser Lyonel, the Humfreys. *Good men all, but are they good enough?* "Where is Raymun?"

"*Ser* Raymun, if you please." He cantered up, a grim smile lighting his face beneath his plumed helm. "My pardons, ser. I needed to make a small change to my sigil, lest I be mistaken for my dishonorable cousin." He showed them all his shield. The polished golden field remained the same, and the Fossoway apple, but this apple was green instead of red. "I fear I am still not ripe . . . but better green than wormy, eh?"

Ser Lyonel laughed, and Dunk grinned despite himself. Even Prince Baelor seemed to approve.

Lord Ashford's septon had come to the front of the viewing stand and raised his crystal to call the throng to prayer.

"Attend me, all of you," Baelor said quietly.

"The accusers will be armed with heavy war lances for the first charge. Lances of ash, eight feet long, banded against splitting and tipped with a steel point sharp enough to drive through plate with the weight of a warhorse behind it."

"We shall use the same," said Ser Humfrey Beesbury. Behind him, the septon was calling on the Seven to look down and judge this dispute, and grant victory to the men whose cause was just.

"No," Baelor said. "We will arm ourselves with tourney lances instead."

"Tourney lances are made to break," objected Raymun.

"They are also made twelve feet long. If our points strike home, theirs cannot touch us. Aim for helm or chest. In a tourney it is a gallant thing to break your lance against a foe's shield, but here it may well mean death. If we can unhorse them and keep our own saddles, the advantage is ours." He glanced to Dunk. "If Ser Duncan is killed, it is considered that the gods have judged him guilty, and the contest is over. If both of his accusers are slain, or withdraw their accusations, the same is true. Elsewise, all seven of one side or the other must perish or yield for the trial to end."

"Prince Daeron will not fight," Dunk said.

"Not well, anyway," laughed Ser Lyonel. "Against that, we have three of the White Swords to contend with."

Baelor took that calmly. "My brother erred when he demanded that the Kingsguard fight for his son. Their oath forbids them to harm a prince of the blood. Fortunately, I am such." He gave them a faint smile. "Keep the others off me long enough, and I shall deal with the Kingsguard."

"My prince, is that chivalrous?" asked Ser Lyonel Baratheon as the septon was finishing his invocation.

"The gods will let us know," said Baelor Breakspear.

A deep expectant silence had fallen across Ashford Meadow.

Eighty yards away, Aerion's grey stallion trumpeted with impatience and pawed the muddy ground. Thunder was very still by comparison; he was an older horse, veteran of half a hundred fights, and he knew what was expected of him. Egg handed Dunk up his shield. "May the gods be with you, ser," the boy said.

The sight of his elm tree and shooting star gave him heart. Dunk slid his left arm through the strap and tightened his fingers around the grip. *Oak and iron, guard me well, or else I'm dead and doomed to hell.* Steely Pate brought his lance to him, but Egg insisted that it must be he who put it into Dunk's hand.

To either side, his companions took up their own lances and spread out in a long line. Prince Baelor was to his right and Ser Lyonel to his left, but the narrow eye slit of the greathelm limited Dunk's vision to what was directly ahead of him. The viewing stand was gone, and likewise the smallfolk crowding the fence; there was only the muddy field, the pale blowing mist, the river, town, and castle to the north, and the princeling on his grey charger with flames on his helm and a dragon on his shield. Dunk watched Aerion's squire hand him a war lance, eight feet long and black as night. *He will put that through my heart if he can.*

A horn sounded.

For a heartbeat Dunk sat as still as a fly in amber, though all the horses were moving. A stab of panic went through him. *I have forgotten*, he thought wildly, *I have forgotten all, I will shame myself, I will lose everything.*

Thunder saved him. The big brown stallion knew what to do, even if his rider did not. He broke into a slow trot. Dunk's training took over then. He gave the warhorse a light touch of spur and couched his lance. At the same time he swung his shield until it covered most of the left side of his body. He held it at an angle, to deflect blows away from him. *Oak and iron guard me well, or else I'm dead and doomed to hell.*

The noise of the crowd was no more than the crash of distant waves. Thunder slid into a gallop. Dunk's teeth jarred together with the violence of the pace. He pressed his heels down, tightening his legs with all his strength and letting his body become part of the motion of the horse beneath. *I am Thunder and Thunder is me, we are one beast, we are joined, we are one.* The air inside his helm was already so hot he could scarce breathe.

In a tourney joust, his foe would be to his left across the tilting barrier, and he would need to swing his lance across Thunder's neck. The angle made it more likely that the wood would split on impact. But this was a deadlier game they played today. With no barriers dividing them, the destriers charged straight at one another. Prince Baelor's huge black was much faster than Thunder, and Dunk glimpsed him pounding ahead through the corner of his eye slit. He sensed more than saw the others. *They do not matter, only Aerion matters, only him.*

He watched the dragon come. Spatters of mud sprayed back from the hooves of Prince Aerion's grey, and Dunk could see the horse's nostrils flaring. The black lance still angled upward. A knight who holds his lance high and brings it on line at the last moment always risks lowering it too far, the old man had told him. He brought his own point to bear on the center of the princeling's chest. *My lance is part of my arm,* he told himself. *It's my finger, a wooden finger. All I need do is touch him with my long wooden finger.*

He tried not to see the sharp iron point at the end of Aerion's black lance, growing larger with every stride. *The dragon, look at the dragon,* he thought. The great three-headed beast covered the prince's shield, red wings and gold fire. *No, look only where you mean to strike,* he remembered suddenly, but his lance had already begun to slide off line. Dunk tried to correct, but it was too late. He saw his point strike Aerion's shield, taking the dragon between two of its heads, gouging into a gout of painted flame. At the muffled *crack,* he felt Thunder recoil under him, trembling with the force of the impact, and half a heartbeat later something smashed into his side with awful force. The horses slammed together violently, armor crashing and clanging as Thunder stumbled and Dunk's lance fell from his hand. Then he was past his foe, clutching at his saddle in a desperate effort to keep his seat. Thunder lurched sideways in the sloppy mud and Dunk felt his rear legs slip out from under. They were sliding, spinning, and then the stallion's hindquarters slapped down hard. *"Up!"* Dunk roared, lashing out with his spurs. *"Up, Thunder!"* And somehow the old warhorse found his feet again.

He could feel a sharp pain under his rib, and his left arm was being pulled down. Aerion had driven his lance through oak, wool, and steel; three feet of splintered ash and sharp iron stuck from his side. Dunk reached over with his right hand, grasped the lance just below the head, clenched his teeth, and pulled it out of him with one savage yank. Blood followed, seeping through the rings of his mail to redden his surcoat. The world swam and he almost fell. Dimly, through the pain, he could hear voices calling his name. His beautiful shield was useless now. He tossed it aside, elm tree, shooting star, broken lance, and all, and drew his sword, but he hurt so much he did not think he could swing it.

Turning Thunder in a tight circle, he tried to get a sense of what was happening elsewhere on the field. Ser Humfrey Hardyng clung to the neck of his mount, obviously wounded. The other Ser Humfrey lay motionless in a lake of bloodstained mud, a broken lance protruding from his groin. He saw Prince Baelor gallop past, lance still intact, and drive one of the Kingsguard from his saddle. Another of the white knights was already down, and Maekar had been unhorsed as well. The third of the Kingsguard was fending off Ser Robyn Rhysling.

Aerion, where is Aerion? The sound of drumming hooves behind him made Dunk turn his head sharply. Thunder bugled and reared, hooves lashing out futilely as Aerion's grey stallion barreled into him at full gallop.

This time there was no hope of recovery. His longsword went spinning from his grasp, and the ground rose up to meet him. He landed with a bruising impact that jarred him to the bone. Pain stabbed through him, so sharp he sobbed. For a moment it was all he could do to lie there. The taste of blood filled his mouth. *Dunk the lunk, thought he could be a knight.* He knew he had to find his feet again, or die. Groaning, he forced himself to hands and knees. He could not breathe, nor could he see. The eye slit of his helm was packed with mud. Lurching blindly to his feet, Dunk scraped at the mud with a mailed finger. *There, that's . . .*

Through his fingers, he glimpsed a dragon flying, and a spiked morningstar whirling on the end of a chain. Then his head seemed to burst to pieces.

When his eyes opened he was on the ground again, sprawled on his back. The mud had all been knocked from his helm, but now one eye was closed by blood. Above was nothing was dark grey sky. His face throbbed, and he could feel cold wet metal pressing in against cheek and temple. *He broke my head, and I'm dying.* What was worse was the others who would die with him, Raymun and Prince Baelor and the rest. *I've failed them. I am no champion. I'm not even a hedge knight. I am nothing.* He remembered Prince Daeron boasting that no one could lie insensible in the mud as well as he did. *He never saw Dunk the lunk, though, did he?* The shame was worse than the pain.

The dragon appeared above him.

Three heads it had, and wings bright as flame, red and yellow and orange. It was laughing. "Are you dead yet, hedge knight?" it asked. "Cry for quarter and admit your guilt, and perhaps I'll only claim a hand and a foot. Oh, and those teeth, but what are a few teeth? A man like you can live years on pease porridge." The dragon laughed again. "No? Eat *this*, then." The spiked ball whirled round and round the sky, and fell toward his head as fast as a shooting star.

Dunk rolled.

Where he found the strength he did not know, but he found it. He rolled into Aerion's legs, threw a steel-clad arm around his thigh, dragged him cursing into the mud, and rolled on top of him. *Let him swing his bloody morningstar now.* The prince tried forcing the lip of his shield up at Dunk's head, but his battered helm took the brunt of the impact. Aerion was strong, but Dunk was stronger, and larger and heavier as well. He grabbed hold of the shield with both hands and twisted until the straps broke. Then he brought it down on the top of the princeling's helm, again and again and again, smashing the enameled flames of his crest. The shield was thicker than Dunk's had been, solid oak banded with iron. A flame broke off. Then another. The prince ran out of flames long before Dunk ran out of blows.

Aerion finally let go the handle of his useless morningstar and clawed for the poniard at his hip. He got it free of its sheath, but when Dunk whanged his hand with the shield the knife sailed off into the mud.

He could vanquish Ser Duncan the Tall, but not Dunk of Flea Bottom. The old man had taught him jousting and swordplay, but this sort of fighting he had learned earlier, in shadowy wynds and crooked alleys behind the city's winesinks. Dunk flung the battered shield away and wrenched up the visor of Aerion's helm.

A visor is a weak point, he remembered Steely Pate saying. The prince had all but ceased to struggle. His eyes were purple and full of terror. Dunk had a sudden urge to grab one and pop it like a grape between two steel fingers, but that would not be knightly. *"YIELD!"* he shouted.

"I yield," the dragon whispered, pale lips barely moving. Dunk blinked down at him. For a moment he could not credit what his ears had heard. *Is it done, then?* He turned his head slowly from side to side, trying to see. His vision slit was partly closed by the blow that had smashed in the left side of his face. He glimpsed Prince Maekar, mace in hand, trying to fight his way to his son's side. Baelor Breakspear was holding him off.

Dunk lurched to his feet and pulled Prince Aerion up after him. Fumbling at the lacings of his helm, he tore it off and flung it away. At once he was drowned in sights and sounds; grunts and curses, the shouts of the crowd, one stallion screaming while another raced riderless across the field. Everywhere steel rang on steel. Raymun and his cousin were slashing at each other in front of the viewing stand, both afoot. Their shields were splintered ruins, the green apple and the red both hacked to tinder. One of the Kingsguard knights was carrying a wounded brother from the field. They both looked alike in their white armor and white cloaks. The third of the white knights was down, and the Laughing Storm had joined Prince Baelor against Prince Maekar. Mace, battle-axe, and longsword clashed and clanged, ringing against helm and shield. Maekar was taking three blows for every one he landed, and Dunk could see that it would be over soon. *I must make an end to it before more of us are killed.*

Prince Aerion made a sudden dive for his morningstar. Dunk kicked him in the back and knocked him facedown, then grabbed hold of one of his legs and dragged him across the field. By the time he reached the viewing stand where Lord Ashford sat, the Bright Prince was brown as a privy. Dunk hauled him onto his feet and rattled him, shaking some of the mud onto Lord Ashford and the fair maid. "Tell him!"

Aerion Brightflame spit out a mouthful of grass and dirt. "I withdraw my accusation."

Afterward Dunk could not have said whether he walked from the field under his own power or had required help. He hurt everywhere, and some places worse than others. *I am a knight now in truth?* he remembered wondering. *Am I a champion?*

Egg helped him remove his greaves and gorget, and Raymun as well, and even Steely Pate. He was too dazed to tell them apart. They were fingers and thumbs and voices. Pate was the one complaining, Dunk knew. "Look what he's done to me armor," he said. "All dinted and banged and scratched. Aye, I ask you, why do I bother? I'll have to cut that mail off him, I fear."

"Raymun," Dunk said urgently, clutching at his friend's hands. "The others. How did they fare?"

He had to know. "Has anyone died?"

"Beesbury," Raymun said. "Slain by Donnel of Duskendale in the first charge. Ser Humfrey is gravely wounded as well. The rest of us are bruised and bloody, no more. Save for you."

"And them? The accusers?"

"Ser Willem Wylde of the Kingsguard was carried from the field insensate, and I think I cracked a few of my cousin's ribs. At least I hope so."

"And Prince Daeron?" Dunk blurted. "Did he survive?"

"Once Ser Robyn unhorsed him, he lay where he fell. He may have a broken foot. His own horse trod on him while running loose about the field."

Dazed and confused as he was, Dunk felt a huge sense of relief. "His dream was wrong, then. The dead dragon. Unless Aerion died. He didn't though, did he?"

"No," said Egg. "You spared him. Don't you remember?"

"I suppose." Already his memories of the fight were becoming confused and vague. "One moment I feel drunk. The next it hurts so bad I know I'm dying."

They made him lie down on his back and talked over him as he gazed up into the roiling grey sky. It seemed to Dunk that it was still morning. He wondered how long the fight had taken.

"Gods be good, the lance point drove the rings deep into his flesh," he heard Raymun saying. "It will mortify unless . . ."

"Get him drunk and pour some boiling oil into it," someone suggested. "That's how the maesters do it."

"Wine." The voice had a hollow metallic ring to it. "*Not* oil, that will kill him, boiling wine. I'll send Maester Yormwell to have a look at him when he's done tending my brother."

A tall knight stood above him, in black armor dinted and scarred by many blows. *Prince Baelor.* The scarlet dragon on his helm had lost a head, both wings, and most of its tail. "Your Grace," Dunk said, "I am your man. Please. Your man."

"My man." The black knight put a hand on Raymun's shoulder to steady himself. "I need good men, Ser Duncan. The realm . . ." His voice sounded oddly slurred. Perhaps he'd bit his tongue.

Dunk was very tired. It was hard to stay awake. "Your man," he murmured once more.

The prince moved his head slowly from side to side. "Ser Raymun . . . my helm, if you'd be so kind. Visor . . . visor's cracked, and my fingers . . . fingers feel like wood . . ."

"At once, Your Grace." Raymun took the prince's helm in both hands and grunted. "Goodman Pate, a hand."

Steely Pate dragged over a mounting stool. "It's crushed down at the back, Your Grace, toward the left side. Smashed into the gorget. Good steel, this, to stop such a blow."

"Brother's mace, most like," Baelor said thickly. "He's strong." He winced. "That . . . feels queer, I . . ."

"Here it comes." Pate lifted the battered helm away. "Gods be good. *Oh gods oh gods oh gods preserve . . .*"

Dunk saw something red and wet fall out of the helm. Someone was screaming, high and terrible. Against the bleak grey sky swayed a tall tall prince in black armor with only half a skull. He could see red blood and pale bone beneath and something else, something blue-grey and pulpy. A queer troubled look passed across Baelor Breakspear's face, like a cloud passing before a sun. He raised his hand and touched the back of his head with two fingers, oh so lightly. And then he fell.

Dunk caught him. "Up," they say he said, just as he had with Thunder in the melee, "up, up." But he never remembered that afterward, and the prince did not rise.

Baelor of House Targaryen, Prince of Dragonstone, Hand of the King, Protector of the Realm, and heir apparent to the Iron Throne of the Seven

Kingdoms of Westeros, went to the fire in the yard of Ashford Castle on the north bank of River Cockleswent. Other great houses might choose to bury their dead in the dark earth or sink them in the cold green sea, but the Targaryens were the blood of the dragon, and their ends were writ in flame.

He had been the finest knight of his age, and some argued that he should have gone to face the dark clad in mail and plate, a sword in his hand. In the end, though, his royal father's wishes prevailed, and Daeron II had a peaceable nature. When Dunk shuffled past Baelor's bier, the prince wore a black velvet tunic with the three-headed dragon picked out in scarlet thread upon his breast. Around his throat was a heavy gold chain. His sword was sheathed by his side, but he did wear a helm, a thin golden helm with an open visor so men could see his face.

Valarr, the Young Prince, stood vigil at the foot of the bier while his father lay in state. He was a shorter, slimmer, handsomer version of his sire, without the twice-broken nose that had made Baelor seem more human than royal. Valarr's hair was brown, but a bright streak of silver-gold ran through it. The sight of it reminded Dunk of Aerion, but he knew that was not fair. Egg's hair was growing back as bright as his brother's, and Egg was a decent enough lad, for a prince.

When he stopped to offer awkward sympathies, well larded with thanks, Prince Valarr blinked cool blue eyes at him and said, "My father was only nine-and-thirty. He had it in him to be a great king, the greatest since Aegon the Dragon. Why would the gods take him, and leave *you*?" He shook his head. "Begone with you, Ser Duncan. Begone."

Wordless, Dunk limped from the castle, down to the camp by the green pool. He had no answer for Valarr. Nor for the questions he asked himself. The maesters and the boiling wine had done their work, and his wound was healing cleanly, though there would be a deep puckered scar between his left arm and his nipple. He could not see the wound without thinking of Baelor. *He saved me once with his sword, and once with a word, even though he was a dead man as he stood there.* The world made no sense when a great prince died so a hedge knight might live. Dunk sat beneath his elm and stared morosely at his foot.

When four guardsmen in the royal livery appeared in his camp late one day, he was sure they had come to kill him after all. Too weak and weary to reach for a sword, he sat with his back to the elm, waiting.

"Our prince begs the favor of a private word."

"Which prince?" asked Dunk, wary.

"This prince," a brusque voice said before the captain could answer. Maekar Targaryen walked out from behind the elm.

Dunk got slowly to his feet. *What would he have of me now?*

Maekar motioned, and the guards vanished as suddenly as they had appeared. The prince studied him a long moment, then turned and paced away from him to stand beside the pool, gazing down at his reflection in the water. "I have sent Aerion to Lys," he announced abruptly. "A few years in the Free Cities may change him for the better."

Dunk had never been to the Free Cities, so he did not know what to say to that. He was pleased that Aerion was gone from the Seven Kingdoms, and hoped he never came back, but that was not a thing you told a father of his son. He stood silent.

Prince Maekar turned to face him. "Some men will say I meant to kill my brother. The gods know it is a lie, but I will hear the whispers till the day I die. And it was my mace that dealt the fatal blow, I have no doubt. The only other foes he faced in the melee were three Kingsguard, whose vows forbade them to do any more than defend themselves. So it was me. Strange to say, I do not recall the blow that broke his skull. Is that a mercy or a curse? Some of both, I think."

From the way he looked at Dunk, it seemed the

prince wanted an answer. "I could not say, Your Grace." Perhaps he should have hated Maekar, but instead he felt a queer sympathy for the man. "You swung the mace, m'lord, but it was for me Prince Baelor died. So I killed him too, as much as you."

"Yes," the prince admitted. "You'll hear them whisper as well. The king is old. When he dies, Valarr will climb the Iron Throne in place of his father. Each time a battle is lost or a crop fails, the fools will say, 'Baelor would not have let it happen, but the hedge knight killed him.' "

Dunk could see the truth in that. "If I had not fought, you would have had my hand off. And my foot. Sometimes I sit under that tree there and look at my feet and ask if I couldn't have spared one. How could my foot be worth a prince's life? And the other two as well, the Humfreys, they were good men too." Ser Humfrey Hardyng had succumbed to his wounds only last night.

"And what answer does your tree give you?"

"None that I can hear. But the old man, Ser Arlan, every day at evenfall he'd say, 'I wonder what the morrow will bring.' He never knew, no more than we do. Well, mighten it be that some morrow will come when I'll have need of that foot? When the *realm* will need that foot, even more than a prince's life?"

Maekar chewed on that a time, mouth clenched

beneath the silvery-pale beard that made his face seem so square. "It's not bloody likely," he said harshly. "The realm has as many hedge knights as hedges, and all of them have feet."

"If Your Grace has a better answer, I'd want to hear it."

Maekar frowned. "It may be that the gods have a taste for cruel japes. Or perhaps there are no gods. Perhaps none of this had any meaning. I'd ask the High Septon, but the last time I went to him he told me that no man can truly understand the workings of the gods. Perhaps he should try sleeping under a tree." He grimaced. "My youngest son seems to have grown fond of you, ser. It is time he was a squire, but he tells me he will serve no knight but you. He is an unruly boy, as you will have noticed. Will you have him?"

"Me?" Dunk's mouth opened and closed and opened again. "Egg . . . Aegon, I mean . . . he is a good lad, but, Your Grace, I know you honor me, but . . . I am only a hedge knight."

"That can be changed," said Maekar. "Aegon is to return to my castle at Summerhall. There is a place there for you, if you wish. A knight of my household. You'll swear your sword to me, and Aegon can squire for you. While you train him, my master-at-arms will finish your own training." The prince gave him a shrewd look. "Your Ser Arlan did all he could for you, I have no doubt, but you still have much to learn.''

''I know, m'lord.'' Dunk looked about him. At the green grass and the reeds, the tall elm, the ripples dancing across the surface of the sunlit pool. Another dragonfly was moving across the water, or perhaps it was the same one. *What shall it be, Dunk?* he asked himself. *Dragonflies or dragons?* A few days ago he would have answered at once. It was all he had ever dreamed, but now that the prospect was at hand it frightened him. ''Just before Prince Baelor died, I swore to be his man.''

''Presumptuous of you,'' said Maekar. ''What did he say?''

''That the realm needed good men.''

''That's true enough. What of it?''

''I will take your son as squire, Your Grace, but not at Summerhall. Not for a year or two. He's seen sufficient of castles, I would judge. I'll have him only if I can take him on the road with me.'' He pointed to old Chestnut. ''He'll ride my steed, wear my old cloak, and he'll keep my sword sharp and my mail scoured. We'll sleep in inns and stables, and now and again in the halls of some landed knight or lesser lordling, and maybe under trees when we must.''

Prince Maekar gave him an incredulous look. ''Did the trial addle your wits, man? Aegon is a prince of the realm. The blood of the dragon. Princes are not made for sleeping in ditches and eating hard salt beef." He saw Dunk hesitate. "What is it you're afraid to tell me? Say what you will, ser."

"Daeron never slept in a ditch, I'll wager," Dunk said, very quietly, "and all the beef that Aerion ever ate was thick and rare and bloody, like as not."

Maekar Targaryen, Prince of Summerhall, regarded Dunk of Flea Bottom for a long time, his jaw working silently beneath his silvery beard. Finally he turned and walked away, never speaking a word. Dunk heard him riding off with his men. When they were gone, there was no sound but the faint thrum of the dragonfly's wings as it skimmed across the water.

The boy came the next morning, just as the sun was coming up. He wore old boots, brown breeches, a brown wool tunic, and an old traveler's cloak. "My lord father says I am to serve you."

"Serve you, *ser*," Dunk reminded him. "You can start by saddling the horses. Chestnut is yours, treat her kindly. I don't want to find you on Thunder unless I put you there."

Egg went to get the saddles. "Where are we going, ser?"

Dunk thought for a moment. "I have never been over the Red Mountains. Would you like to have a look at Dorne?"

Egg grinned. "I hear they have good puppet shows," he said.

PERN

Anne McCaffrey

DRAGONRIDERS OF PERN TRILOGY:

DRAGONFLIGHT (1969)
DRAGONQUEST (1971)
THE WHITE DRAGON (1978)

HARPER HALL TRILOGY:
DRAGONSONG (1976)
DRAGONSINGER (1977)
DRAGONDRUMS (1978)

OTHER PERN NOVELS:

MORETA, DRAGONLADY OF PERN (1983)
NERILKA'S STORY (1986)
DRAGONSDAWN (1988)
THE RENEGADES OF PERN (1989)
ALL THE WEYRS OF PERN (1991)
THE CHRONICLES OF PERN (1992)
THE DOLPHINS OF PERN (1994)
DRAGONSEYE (1996)
THE MASTERHARPER OF PERN (1998)

Dissatisfied with life on technologically advanced Earth, hundreds of colonists traveled through space to the star Rukbat, which held six planets in orbit around it, five in stable trajectories, and one that looped wildly around the others. The third planet was capable of sustaining life, and the spacefarers settled there, naming it Pern. They cannibalized their spaceships for material and began building their homes.

Pern was ideal for settlement, except for one thing. At irregular intervals, the sixth planet of its system would swing close to it and release swarms of deadly mycorrhizoid spores, which devoured anything organic that they touched and rendered the ground where they landed fallow for years. The colonists immediately began searching for a way to combat the Thread, as the spores were named. For defense, they turned to the dragonets, small flying lizards that the colonists had tamed when they first landed. The fire-breathing ability of these reptiles had been a great help in the first Threadfall. By genetically enhancing and selectively breeding these reptiles through the generations, the colonists created a race of full-sized dragons.

With the dragons and their riders working together, the Pern colonists were able to fight Thread effectively and establish a firm hold on the planet. They settled into a quasi-feudal agricultural society, building Holds for the administrators and field workers, Halls for the craftsmen, and Weyrs for the dragons and riders to inhabit.

Many of the Pern novels detail the politics of the Holds and Weyrs between Threadfalls. The entire line of books spans over twenty-five hundred years, from the first landing of the settlers to their descendants' discovery of the master ship's computer centuries later.

Dragonflight, the first of the Dragonriders of Pern books, tells of a time twenty-five hundred years after the initial landing. The Thread has not been seen in four centuries, and people are starting to be skeptical of the old warnings. Three dragonriders, Lessa, F'lar, and F'nor, believe that the Thread is coming back, and try to mobilize the planetary defenses. Lessa, knowing that there are not enough dragons to combat the Thread effectively, time-travels back four hundred years to a point just after the last Threadfall, when that era's Dragonriders are growing restless and bored from lack of activity. Lessa convinces most of them to come back with her to combat Thread in her time. They arrive and fight off the Thread.

Dragonquest, the second book, picks up seven

years after the end of the first book. Relations between the Oldtimers, as the time-traveling dragonriders are called, and the current generation are growing tense. After getting into a fight with one of the old dragonriders, F'nor is sent to Pern's Southern Continent to recover from his wound. There he discovers a grub that neutralizes the Thread after it burrows into the ground. Realizing they have discovered a powerful new weapon against Thread, F'nor begins planning to seed the grubs over both continents.

Meanwhile, an unexpected Threadfall is the catalyst for a duel between F'lar, the Benden Weyrleader, and T'ron, the leader of the Oldtimers. F'lar wins and banishes all dragonriders who will not accept his role as overall Weyrleader. The banished go to the Southern Continent. The book ends with the grubs being bred for distribution over Pern.

The third book, *The White Dragon,* chronicles the trials of young Jaxom as he raises the only white dragon on Pern, a genetic anomaly. Jaxom encounters prejudice and scorn from other dragonriders because his dragon is smaller than the rest. He is also scheduled to take command of one of the oldest Holds on Pern, and there are those who doubt his ability to govern. Both Jaxom and his dragon, Ruth, rise to the challenges and succeed in proving that bigger is not necessarily better. Jaxom commands his Hold, gets the girl, and all is set right with the world.

The Harper Hall trilogy (*Dragonsong, Dragonsinger, Dragondrums*) is aimed at young readers, and deals with a girl named Menolly and her rise from unappreciated daughter to Journeywoman Harper and keeper of fire-lizards.

In many subsequent novels, and in the short novel published here, McCaffrey has examined various other aspects of life on Pern from the earliest days of its colonization by humans.

RUNNER OF PERN

∞

Anne McCaffrey

Tenna topped the rise and paused to catch her breath, leaning forward, hands on her knees to ease her back muscles. Then, as she had been taught, she walked along the top on what flat space there was, kicking out her legs and shaking the thigh muscles, breathing through her mouth until she stopped panting. Taking her water bottle from her belt, she allowed herself a swig, swishing it around in her mouth to moisturize the dry tissue. She spat out that mouthful and took another, letting this one slowly trickle down her throat. The night was cool enough to keep her from sweating too heavily. But she wouldn't be standing around long enough to get a chill.

It didn't take long for her breath to return to normal, and she was pleased by that. She was in good shape. She kicked out her legs to ease the strain she had put on them to make the height. Then, settling her belt and checking the message pouch, she started down the hill at a rapid walking pace. It was too dark—Belior had not yet risen above the plain to give her full light for the down side of the hill—to be safe to run in shadows. She only knew this part of the trace by word of mouth, not actually footing it. She'd done well so far during this, her second Turn of running, and had made most of her first Cross by the suggested easy laps. Runners watched out for each other, and no station manager would overtax a novice. With any luck, she'd've made it all the way to the Western Sea in the next sevenday. This was the first big test of her apprenticeship as an express runner. And really she'd only the Western Range left to cross once she got to Fort Hold.

Halfway down from the top of the rise, she met the ridge crest she'd been told about and, with the usual check of the pouch she carried, she picked up her knees and started the ground-eating lope that was the pride of a Pernese runner.

Of course, the legendary "lopers"—the ones who had been able to do a hundred miles in a day—had perished ages ago, but their memory was kept alive. Their endurance and dedication were an example to everyone who ran the traces of Pern. There hadn't been many of them, according to the legend, but they had started the runner stations when the need for the rapid delivery of messages arose, during the First Fall of Thread. Lopers had been able to put themselves in some sort of trance which not only allowed them to run extended distances but kept them warm during snowstorms and in freezing temperatures. They had also planted the original traces, which now were a network crisscrossing the entire continent.

While only Lord Holders and Craftmasters could afford to keep runnerbeasts for their couriers, the average person, wanting to contact crafthalls, relatives, or friends across Pern, could easily afford to express a letter across the continent in runner pouches, carried from station to station. Others might call them "holds," but runners had always had "stations," and station agents, as part of *their* craft history. Drum messages were great for short messages, if the weather was right and the winds didn't interrupt the beat, but as long as folks wanted to send written messages there'd be runners to take them.

Tenna often thought proudly of the tradition she was carrying on. It was a comfort on long solitary journeys. Right now, the running was good: the ground was firm but springy, a surface that had been assiduously maintained since the ancient runners had planted it. Not only did the mossy stuff make running easier but it identified a runner's path. A runner would instantly feel the difference in the surface, if he, or she, strayed off the trace.

Slowly, as full Belior rose behind her, her way became illuminated by the moon's light and she picked up her pace, running easily, breathing freely, her hands carried high, chest height, with elbows tucked in. No need to leave a "handle," as her father called it, to catch the wind and slow the pace. At times like these, with good footing, a fair light, and a cool evening, you felt like you could run forever. If there weren't a sea to stop you.

She ran on, able to see the flow of the ridge, and by the time the trace started to descend again, Belior was high enough to light her way. She saw the stream ahead and slowed cautiously . . . though she'd been told that the ford had a good pebbly surface . . . and splashed through the ankle-high cold water, up onto the bank, veering slightly south, picking up the trace again by its springy surface.

She'd be over halfway now to Fort Hold and should make it by dawn. This was a well-traveled route, southwest along the coast to the farther Holds. Most of what she carried right now was destined for Fort Holders, so it was the end of the line for both the pouch and herself. She'd heard so much about the facilities at Fort that she didn't quite believe it. Runners tended to understatement rather than exaggeration. If a runner told you a trace was dangerous, you believed it! But what they said about Fort was truly amazing.

Tenna came from a running family: father, uncles, cousins, grandfathers, brothers, sisters, and two aunts were all out and about the traces that crisscrossed Pern from Nerat Tip to High Reaches Hook, from Benden to Boll.

"It's bred in us," her mother had said, answering the queries of her younger children. Cesila managed a large runner station, just at the northern Lemos end of the Keroon plains where the immense sky-broom trees began. Strange trees that flourished only in that region of Pern. Trees that, a much younger Tenna had been sure, were where the Benden Weyr dragons took a rest in their flights across the continent. Cesila had laughed at Tenna's notion.

"The dragons of Pern don't need to rest anywhere, dear. They just go *between* to wherever they need to go. You probably saw some of them out hunting their weekly meal."

In her running days, Cesila had completed nine full Crosses a Turn until she'd married another runner and started producing her own bag of runners-to-be.

"Lean we are in the breeding, and leggy, most of us, with big lungs and strong bones. Ah, there now, a few come out who're more for speed than distance but they're handy enough at Gathers, passing the winning line before the others have left the starting ribbon. We have our place on the world same as holders and even Weyrfolk. Each to his, or her, own. Weaver and tanner, and farmer, and fisher, and smith and runner and all."

"That's not the way we was taught to sing the Duty Song," Tenna's younger brother had remarked.

"Maybe," Cesila had said with a grin, "but it's the way I sing it and you can, too. I must have a word with the next harper through here. He can change his words if he wants us to take his messages." And she gave her head one of her emphatic shakes to end that conversation.

As soon as runner-bred children reached full growth, they were tested to see if they'd the right Blood for the job. Tenna's legs had stopped growing by the time she'd reached her fifteenth full Turn. That was when she was assessed by a senior runner of another Bloodline. Tenna had been very nervous, but her mother, in her usual offhanded way, had given her lanky daughter a long knowing look.

"Nine children I've given your father, Fedri, and four are already runners. You'll be one, too, never fear."

"But Sedra's . . ."

Cesila held up her hand. "I know your sister's mated and breeding but she did two Crosses before she found a man she had to have. So she counts, too. Gotta have proper Bloodlines to breed proper runners and it's us who do that." Cesila paused to be sure Tenna would not interrupt again. "I came from a hold with twelve, all of them runners. And all breeding runners. You'll run, girl. Put your mind at ease. You'll run." Then she'd laughed. "It's for how long, not will you, for a female."

Tenna had decided a long time ago—when she had first been considered old enough to mind her younger siblings—that she'd prefer running to raising runners. She'd run until she could no longer lift her knees. She'd an aunt who'd never mated: ran until she was older than Cesila was now and then took over the management of a connecting station down Igen way. Should something happen and she couldn't run any more, Tenna wouldn't mind managing a station. Her mother ran hers proper, always had hot water ready to ease a runner's aching limbs, good food, comfortable beds, and healing skills that rivaled what you could find in any Hold. And it was always exciting, for you never knew who might run in that day, or where they'd be going. Runners crossed the continent regularly, bringing with them news from other parts of Pern. Many had interesting tales to tell of problems on the trace and how to cope with them. You heard all about other Holds and Halls, and the one dragonweyr, as well as what interested runners most specifically: what conditions were like and where traces might need maintenance after a heavy rain or landslide.

She was mightily relieved, however, when her father said he had asked Mallum of the Telgar station to do her assessment. At least Tenna had met the man on those occasions when he'd been through to their place on the edge of Keroon's plains. Like other runners, he was a lanky length of man, with a long face and graying hair that he tied back with his sweatband as most runners did.

Her parents didn't tell her when Mallum was expected, but he turned up one bright morning, handing in a pouch to be logged on the board by the door and then limping to the nearest seat.

"Bruised the heel. We'll have to rock that south trace again. I swear it grows new ones every Turn or two," he said, mopping his forehead with his orange sweatband and thanking Tenna for the cup of water. "Cesila, got some of that sheer magic poultice of yours?"

"I do. Put the kettle to heat the moment I saw you struggling up the trace."

"Was not struggling," Mallum said in jovial denial. "Was careful not to put the heel down was all."

"Don't try to fool me, you spavined gimper," Cesila replied as she was dipping a poultice sack into the heated water, testing it with a finger.

"Who's to run on? Some orders in that need to be got south smartly."

"I'm taking it on," Fedri said, coming out of his room and tying on his sweatband. "How urgent?" His runner's belt was draped over his shoulder. "I've others to add from the morning's eastern run."

"Hmmm. They want to make the Igen Gather."

"Ha! It'll be there betimes," Fedri said, reaching for the pouch and carefully adding the other messages to it before he put it through the belt loops. Settling it in the small of his back with one hand, he chalked up the exchange time with the other. "See you."

Then he was out the door and turning south, settling into his long-distance stride almost as soon as his foot hit the moss of the trace.

Tenna, knowing what was needed, had already pulled a footstool over to Mallum. She looked up at him for permission and, with his nod, unlaced the right shoe, feeling the fine quality of the leather. Mallum made his own footwear and he had set the stitching fine and tight.

Cesila knelt beside her daughter, craning her head to see the bruise.

"Hmmm. Hit it early on, didn'tcha?"

"I did," Mallum said, drawing his breath in with a hiss as Cesila slapped the poultice on. "Oooooh! Shards . . . you didn't get it too hot, didja?"

Cesila sniffed denial in reply as she neatly and deftly tied the packet to his foot.

"And is this the lass of yours as is to be taken for a run?" he asked, relaxing his expression from the grimace he'd made when the poultice was first applied. "Prettiest of the bunch." And he grinned at Tenna.

"Handsome is as handsome does," Cesila said. "Looks is all right but long legs is better. Tenna's her name."

"Handsome's not a bad thing to be, Cesila, and it's obvious your daughter takes after you."

Cesila sniffed again but Tenna could see that her mother didn't mind Mallum's remarks. And Cesila was a handsome woman: lithe still and slender, with graceful hands and feet. Tenna wished she were more like her mother.

"Nice long line of leg," Mallum went on approvingly. He beckoned for Tenna to come closer and had a good look at the lean muscles, then asked to see her bare feet. Runners tended to walk barefooted a lot. Some even ran barefooted. "Good bone. Hmmm. Nice lean frame. Hmm. Not a pick on you, girl. Hope you can keep warm enough in winter like that.'' That was such an old runner comment, but his jollity was encouraging and Tenna was ever so glad that Mallum was her assessor. He was always pleasant on his short stops at Station 97. ''We'll take a short one tomorrow when this foot's eased.''

More runners came in so Cesila and Tenna were busy, checking in messages, sorting the packets for the changeovers, serving food, heating water for baths, tending scratched legs. It was spring of the year and most runners only used leggings during the coldest months.

Enough stayed the night so there was good chatter and gossip to entertain. And prevent Tenna from worrying about satisfying her assessor on the morning.

A runner had come in late that night, on her way north, with some messages to be transferred to an eastern route. His heel bruise much eased, Mallum thought he could take those on.

''It's a good testing trot,'' he said, and gestured for Tenna to slip the message pouch on her belt. ''I'll travel light, girl.'' His grin was teasing, for the pouch weighed little more than the wherhide it was made from. ''First, lemme see what you wear on your feet.''

She showed him her shoes, the most important part of a runner's gear. She'd used her family's special oils to soften the wherhide and then formed it on the lasts that had been carved for her feet by her uncle who did them for her Bloodline. Her stitches were neat but not as fine as Mallum's. She intended to improve. Meanwhile, this pair wasn't a bad effort and fit her feet like gloves. The spikes were medium length as fit for the present dry trace conditions. Most long-distance runners carried an extra pair with shorter spikes for harder ground, especially during spring and summer. She was working on her winter footwear, hoping she'd need it, for those boots came up to midcalf and required a lot more conditioning. Even they were of lighter weight than the footgear holders would use. But then most holders plodded and the thicker leather was suitable for their tasks as fine soft hide was right for a runner's foot.

Mallum nodded in approval as he handed back her shoes. Now he checked the fit of her belt to be sure it was snug enough not to rub against the small of her back as she ran, and made certain that her short trunks would not pull against her leg and that her sleeveless top covered her backside well below her waist to help prevent her getting a kidney chill. Stopping often from a need to relieve oneself ruined the rhythm of a run.

"We'll go now," Mallum said, having assured himself that she was properly accoutred.

Cesila stood in the door, gave her daughter a reassuring nod, and saw them off, up the eastern trace. Before they were out of sight, she gave the particular runner yodel that stopped them in their tracks. They saw her pointing skyward: at the arrow formation of dragons in the sky, a most unusual sight these days when the dragons of Benden Weyr were so rarely seen.

To see dragons in the sky was the best sort of omen. They were there . . . and then they weren't! She smiled. Too bad runners couldn't just *think* themselves to their destinations the way dragons could. As if he had shared her thought, Mallum grinned back at her and then turned to face the direction in which they were headed, and any nervousness Tenna had had disappeared. When he sprang off again, she was in step with him by the third stride. He nodded again approvingly.

"Running's not just picking up your heels and showing them to those behind you," Mallum said, his eyes watching the trace ahead, though he must have known it as well as Tenna did. "A good bit of proper running is learning to pace yourself and your stride. It's knowing the surfaces of the traces you have to traverse. It's knowing how to save your strength so you'll last the longer hauls. When to ease back to a walk, when and how to drink and eat so's you're not too gutty to run right. It's learning the routes of the various Crosses and what sort of weather you might have to run through . . . and learning to maneuver on snowrunners on the northern Crosses. And, most important, when to take cover and just let the weather have its way with the world and you safe out of it. So's the messages and the packets you carry will get through as soon as possible.''

She had responded with a nod of appreciation. Not that she hadn't heard the same lecture time and again in the station from every relative and runner. But this time it was for her benefit and she owed Mallum the courtesy of listening closely. She did watch Mallum's stride, though, to be sure his heel wasn't bothering him. He caught her glance once and gave her a grin.

''Be sure you carry a wedge of that poultice on any long laps, girl. You never know, you know, when you might need it. As I just did.'' And he grimaced, reminding Tenna that even the best runner can put a foot wrong.

While no runner carries much, the long-tailed orange sweatband that runners invariably wore could be used to strap a strain or sprain. An oiled packet, no larger than the palm of a hand, had a cloth soaked in numbweed which both cleansed and eased the scratches one could acquire from time to time. Simple remedies for the most common problems. A wedge of poultice could be added to such travel gear and be well worth its weight.

Tenna had no trouble making that lap with Mallum even when he picked up the pace on the flat section.

"Running with a pretty girl's not hard to do," he told her when they took one brief pause.

She wished he didn't make so much of her looks. They wouldn't help her run any better or help her become what she wanted to be: a top runner.

By the time they reached Irma's station at midday, she was not even breathing very hard. But the moment Mallum slowed, he limped slightly with his full weight on the heel.

"Hmm. Well, I can wait out the day here with more poultice," he said, pulling the little wedge from one of the pockets of his belt. "See," and he displayed it to Tenna, "handy enough."

She tapped her aid pocket and smiled.

Old Irma came out with a grin on her sun-dried face for them.

"Will she do, Mallum?" the old woman asked, handing each a cup.

"Oh, aye, she'll do. A credit to her Bloodline and not a bother to run with!" Mallum said with a twinkle in his eyes.

"I pass, do I, Mallum?" Tenna asked, needing to have a direct answer.

"Oh, aye," and he laughed, walking about and shaking his legs to get the kinks out even as she was doing. "No fear on that. Any hot water for m'poultice, Irm?"

"Coming up." She ducked back into her station and came out with a bowl of steaming water which she set down on the long bench that was an inevitable fixture of every station. The overhang of the roof provided a shelter from sun and rain. Most runners were obsessed with watching the traces to see who was coming and going. The long bench, its surface smoothed by generations of bums sliding across it, was placed so that it commanded a good view of the four traces linking at Irma's.

Automatically, Tenna pulled a footstool from under the bench and held out her hand to receive Mallum's right foot. She untied the shoe, and placed the now moistened poultice on the bruise while Irma handed her a bandage to fix it in place, taking a good look at the injury in the process.

" 'Nother day'll do it. Shoulda stayed off it this mornin', too."

"Not when I'd a chance to run with such a pretty girl," Mallum said.

"Just like a man," Irma said dismissively.

Tenna felt herself blushing, although she was beginning to believe he wasn't just teasing. No one else had ever commented on her looks.

"It wasn't a taxing leg, Irma. It's level most of the way and a good surface," she said, grinning shyly at Mallum as she tried to divert Irma's criticism.

"Humph! Well, a hill run would've been downright foolish and it is flat this a way."

"Anything for Tenna to take back," Mallum asked, getting back to business, "to make her first round-trip as a runner?"

"Should be," Irma said, winking at Tenna for this informal inclusion into the ranks of Pern runners. "You could eat now . . . soup's ready and so's the bread."

"Wouldn't mind a bit myself," Mallum said, carefully shifting his position as if easing the heat from the poultice, since the heat probably penetrated even the toughened sole of his foot.

By the time Tenna had eaten the light meal, two runners came in: a man she didn't know by sight, on a long leg from Bitra with a pouch to go farther west; and one of Irma's sons.

"I can run it to Ninety-Seven," she said, the official designation of her family's station.

"That'll do," the man said, panting and heaving from his long haul. "That'll do fine." He gasped for more breath. "It's an urgent," he got out. "Your name?"

"Tenna."

"One . . . of . . . Fedri's?" he asked and she nodded. "That's good . . . enough for me. Ready to . . . hit the trace?"

"Sure." She held out her hand for the pouch that he slipped off his belt, pausing only to mark the pass-over time on the flap as he gave it into her keeping. "You are?" she asked, sliding the pouch onto her own belt and settling it in the small of her back.

"Masso," he said, reaching now for the cup of water Irma had hastened to bring him. He whooshed her off to the westward trace. With a final grateful farewell wave to Mallum, she picked up her heels as Mallum cheered her on with the traditional runner's "yo-ho."

She made it home in less time than it had taken her to reach Irma's, and one of her brothers was there to take the pouch on the next westward lap. Silan nodded approval at the pass-over time, marked his own receipt, and was off.

"So, girl, you're official," her mother said, and embraced her. "And no need to sweat it at all, was there?"

"Running's not always as easy," her father said from the bench, "but you made good time and that's a grand way to start. I hadn't expected you back before midafternoon."

Tenna did the short legs all around Station 97 for the first summer and into that winter, building her stamina for longer runs and becoming known at all the connecting stations. She made her longest run to Greystones, on the coast, just ahead of a very bad snowstorm. Then, because she was the only runner available in Station 18 when the exhausted carrier of an urgent message came in, she had to carry it two stations north. A fishing sloop would be delayed back to port until a new mast could be stepped. Since the vessel was overdue, there were those who'd be very glad to get the message she carried.

Such emergency news should have been drummed ahead, but the high winds would tear such a message to nonsense. It was a tough run, with cold as well as wind and snow across a good bit of the low-lying trace. Pacing herself, she did take an hour's rest in one of the Thread shelters that dotted a trace. She made the distance in such good time in those conditions that she got extra stitches on her belt, marking her rise toward journeyman rank.

This run to Fort Hold would be two more stitches on her belt if she finished in good time. And she was sure she would . . . with the comforting sort of certainty that older runners said you began to sense when you'd been traveling the traces awhile. She was also now accustomed to judging how long she had run by the feeling in her legs. There was none of the leaden feeling that accompanied real fatigue, and she was still running easily. So long as she had no leg cramp, she knew she could continue effortlessly at this good pace until she reached Station 300 at Fort. Leg cramp was always a hazard and could strike you without warning. She was careful to renew the tablets a runner chewed to ease off a cramp. And was not too slow about grabbing a handful of any useful herbs she spotted which would help prevent the trouble.

She oughtn't to be letting her mind wander like this, but with an easy stride and a pleasant night in which to travel, it was hard to keep her mind on the job. She would, smartly enough, if there were complications like bad weather or poor light. This was also far too well traveled country for there to be dangers like tunnel snakes, which were about the worst risk that runners encountered—usually at dawn or dusk, when the creatures were out hunting. Of course, renegades, while not as common as tunnel snakes, were more dangerous, since they were human, not animal, but that distinction was often moot. As runners rarely carried marks, they were not as likely to be waylaid as were messengers on runnerbeasts, or other solitary travelers. Tenna hadn't heard of any renegade attacks this far west, but sometimes those people were so vicious that they might pull up a runner just for spite and malice. In the past three turns, there had been two cases—and those up in northern Lemos and Bitra—where runners had been hamstrung out of sheer malevolence.

Once in a while, in a bad winter, a flock of very hungry wherries might attack a runner in the open, but the instances were rare enough. Snakes were the most likely danger encountered, particularly midsummer, when there were newly hatched clutches.

Her father had had injuries two summers back with such a hazard. He'd been amazed at how fast the adult tunnel snake could move when alarmed. Mostly they were torpid creatures, only hunger quickening them. But he'd stepped in the midst of an ill-placed nest and had had the hatchlings swarming up his legs, pricking the skin in innumerable places and even managing to get as high as his crotch. (Her mother had stifled a giggle and remarked that it had been more than her father's pride that had been wounded.) But he'd scars from claw and tooth that he could show.

Moonlit nights like this one were a joy to run in, with the air cool enough to dry the sweat on her face and chest, the trace springy underfoot and clear ahead of her. And her thoughts could wander.

There would be a Gather shortly after she reached her destination; she knew she was carrying some orders for Crafts displaying at Fort Hold. Pouches were invariably fuller going to or coming from a Gather—orders from those unable to attend, wishing to contact a Mastercraftsman. Maybe, if she was lucky, she could stay over for the Gather. She hadn't been to one in a long while and she did want to find well-tanned leathers for a new pair of running shoes. She'd enough money to her credit to give a fair price for the right hides: she'd checked the books her mother kept of her laps. Most Halls were quite willing to take a runner-station chit. She'd one in a belt pocket. If she found just the right skins, she'd a bit of leeway to bargain, above and beyond the surface value of the chit.

A Gather would be fun, too. She loved dancing, and was very good at the toss dance, if she could find someone who could properly partner her in it. Fort was a good Hold. And the music would be special, seeing as how the Harper Hall was right there in Fort.

She ran on, tunes of harper melodies flitting through her mind even if she'd no breath to sing them.

She was running along a long curve now, around an upthrust of rock—most traces were as straight as possible—and brought her mind back to her directions. Just around this curve, she should find a trace turning off to the right, inland, toward Fort. She must pay attention now so she wouldn't have to break stride and backtrack.

Suddenly she could feel vibrations through her feet, though she could see nothing around the vegetation banking the curve. Listening intently, she could now hear an odd *phuff-phuff* sound, coming closer, getting louder. The sound was just enough of a warning for her to move left, out of the center of the trace, where she'd have just that much more of a glimpse of what was making the sound and the vibrations. This was a runner track, not a trail or road. No runner made those sounds, or hit the ground that hard to make vibrations. She saw the dark mass bearing down on her, and flung herself into the undergrowth as runnerbeast and rider came within a finger span of knocking into her. She could feel the wind of their passing and smell the sweat of the beast.

"*Stupid!*" she shouted after them, getting branches and leaves in her mouth as she fell, feeling needly gouges in the hands she had put out to break her fall. She spent the next minute struggling to her feet and spitting bitter leaves and twigs out of her mouth. They left behind an acrid, drying taste: sticklebush! She'd fallen into a patch of sticklebush. At this time of the Turn, there were no leaves yet to hide the hairlike thorns that coated twig and branch. A nuisance which balanced out their gift of succulent berries in the autumn.

Nor did the rider falter, or even pull up, when the least he could have done was return to be sure she hadn't been injured. Surely he'd seen her? Surely he'd heard her outraged shout. And what was *he* doing, using a runner trace in the first place? There was a good road north for ordinary travelers.

"I'll get you!" she called, shaking her fist with frustration.

She was shaking with reaction to such a near miss. Then she became uncomfortably aware of the scratches on hands, arms, legs, chest, and two on one cheek. Stamping with fury, she got the numbweed from her belt pocket and daubed at the cuts, hissing as the solution stung. But she didn't want the sap to get into her blood. Nor did she want the slivers to work in. She managed to pick the ones out of her hands, daubing the numbweed into those. She couldn't really see the extent of her injuries, some being down the back of her arm. She picked out what slivers she could and carefully pressed in the pad until all the moisture was gone from it. Even if she had avoided infection, she was likely to be teased about falling when she got to the station. Runners were supposed to keep *on* their feet, and in balance. Not that a rider had any business on the trace. Surely that would also help her find out who the rider had been, besides being bold enough to ride a runner trace. And if she wasn't around to give him a fat lip, maybe another runner would give the lesson in her place. Runners were not above complaining to Lord Holders or their stewards if someone abused their rights.

Having done as much as she could then, she stifled her anger: that didn't get the pouch to its destination. And she mustn't let her anger get the better of common sense. The brush with disaster, close as it was, had resulted in very minor problems, she told herself firmly. What were scratches! But she found it hard to regain her stride. She'd been going so smoothly, too, and so close to the end of this lap.

She could have been killed, smacking into a runnerbeast at the speeds they'd both been traveling. If she hadn't thought to move out of the center of the trace ... where she had every right to be, not him ... if she hadn't felt the hoofbeats through her shoes and heard the animal's high breathing ... Why, both sets of messages could have been delayed! Or lost.

Her legs felt tired and heavy and she had to concentrate hard to try to regain the rhythm. Reluctantly she realized that she was unlikely to and settled for conserving her energy.

Running into the end of night, the dawn behind her, was not as much a pleasure as it could have been, and that annoyed Tenna even more. Just wait till she found out who that rider was! She'd tell him a thing or two. Though common sense told her that she was unlikely to encounter him. He was outbound and she was inbound. If he'd been in that much of a hurry, he might be a relay rider, bound for a distant location. Lord Holders could afford such services and the stabling of fast runnerbeasts along the way. But he shouldn't have been on a runner trace. There were roads for beasts! Hooves could tear up the surface of the trace and the station manager might have to spend hours replacing divots torn up by shod hooves. Traces were for runners. She kept returning to that indignant thought. She just hoped any other runner on the trace would hear him in time! *That's one reason you keep your mind on your run, Tenna.* Even if you'd no reason to suspect you weren't alone with the night and the moon on a runner trace.

The runner station was just below the main entrance to Fort Hold. History had it that Fort had started runners as short-distance messengers, hundreds and hundreds of turns ago, even before drum towers were built. Fort Hold had utilized the skills of runners for many tasks, especially during Threadfall, when runners had accompanied all ground crews, vital as couriers in emergencies. The installation of the drum towers and the development of runnerbeasts had not put an end to the need for the runners of Pern. This main connecting hold was the largest ever built just to house and care for runners. Three levels high, she'd been told, and several back into the Fort cliff. It also boasted one of the best bathing facilities on the continent: hot running water in deep tubs that had eased centuries of runner aches and pains. Cesila had highly recommended that Tenna try for Fort when she got that far west. And here she was and right ready to appreciate the accommodations.

She was very weary and not only out of pace but jarring herself with every step down the broader avenue that led to her destination. Her hands stung from the sap and she hoped she hadn't any slivers left in them. But hands were a long way from the feet.

Beastholders, up early to feed stock, gave her cheery waves and smiles, and their courtesies somewhat restored her good humor. She did not care to arrive petulant as well as scratched, not on her first visit here.

Almost as if the manager had a special sensitivity to incoming runners, the double door was thrown open as she came to a rough, gasping halt, hand raised to catch the bell cord.

"Thought I heard someone coming." The man, a welcoming grin on his face, put out both hands to steady her. He was one of the oldest men she had ever seen: his skin was a network of wrinkles and grooves, but his eyes were bright—for this hour—and he looked to be a merry man. "New one, too, at that, for all you look familiar to me. A pretty face is a great sight on a fine morning."

Sucking in breath enough to give her name, Tenna paced into the large entry room. She unbuckled her message pouch as she eased the tension in her leg muscles.

"Tenna passing Two-Oh-Eight with eastern messages. Fort's the destination for all."

"Welcome to Three Hundred, Tenna," he said, taking the pouch from her and immediately chalking up her arrival on the heavy old board to the left of the station door. "All for here, huh?" He passed her a cup before he opened the pouch, to check the recipients.

With cup in hand, she went out again, still flicking her legs to ease the muscles. First she rinsed her mouth, spitting out that first mouthful onto the cobbles. Then she would sip to swallow. Nor was this just water but some sort of fresh-tasting drink that refreshed dry tissues.

"You're a mite the worse for the run," the man said, standing in the door and pointing to the bloody smears on her bare skin. "What'd you run into?"

"Sticklebush," she said through gritted teeth. "Runnerbeast ran me off round the hill curve . . . galloping along a *runner* trace like he must know he shouldn't." She was astonished at the anger in her voice when she'd meant to sound matter-of-fact.

"That'd be Haligon, more'n likely," the station keeper said, nodding with a disapproving scowl. "Saw him peltin' down to the beasthold an hour or so ago. I've warned him myself about using the traces but he says it cuts half an hour off a trip and he's conducting an ex-per-i-ment."

"He might have killed me," she said, her anger thoroughly fanned.

"You'd better tell him. Maybe a pretty runner'll get it through his thick skull because the odd crack or two hasn't."

His reaction made Tenna feel that her anger was righteous. It's one thing to be angry on your own, another to have confirmation of your right to be angry. She felt redeemed. Though she couldn't see why being pretty would be an advantage if you were giving someone what-for. She could hit just as hard as the ugliest runner she'd ever met.

"You'll need a long soak with sticklebush slivers in you. You did have something to put on 'em right then, didn't you?" When she nodded, now annoyed because he implied that she might not have that much sense, he added, "I'll can send m'mate to look at those cuts. Wrong time of the Turn to fall into sticklebush, ya know." And she nodded her head vigorously. "All in all, you made a good time from Two-Oh-Eight," he added, approvingly. "Like that in a young runner. Shows you're not just a pretty face. Now, go up the stairs there, take your first right, go along the corridor, fourth door on the left. No one else's up. Towels on the shelves. Leave your clothes: they'll be washed and dry by evening. You'll want a good feed after a night run and then a good long sleep. We've all for you, runner."

She thanked him, turned to the stairs, and then tried to lift the wooden blocks her legs had become up the steps. Her toes dragged as she made her feet move, and she was grateful for the carpeting that saved the wooden stairs from her spikes. But then this place was for runners, shoes, spikes, and all.

"Fourth door," she murmured to herself, and pushed against a portal that opened into the most spacious bathing room she'd ever seen. And pungent with something pleasantly astringent. Nothing as grand as this even at Keroon Hold. Five tubs

ranged along the back wall with curtains to separate
them if one needed privacy. There were two massage tables, sturdy, padded, with shelves of oils and
salves underneath. They would account for the nice
smells. The room was hot and she began to sweat
again, a sweat that made her nicks and scratches
itch. There were changing cubicles, too, to the right
of the door . . . and behind her she found oversized
towels in stacks higher than her head, and she
wasn't short. There were cubbies holding runner
pants and shirts for all weathers and the thick anklets that cushioned and warmed weary feet. She
took a towel, her fingers feeling the thick, soft nap.
It was as big as a blanket.

In the cubicle nearest the tubs, she shucked off
her garments, automatically folding them into a
neat pile. Then, looping the towel over the hook
set by the side of the tub for that purpose, she eased
herself into the warm water. The tub was taller than
she was and she let herself down to touch a floor,
a full hand of water above her head when she did.
Amazing!

This was sheer luxury. She wondered how often
she could draw a run to Fort Hold. The water made
her scratches sting, but that was nothing to the
comfort it was giving her tired muscles. Swishing
around in the large square tub, her hand connected
with a ledge, sort of curved, a few inches below

the surface. With a grin she realized that she could rest her head on it and be able to float safely. Which was exactly what she did, arms out to her sides, legs dangling. She hadn't known bathing could be so . . . so splendid. She let every muscle in her body go limp. And lay suspended in the water.

"Tenna?" a woman's voice called gently, as if not to startle the lone bather. "I'm Penda, Torlo's mate. He sent me up. I've some herbs for the bath that'll help those scratches. Wrong time of the Turn to fall into sticklebush."

"I know," Tenna agreed dourly. "Be glad of any help." Tenna didn't really want to open her eyes or move but she politely swished herself across the water to the edge of the tub.

"Lemme see them cuts so's I can see didja get any punctures like. That'd be no good with the sap rising," Penda said. She walked quickly to the tub with a odd sideways gait, so whatever had injured her hip had happened a long time ago and she had learned to cope with it. She grinned at Tenna. "Pretty runner girl, you are. You give Haligon what-for next time you see him."

"How'll I know him?" Tenna asked acerbically, though she dearly wished a confrontation with the rider. "And why is 'pretty' a help?"

"Haligon likes pretty girls." Penda gave an exaggerated wink. "We'll see you stay about long enough to give him what-for. *You* might do some good."

Tenna laughed and, at Penda's gesture, held out her hands and turned her left arm where Penda could see it.

"Hmmm. Mostly surface but there's punctures on the heels of both hands." She ran oddly soft fingers across Tenna's hands, catching on three slivers so that Tenna shivered with the unpleasant sensation. "Soaking'll do the most good. Loosen them up in your skin. Prolly clean 'em all out. Stickle's a clever bush, harming you so, but this'll help," she said, and took a collection of bottles from the deep pocket in her apron and selected one. "Got to leave nothing to chance, ya know," she added as she deftly splashed about twenty drops into the tub water. "Don't worry about emptying the tub, either. It'll run clear and'll be fresh water by the time someone else climbs in. I'll take out the slivers when you've soaked. You want a rub then? Or would you rather sleep first?"

"A bit of a rub would be marvelous, thanks. And before I sleep."

"I'll be back with some food."

Tenna thought of the bathing room in her parents' station and grinned. Nothing to compare to this, though she'd always thought her station was lucky to have a tub so long you could lie out flat in it: even the tallest runners could. But you had to keep the fire going under the tank all the time to be sure there was enough for when a bath was needed. Not like this—the water already hot and you only needing to step into the tub. The herbs scented the steamy water, making it feel softer against her skin. She lay back again.

She was nearly asleep when Penda returned with a tray containing klah, fresh-baked bread, a little pot of, appropriately enough, stickleberry preserve, and a bowl of porridge.

"Messages've already been handed over to them they was sent to, so you can sleep good, knowing the run's well ended."

Tenna consumed her meal, down to the last scrap. Penda was making quite a mixture with the massage oils, and the runner inhaled the scent of them. Then Tenna climbed on the table, letting her body go limp while Penda used a tweezer on the slivers still caught in her flesh. Penda counted as she deposited the wicked hairs. Nine, all told. She applied more medication and the last of the itching and discomfort vanished. Tenna sighed. Then Penda soothed tired muscles and tendons. Her touch was sure but gentle. She did announce that there were more punctures on the backs of Tenna's arms and legs and proceeded go at them with the

RUNNER OF PERN

tweezers to remove the slivers. That done, her motions became more soothing and Tenna relaxed again.

"There y'are. Just go along to the third door down on your left, Tenna," Penda said softly when she had finished.

Tenna roused enough from the delightful, massage-induced stupor and wrapped the big towel tightly around her chest. Like most runner females, she didn't have much of a bust, but that was an advantage.

"Don't forget these," Penda said, shoving the laces of her running shoes at her. "Clothes'll be clean and dry when you wake."

"Thanks, Penda," Tenna said sincerely, astonished that she'd been drowsy enough to forget her precious shoes.

She padded down the hall in the thick anklets that Penda had slipped on her feet and pushed in the third door. Light from the corridor showed her where the bed was, straight across the narrow space, against the wall. Closing the door, she made her way to it in the dark. Dropping the towel, she leaned down to feel for the edge of the quilt she'd seen folded on the foot of the bed. She pulled it over her as she stretched out. Sighed once and fell asleep.

* * *

Good-natured laughter and movement down the hall roused her. Someone had half-opened the glowbasket, so she saw her own clothes, clean, dry, and neatly folded on the stool where she'd dropped her running shoes. She realized she hadn't even taken off the anklets before she got into bed. She wriggled her toes in them. No tenderness there. Her hands were stiff but cool, so Penda'd gotten out all the slivers. The skin of her left arm and leg was stiff, though, and she threw back the quilt and tried to see the injuries. She couldn't, but there was a little too much heat in the skin on the back of her left arm for her liking, and her right leg. Five sort-of-sore spots she couldn't really check at all other than identifying them as "sore." And, when she checked her legs, two bad red bumps on her thigh, one in the left calf and two on the fleshy part of her right leg by the shinbone. She had suffered more hurt than she'd realized. And stickle slivers could work their way through your flesh and into your blood. If one got to your heart, you could die from it. She groaned and rose. Shook out her legs, testing the feel of her muscles, and, thanks to Penda's massage, they didn't ache. She dressed and then carefully folded the quilt, placing it just as she'd found it on the bed.

Making her way back to the stairs, she passed the bathing room and heard the hum of masculine voices, then a laugh that was clearly from a female runner. As she came down the stairs, she was aware of the smell of roasting meats. Her stomach rumbled. One long narrow window lit the hall that led to the main room, and she gauged that she had slept most of the day. Perhaps she ought to have had a healer check out the scratches, but Penda knew what to do as well as any Hall-trained healer . . . probably better, since she was a station manager's mate.

"Now, here's a one who's prompt for her supper," Torlo said, calling the attention of the runners sitting around the room to Tenna's appearance. He introduced her. "Had a brush with Haligon early this morning," he added, and Tenna did not fail to note that this brash personage was known to them all from the nods and grimaces on their faces.

"I tol' Lord Groghe myself," one of the older runners said, nodding his head and looking solemn, "that there'd be an accident . . . then what'd he say to that? I asked him. Someone hurt because a wild lad won't respect what's our rights and propitty." Then he nodded directly at Tenna. "You aren't the only one he's knocked aside. Dinncha hear him coming?"

"Met him on the hill curve, she said," Torlo answered before Tenna could open her own mouth.

"Bad place, bad place. Runner can't see around

it,'' a second man said, and nodded his sympathy to her. ''See you've scratches? Penda put her good junk on ya?'' Tenna nodded. ''You'll be right then. I've seen your kin on the traces, haven't I? Betchur one of Fedri and Cesila's, aincha?'' He smiled knowingly at the others. ''You're prettier than she was and she was some pretty woman.''

Tenna decided to ignore the compliment and admitted to her parentage. ''Have you been through Station Ninety-Seven?''

''A time or two, a time or two,'' he said, grinning amiably. His runner's belt was covered with stitches.

Torlo had come up beside her and now took her left arm to peer at the side she couldn't really see well.

''Punctures,'' he said in a flat tone.

The other runners came to be sure his verdict was correct. They all nodded sagely and resumed their seats.

''Sometimes I wonder if all those berries're worth the risk of them slivers in spring,'' the veteran runner said.

''Worse time of the Turn to fall into them,'' she was told again.

''Misler, you run over to Healer Hall,'' Torlo said to one of them.

''Oh, I don't think that's necessary,'' Tenna said,

because you had to pay healers and she then wouldn't have enough for good leathers.

"Being as how it was the Lord Holder's runnerbeast knocked you in, he'll pay for it," Torlo said, sensing her reluctance and winking at her.

"One of these days he'll have to pay out blood money iffen he doesn't bring that Haligon up short and *make* him quit our traces. Did those shod hooves leave many holes?" another man asked her.

"No," she had to admit. "Surface sprang right back up."

"Hmmm, that's what it's supposed to do."

"But we don't need Haligon galloping up and down like traces was put there for *his* benefit."

Misler departed on his errand and then, after each runner spoke his or her name and home station, a glass of wine was poured for her. She started to demur but Torlo eyed her sternly.

"You're not on the run list this day, girl."

"I need to finish my first Cross," she said wistfully as she took the glass and found an empty seat.

"You will, lass, you will," the first man—Grolly—said so assuredly as he held his glass up that she was heartened. The others all seconded his words.

A few scratches and maybe the three-four punctures were not going to keep her from reaching the western seashore. She sipped her wine.

The runners who'd been bathing descended now and were served their wine by the time Misler came trotting back, a man in healer colors following behind, with a hop and a skip to keep up with his long-legged escort.

Beveny introduced himself and asked for Penda to join him—a nicety that pleased Tenna and gave her a very good opinion of the journeyman. The consultation was conducted right there in the main hall since the injuries were to visible portions of her body. And the other runners were genuinely interested in knowing the worst of her condition and offered suggestions, most of them knowledgeable as to which herbs should be used and how efficacious they had been on such and such an occasion. Beveny kept a grin on his face as if he was well used to runner chaffering. As he probably was.

"I think this one, and the two on your leg, may still have slivers in them," Beveny said at length. "Nothing a poultice won't draw out overnight, I'm sure."

There were approving nods and wise smiles from the audience. Poultices were then discussed again and at length and the appropriate one decided on. During this part of the consultation, Tenna was installed in a comfortable, padded chair, a long stool affair attached to the front of it so her legs could stretch out. She'd never been fussed over so much

in her life, but it was a runner thing: she'd seen her
mother and father take the same personal care of
anyone arriving at their station with an injury. But
to be the center of so much attention—and at Fort
Station—was embarrassing in the extreme for
Tenna and she kept trying to discount the urgency
of such minor wounds. She did offer her packet of
her mother's poultice, and three of the runners remarked favorably on Cesila's famous poultice, but
hers was clearly for bruises, not infections, so the
healer told her to keep it for emergencies.

"Which I hope you won't have, of course," he
said, smiling at her as he mixed—with the hot water Penda fetched—an aromatic concoction that
everyone now in the room had to approve.

Keenly aware that she must be properly modest
and forbearing, as well as brave, Tenna braced herself for the treatment. Hot poultices, however ther-
apeutic, could be somewhat uncomfortable. Then
the mixture was ready. With deft fingers, Healer
Beveny deposited neat blobs, no larger than his
thumbnail, on the sore spots. He must have judged
the heat just right, because none were too hot. He
made sure to position the patches right over each
blob before securing them with bandage strips that
Penda had produced. Tenna felt each of the ten hot
spots, but the sensation was not all that unpleasant.

"I'll check tomorrow, Tenna, but I don't think

we have to worry about any of them," Beveny said with such conviction that Tenna was relieved.

"Nor do you, here at Fort Station with the Healer Hall a stretch away," said Torlo, and courteously saw Beveny to the door and watched a polite few moments until the healer was halfway to his Hall.

"Nice fella," he said to anyone listening, and smiled at Tenna. "Ah, here's the food."

Evidently that meal had been held up for her to be treated, because now Penda led in the drudge carrying the roast platter with others behind him, laden with large bowls of steaming food.

"Rosa," she said, pointing to one of the female runners, "get the board. Spacia, grab a fork and spoon for Tenna. She's not to move. Grolly, her glass is empty. . . ." As she directed the others to serve the injured runner, she herself carved fine slices from the roasted ribs of herdbeast. "The rest of you, get on line."

Tenna's embarrassment returned, waited on as she was by Rosa and Spacia, who cheerfully performed their assigned tasks. Always she had been the one to help, so this situation was quite novel. Of course, it was also a runner thing, to be cosseted in need, but she'd never been the recipient before.

Two more batches of runners arrived in from south and east. When they came back from bathing, they had to be told all about Haligon's forcing Tenna off the trace and how she had sticklebush punctures that were severe enough to require a healer. She got the distinct impression that almost everyone had had a run-in with this infamous Haligon, or knew someone who had. Eventually the tale had been told to everyone and the conversation changed to talk of the Gather three days hence.

Tenna sighed softly to herself. Three days? She'd be fully recovered by then and have to run on. She really did want to get the extra stitches for her first Cross. A Gather, even one at Fort, was not as important as upgrading herself. Well, nearly. It wasn't as if this were the last Gather she'd ever have a chance to attend, even if it was the first for her at the First Hold on Pern.

This was home station for two girls. Rosa had a cap of very tight dark curls and a pert face with mischievous eyes. Spacia, with long blond hair tied back, runner-wise, had a more dignified way about her although she kept up a wickedly bantering conversation with the younger male runners among others there. Then there was an informal concert for Tenna, some of the newer songs that the Harper Hall was airing. Rosa led, Spacia adding an alto line while three of the other runners joined in, one with a little whistle and the others with their voices. The evening became quite enjoyable, especially as either Grolly or Torlo kept filling Tenna's wine-glass.

Rosa and Spacia helped her up the stairs, one on either side of her, with the excuse that the bandages mustn't loosen. They chattered about what they intended to wear to the Gather and who they hoped to dance with.

"We're on line tomorrow," Rosa said as they got her to her bed, "so we'll probably be off before you get down. Those poultices ought to do the trick."

They both wished her a good night's sleep. Her head was spinning as she lay down, but pleasantly, and she drifted into sleep very quickly.

Torlo arrived with a tray of food just as she was waking up.

"Not as sore today?"

"Not all over but my leg . . ." She pulled the quilt back so he could see.

"Hmmm. Need more on that one. Went in at an angle. I'm calling Beveny."

"Oh, really . . . I'd rather . . . Surely Penda knows what the healer made up for me . . ."

"She does, but we want the healer to speak about your injuries to Lord Groghe."

Tenna was dismayed now. A runner didn't go to the Lord Holder without *real* cause for complaint, and her injuries were not that serious.

"Now, see here, young runner," and Torlo waggled a finger at her, "I'm station master and I say we take this to the Lord Holder on account of it shouldna happened at all."

Beveny recommended a long soak in the tub and provided her with an astringent to use in the water.

"I'll leave more poultice with Penda. We want that final sliver out. See . . ." and he pointed to the thin, almost invisible hairs of the sticklebush which had come from the arm puncture. "We want another of these fellows on the pad, not in you."

Two more had also erupted from the puncture wounds, and he carefully covered all three pads with glass slides, which he tied together.

"Soak at least an hour, Tenna," he told her. "You're to take it very handy today, too. Don't want that sliver to work any further down in your flesh."

She shuddered at the thought of an evil-looking hair loose in her body.

"Don't worry. It'll be out by evening," Beveny said, grinning reassuringly. "And you'll be dancing with us."

"Oh, I'll have to run on as soon as I'm able," she said earnestly.

Beveny's grin broadened. "What? And do me out of my dance with you?" Then his expression turned professional. "I can't release you as fit to run yet, you know. I'd want to see those puncture marks healing. Especially in the shin, where just the dirt and dust of a run could be embedded and cause a repeat infection. The wounds may seem," and he emphasized the word, "insignificant but I've tended a lot of runners and I know the hazards of the trace."

"Oh," Tenna said meekly.

"Right. Oh!" And he grinned again, pressing her shoulder with a kindly squeeze. "You will make your first Cross. Now rest. You runners are a breed apart, you know."

With that reminder, he left her to make her way to the bathing room.

Rosa, Spacia, Grolly—in fact, all the runners at the Fort Station—were in and out, groaning over the special messages that needed to be delivered to the Fort crafthalls, the Lord Holder, the Harper Hall, coming from the "backside of beyond" as Rosa termed it.

"Don't mind us," Rosa said when Tenna began to feel as if she ought to be doing her share. "It's always like this just before a Gather and we always complain, but the Gather makes up for it. Which reminds me, you don't have anything to wear."

"Oh, no, don't worry about me...."

"Nonsense," Spacia said. "We will if we want

to and we do.'' She gave Tenna's long frame an intent look and then shook her head. ''Well, nothing we have would fit.'' Both girls were shorter than Tenna by a full head and, while neither carried much flesh, they were stockier than the eastern girl.

Then both turned to each other in the same instant and snapped their fingers. ''Silvina!'' they exclaimed in chorus.

''C'mon,'' Spacia said, and reached for Tenna's hand. ''You can walk, can't you?''

''Oh, yes, but . . .''

''On your feet then, runner,'' Rosa said, and took Tenna's other arm, assisting her to an upright position. ''Silvina's headwoman at the Harper Hall and she always has good things. . . .''

''But . . . I . . .'' and then Tenna gave up protesting. It was obvious from the determined expressions on the two runners' faces that they would brook no argument.

''You're taking her to Silvina?'' Penda asked, sidling out of the kitchen. ''Good. I've nothing here to fit her and she's got to look her best when she meets that wretch Haligon.''

''Why?'' Tenna suspiciously wanted to know. Why would she need to look her best just to give Haligon what-for?

''Why, to maintain the reputation of Fort Station, of course,'' Rosa said with an impish grin. ''We've our pride, you know, and you may be a visitor but you're here, now,'' and she pointed emphatically to the ground, ''and must be presentable.''

''Not that you aren't,'' Spacia hastily added, being slightly more tactful than Rosa, ''except we want you more so than ever.''

''After all, it *is* your first Fort Gather . . .''

''And you nearly finishing your first Cross, too.''

Their chatter was impossible to resist and there was no way Tenna could appear at a Gather in runner gear, which was all she had of her own to wear.

At this evening hour, they found Silvina checking day-records in her office at the Harper Hall and she was more than delighted that she had been approached. She led them down to the storage rooms underneath the Harper Hall.

''We keep quite a few performance dresses in case a soloist wants to wear harper colors. You wouldn't mind wearing blue, would you?'' Silvina said as she paused by the second of a line of locked doors. ''Actually, I think blue would be a very good color for you.'' She had such a lovely speaking voice that Tenna was listening more to her tone than what she was saying. ''And I've one that I think might be just the thing for you.''

She opened a large wardrobe and, from the many there, she brought out a long gown with full sleeves and some fine embroidered trim that made all three girls gasp.

"It's lovely. Oh, I couldn't wear something this valuable," Tenna exclaimed, backing away.

"Nonsense," Silvina said, and gestured for Tenna to slip out of her runner top.

When Tenna carefully slipped on the dress, the softness of the fabric against her skin made her feel . . . special. She tried a little spin and the long skirt swirled about her ankles while the full sleeves billowed about her arms. It was the most flattering dress she'd worn and she examined it thoroughly, committing the details of its design to her mind so that she could reproduce it the next time she had marks enough for a Gather dress. The one she had at home was nowhere near as splendid as this. Could she, should she dance, in something as elegant as this? What if she spilled something on it?

"I'm not sure . . ." she began as she faced her companions.

"Not *sure*!" Rosa was indignant. "Why, that deep blue shows up your lovely skin and your eyes . . . they are blue, aren't they, or is it the dress makes them so? And it fits like it was made for *you*!"

Tenna looked down at the low-cut front of the bodice. Whoever it had been made for had had a lot more breast. She didn't fill it out properly. Silvina was rummaging through another box.

"Here," she said, and stuffed two pads in the

front, settling them with such a practiced hand that the adjustment was done before Tenna could protest.

"*There*! That's much better," Spacia said, and then giggled. "I have to pad, too. But it'd be worse for us as runners to be heavy, bumping around all the time."

Tenna tentatively felt her newly improved form but, as she looked at herself in the mirror, she could see that the fit of the top was vastly improved and she looked more . . . more . . . well, it fit better. The fabric was so smooth to the touch, it was a pleasure just to feel the dress on her. And this shade of blue . . .

"This is harper blue," she said with surprise.

"Of course it is," Silvina said with a laugh. "Not that it matters. You'll be wearing runner cords . . . though right now," and Silvina's appreciative grin broadened, "you don't look runnerish . . . if you'll forgive my frankness."

Tenna couldn't help admiring how much better her figure looked with that little alteration. She had a slim waist and the dress hugged it before flaring out over hips that she knew to be too bony and best covered.

"The pads won't . . . pop out . . . will they, when I'm dancing?"

"If you'll take off the dress, I'll put a few

stitches to secure them where they should stay,"
Silvina said.

That was done so quickly that Silvina was folding the lovely dress over Tenna's arm before she realized it.

"Now, shoes?" Spacia asked. "She can't wear spikes...."

"She might better wear them," Rosa said dourly, "with some of those louts who come to a Fort Gather. Haligon's not the only one who'll home in on her, looking that way."

Silvina had cast a measuring glance at Tenna's long, narrow feet and now took a long box down from one of the many shelves in this huge store-room.

"Should have something to fit even narrow runner feet..." she murmured, and came up with a pair of soft, ankle-high, black suede boots. "Try these."

They did not fit. But the fourth pair—in dark red—were only slightly too long.

"Wear thick anklets and they'll fit fine," Spacia suggested.

And the three girls left, Tenna carefully transporting the dress to the station. Rose and Spacia insisted on sharing the burden of the boots and the underskirt that Silvina had offered to complete the costume.

* * *

The last sliver of sticklebush was on the pad the next morning and Beveny added it to the others, handing the evidence packet over to Torlo, who grinned in satisfaction.

"This'll make Lord Groghe see that we've a legitimate complaint," he said, and nodded emphatically at Tenna. She was about to protest when he added, "But not until after the Gather, for he's too busy to be approached right now. And he'll be in a much better mood after a good Gather." He turned to Tenna. "So you have to stay till after and that's that."

"But I could run short distances now, couldn't I?"

"Mmm," Torlo said, nodding. "Iffen a run comes up. Don't like to be idle, do you, girl?" She shook her head. "Wal, Healer, is she fit?"

"Short run and no hills," Beveny said, "and nowhere Haligon might ride." He grinned mischievously at her and took his leave.

Just before midday, Torlo called her from the front bench where she'd been watching the Gather stalls being erected.

"Run down to the port for me, will you? A ship just was drummed in and has cargo for the Gather. We're to get its manifests." He took her by the arm and showed the route to her on the big map of Fort Hold that displayed local traces and roads. "Straight run . . . downhill all the way to the port. And not too steep on the way back."

It was good to be running again and, though the spring weather had turned chilly, she soon worked up enough heat to keep warm. The captain was muchly relieved to deliver the manifests to her. The cargo was being unloaded and he was anxious to get it up the road to the Hold in time for the Gather. He was equally anxious to receive payment for the deliveries, and she could promise she'd have the manifests in the designated hands before dinnertime.

He also had a pouch of letters from the eastern seacoast on board which were addressed to Fort Hold. So she carried a full belt back. Her legs felt the slight incline but she didn't decrease her pace despite a slight soreness in the right leg at the shin.

Well, a warm bath in one of those incredible tubs would take care of that. And the Gather was tomorrow.

Fort Station was full that night, with runners coming from other stations for the Gather the next day. Tenna bunked in with Rosa and Spacia and a southern runner, Delfie, took the fourth bed in their room. It was a front room with a window, and you heard the traffic on the road, but Tenna was tired enough to sleep through anything.

"Which is as well because the comings and goings up the main track kept up all night long," Rosa said with cheerful disgust. "Let's eat outside. It's so crowded in here." So they all sat on the front benches to eat.

Spacia gave Tenna a conspiratorial wink as Tenna followed the others outside. There had been a few spare seats but not all together. It would be nicer to eat outside instead of the packed tables. Penda and her drudges had their hands full pouring klah and distributing bread, cheese, and porridge.

Actually, it was much more interesting to sit outside to eat. There was so much going on. Gather wagons kept arriving from both directions and rolled onto the field set aside for their use. Stalls which had been bare boards and uprights last night were being decorated with Hall colors and craft insignia. And more stalls were being erected on the wide court in front of the Hold. The long tongue and groove boards for the dancing surface were being slotted into place in the center and the harpers' platform erected. Tenna wanted to hug herself with delight at all the activity. She'd never actually seen a Gather gathering before . . . especially in such a big Hold as Fort. Since she had run yesterday, she felt a little better about not having made a push to finish her first Cross. And she had the chance to see the dragonriders pop into the air above Fort Hold.

"Oh, they are so beautiful," she said, noticing that Rosa and Spacia were also watching the graceful creatures landing, and the elegantly clad dragonriders dismounting.

"Yes, they are," Rosa said in an odd tone. "I just wish they wouldn't keep going on about Thread coming back." She shuddered.

"You don't think it will?" Tenna said, for she had recently had several runs into the Benden Station and knew that Weyrfolk were certain that Thread would return. Hadn't the Red Star been seen in the Eye Rock at the winter solstice?

Rosa shrugged. "It can for all of me but it's going to interfere with running something fierce."

"I noticed that the Benden Thread halts are all repaired," Tenna said.

Spacia shrugged. "We'd be fools to take any chances, wouldn't we?" Then she grimaced. "I'd really hate to be stuck in one of those boxes with Thread falling all around me. Why, the wardrobe in Silvina's storeroom is larger. What if it got in a crack, Thread got in, and I couldn't get out?" She pantomimed terror and revulsion.

"It'll never come to that," Rosa said confidently.

"Lord Groghe certainly got rid of all the greenery around the Hold," Spacia remarked, gesturing around.

ANNE MCCAFFREY

"That was as much for the Gather as because the dragonriders said he had to," Rosa said dismissively. "Oh, here come the Boll runners. . . ." She jumped to her feet, waving at the spearhead of runners who had just appeared on the southern road.

They were running effortlessly, their legs moving as if they had drilled that matched stride. They certainly made a fine sight, Tenna thought, pride swelling in her chest and catching her breath.

"They must have started last night," Rosa said. "Oh, d'you see Cleve, Spacia?"

"Third rank from the rear," Spacia said pointing. "As if anyone could miss *him!*" she added in a slightly derisive tone, winking at Tenna. Then she murmured, behind her hand for Tenna's ears only, "She's been so sure he wouldn't come . . . Ha!"

Tenna grinned, now understanding why Rosa had wanted to sit outside that morning and why she had sent Spacia in when they needed more klah.

Then, all of a sudden, as if the arrival of that contingent had been the signal, the Gather was ready. All stalls were up and furnished, the first shift of harpers on the platform and ready to entertain. Then Rosa pointed to the wide steps leading down from the entrance to the Hold and there were the Lord and Lady, looking exceedingly grand in brown Gather finery, descending to the court to formally open the Gather Square. They were accompanied by the dragonriders as well as a clutch of folk, young and old and all related to the Lord Holder. According to Rosa, Lord Groghe had a large family.

"Oh, let's not miss the opening," Spacia told Tenna. Rosa had accompanied Cleve into the station and was helping Penda serve the Boll group a second breakfast after their long run.

So the two girls had excellent seats to watch the two Lord Holders do the official walk through the Gather.

"There's Haligon," Spacia said, her tone hard, pointing.

"Which one?"

"He's wearing brown," Spacia said.

Tenna was none the wiser. "There are a lot of people wearing brown."

"He's walking just behind Lord Groghe."

"So are a lot of other people."

"He's got the curliest head of hair," Spacia added.

There were two who answered that description, but Tenna decided it was the shorter of the young men, the one who walked with a definite swagger. That had to be Haligon. He was handsome enough, though she liked the appearance of the taller man in brown more: not as attractive perhaps, but with a nicer grin on his face. Haligon obviously thought himself very much the lad, from the smug expression on *his* face.

Tenna nodded. She'd give him what-for, so she would.

"C'mon, we should change before the mob get upstairs," Spacia said, touching Tenna's arm to get her attention.

Now that she had identified Haligon, Tenna was quite ready to be looking her very best. Spacia was also determined to assist and took pains with Tenna's appearance, fluffing her hair so that it framed her face, helping her with lip color and a touch of eye shadow.

"Bring out the blue in 'em, though your eyes are really gray, aren't they?"

"Depends on what I'm wearing." Tenna gave a little twirl in front of the long mirror in the room, watching the bias-cut swirl around her ankles. As Spacia had suggested, the anklets took up the spare room in the toes of the borrowed boots. Nor did they look ungainly on the end of her legs as her long feet usually did. She was really quite pleased with her looks. And had to admit, with a degree of satisfaction, that she looked "pretty."

Then Spacia stood beside her, the yellow of her gown an attractive contrast to Tenna's deep blue.

"Ooops, I'd better find you some spare runner

cords or everyone'll think you're new in the Harper Hall.''

No spare cords were found, though Spacia turned out all the drawers.

"Maybe I should be Harper Hall," Tenna said thoughtfully. "That way I can deal with Haligon as he deserves before he suspects."

"Hmm, that might be the wiser idea, you know," Spacia agreed.

Rosa came rushing in, pulling at her clothes in a rush to change.

"Need any help?" Spacia asked as Rosa pulled her pink, floral-printed Gather dress from its hanger.

"No, no but get down there and keep Felisha from Cleve. She's determined to get him, you know. Waltzed right in before he'd finished eating and started hanging on his arm as if they were espoused.'' Rosa's voice was muffled as she pulled the dress over her head. They all heard a little tearing and Rosa cried out in protest, standing completely still, the dress half on. "Oh, no, no! What did I rip? What'll I do? How bad is it? Can you see?"

While the seam had only parted a bit, and Spacia was threading a needle to make the repairs, Rosa was so disturbed at the thought of her rival that Tenna volunteered to go down.

"You know which one Cleve is?" Rosa asked anxiously, and Tenna nodded and left the room.

She identified Felisha before she did Cleve. The girl, with a mop of curly black tangles half-covering her face, was flirting outrageously with the tall, lantern-jawed runner. He had an engaging smile, though a trifle absent, as he kept looking toward the stairs. Tenna chuckled to herself. Rosa needn't worry. Cleve was obviously uncomfortable with Felisha's coy looks and the way she kept tossing her hair over her shoulder, letting it flick into his face.

"Cleve?" she asked as she approached them. Felisha glared at her and gave her head a perceptible tilt to indicate to Tenna to move on.

"Yes?" Cleve moved a step closer to Tenna, and farther from Felisha, who then altered her stance to put her arm through his in a proprietary fashion that obviously annoyed Cleve.

"Rosa told me that you'd had a run-in with Haligon, too?"

"Yes, I did," Cleve said, seizing on the subject and trying to disentangle himself. "Ran me down on the Boll trace six sevendays ago. Got a nasty sprain out of it. Rosa mentioned he pushed you into sticklebush and you had some mean slivers. Caught you on the hill curve, did he?"

Tenna turned up her hands to show the mottled

sliver pricks still visible from that encounter.

"How terrible!" Felisha said insincerely. "That boy's far too reckless."

"Indeed," Tenna said, not liking this girl at all, though she smiled amiably. Surely she was too heavyset to be a runner. Her mop of hair covered whatever Hall or Hold cords she might be wearing. Tenna turned to Cleve. "Spacia told me that you know a lot about the local leathers and I need new shoes."

"Don't they tan hides wherever you come from?" Felisha asked snidely.

"Station Ninety-Seven, isn't it?" Cleve said, grinning. "Come, I've a mind to look for new leathers myself and the bigger the Gather the more chance at a good price, right?" He brushed free of Felisha and, taking Tenna by the arm, propelled her across to the door.

Tenna had a brief glance at the furious look on Felisha's face as they made their escape.

"Thank *you*, Tenna," Cleve said, exhaling with exaggeration as they strode across the court to the Gather Square. "That girl's a menace."

"Is she a Boll runner? She didn't introduce herself."

Cleve chuckled. "No, she's Weaver Hall," he said dismissively, "but my station runs messages for her Craftmaster." He grimaced.

"Tenna?" Torlo called from the door, and they both stopped, allowing him to catch up with them.

"Anyone point out Haligon to you yet?" he asked.

"Yes, Rosa and Spacia did. He was behind the Lord Holder. I'll have a word with him when we meet."

"Good girl, good girl," Torlo said, pressing her arm firmly in encouragement, and then he returned to the station.

"Will you?" Cleve asked, eyes wide with surprise.

"Will I what? Give him what-for? Indeed I will," Tenna said, firming her mind with purpose. "A bit of what he gave me."

"I thought it was sticklebushes you fell into?" Cleve asked, taking it all literally. "There're none of those in a Square."

"Measuring his length on a Gather floor will do nicely, I think," she replied. It ought to be rather easy to trip someone up with such a crowd around. And she had committed herself rather publicly to giving this Haligon a visible lesson. Even Healer Beveny was helping her. She was obliged to act. She certainly didn't wish to lose respect in the station. She took a deep breath. Would tripping him be sufficient? At least on the personal level. There'd still be the charge of reckless behavior leveled against him with the healer-verified proof of her injuries. These had certainly kept her from running for three days—loss of income.

"Oh!" she said, seeing the display for fabrics draped on the Weaver Hall booth: brilliant colors, and floral prints, as well as stripes in both bold and muted colors. She put her hands behind her back because the temptation to finger the cloth was almost irresistible.

Cleve wrinkled his nose. "That's Felisha's Hall's stuff."

"Oh, that red is amazing. . . ."

"Yeah, it's a good Hall. . . ."

"In spite of her?" Tenna chuckled at his reluctant admission.

"Yes . . ." and he grinned ruefully.

They passed the Glasscraft display: mirrors with ornate frames and plain wood, goblets and drinking glasses in all shapes and colors, pitchers in all sizes.

Tenna caught a reflection and almost didn't recognize herself except for that fact that there was Cleve beside her. She straightened her shoulders and smiled back at the unfamiliar girl in the glass.

The next stand was a large Tailor Hall display with finished goods in tempting array: dresses, shirts, trousers, and more intimate garments— enticing merchandise, to be sure, and this one was already packed out with buyers.

"What's keeping Rosa?" Cleve asked, glancing back over his shoulder toward the station, which would be visible until they turned the corner.

"Well, she wanted to look extra nice for you," Tenna said.

Cleve grinned. "She always looks nice." And he blushed suddenly.

"She's a very kind and thoughtful person," Tenna said sincerely.

"Ah, here we are," he said, pointing to the hides displayed at the stall on the corner of the square. "Though I think there are several stalls. Fort Gathers're big enough to attract a lot of crafthalls. Let's see what's available everyplace. Are you good at haggling? If you're not, we can leave it to Rosa. She's very good. And they'd know she means business. You being unknown, they might think they could put one over on you."

Tenna grinned slyly. "I plan to get the most for my mark, I assure you."

"I shouldn't teach you how to run traces, then, should I?" Cleve said with a tinge of rueful apology in his voice.

Tenna smiled back and began to saunter aimlessly past the leather stall. Just then Rosa caught up with them, giving Tenna a kiss as if they hadn't parted company fifteen minutes before. Cleve threw one arm about Rosa's shoulders and whispered in her ear, making her giggle. Other shoppers walked around the three, standing in the middle of the wide aisle. Tenna didn't object to the chance to examine the leather goods without appearing to do so. The journeyman behind the counter pretended not to see her not looking at his wares. She was also trying to see if she could spot Haligon among those promenading about the Square.

By the time the three of them had done their first circuit of the Gather, it was almost impossible to move for the crowds. But a goodly crowd also added to the "Gather feeling," and the trio of runners were exhilarated by the atmosphere. They spent so many hours in work that was solitary and time-consuming, often at hours when most other folk had finished their labors and were enjoying companionship and family life. True, they had the constant satisfaction of knowing that they provided an important service, but you didn't think of that running through a chilling rain or battling against a fierce gale. You thought more of what you *didn't* have and what you were missing.

Refreshment stalls displayed all kinds of drink and finger edibles. So, when they had finished their circuit, they bought food and drink and sat at the tables about the dance square.

"There he is!" Rosa said suddenly, pointing across the square to where a group of young men were surveying girls parading in their Gather finery. It was a custom to take a Gather partner, someone with whom to spend the occasion—which could include the day, the evening meal, the dancing, and whatever else was mutually decided. Everyone recognized the limitation and made sure that the details were arranged ahead of time so that there wouldn't be a misunderstanding of intent.

This would be an ideal situation in which to make Haligon suffer indignity. The area where he was standing with his friends was at the roadside, dusty and spotted with droppings from all the draft animals pulling Gather wagons past it. He'd look silly, his good clothes mussed. With any luck, she could get his fancy Gather clothing soiled as well as dusty.

"Excuse me," Tenna said, putting down her drink. "I've a score to settle."

"Oh!" Rosa's eyes went wide but an encouraging "yo-ho" followed Tenna as she cut diagonally across the wooden dancing floor.

Haligon was still in the company of the taller man, laughing at something said and eyeing the girls who were parading conspicuously along that side of the Gather Square. Yes, this was the time to repay him for her fall.

Tenna went right up to him, tapped him on the shoulder, and when he turned around in response, the arch smile on his face turned to one of considerable interest at her appearance, his eyes lighting as he gave her a sweeping look of appreciation. He was looking so boldly that he did not see Tenna cock her right arm. Putting her entire body into the swing, she connected her fist smartly to his chin. He dropped like a felled herdbeast, flat on his back and unconscious. And right on top of some droppings. Although the impact of her fist on his chin had rocked her back on her heels, she brushed her hands together with great satisfaction and, pivoting on the heel of her borrowed red shoe, retraced her steps.

She was halfway back to Rosa and Cleve when she heard someone rapidly overtaking her. So she was ready when her arm was seized and her progress halted.

"What was that all about?" It was the tall lad in brown who pulled her about, a look of genuine surprise on his face. And his eyes, too, surveyed her in her formfitting blue dress.

"I thought he ought to have a little of what he deals out so recklessly," she said, and proceeded.

"Wait a minute. What was he supposed to have done to you? I've never seen you around Fort before and he's never mentioned meeting someone like you. And he would!" His eyes glinted with appreciation.

"Oh?" Tenna cocked her head at him. They were nearly at eye level. "Well, he pushed me into sticklebushes." She showed him her hands and his expression altered to one of real concern.

"Sticklebushes? They're dangerous at this season."

"I do know that . . . the hard way," she replied caustically.

"But where? When?"

"That doesn't matter. I've evened the score."

"Indeed," and his grin was respectful. "But are you sure it was my brother?"

"Do you know all Haligon's friends?"

"Haligon?" He blinked. After a pause in which his eyes reflected a rapid series of considerations, he said, "I thought I did." And he laughed nervously. Then he gestured for her to continue on her way. She could see that he was being careful not to annoy her, and that provided her with further amused satisfaction.

"There is a lot about Haligon that he would want kept quiet," she said. "He's a reckless sort."

"And you're the one to teach him manners?" He had to cover his mouth, but she could see that his eyes were brimming with laughter.

"Someone has to."

"Oh? Just what offense did he give you? It's not often . . . Hali-gon . . . measures his length.

Couldn't you have found a less public spot to deliver your lesson? You've ruined his Gather clothes with muck."

"Actually, I chose the spot deliberately. Let him feel what it's like to be flattened unexpectedly."

"Yes, I'm sure. But where did you encounter him?"

"He was using a runner trace, at a gallop, in the middle of the night. . . ."

"Oh," and he stopped dead in his tracks, an odd, almost guilty look on his face. "When was this?" he asked, all amusement gone.

"Four nights ago, at the hill curve."

"And?"

"I was knocked into sticklebushes." With those words, she held out her right leg and pulled her skirt up high enough to expose the red dots of the healing injuries. And again displayed her free hand and its healing rack of punctures.

"They got infected?" He was really concerned now and obviously knew the dangers of the sticklebush.

"I've saved the slivers," she said in a firm tone. "Healer Beveny has them for proof. I wasn't able to continue working and I've been laid up three days."

"I'm sorry to hear that." And he sounded sincere, his expression somber. Then he gave his head a little shake and smiled at her, a trifle warily, but there was a look in his eyes that told her he found her attractive. "If you promise not to drop me, may I say that you don't look at all like most runners I've met." His eyes lingered only briefly on her bodice, and then he hastily cleared his throat. "I'd better get back and see . . . if Haligon's come to."

Tenna spared a glance at the little knot of people clustered around her victim and, giving him a gracious nod, continued on her way back to Rosa and Cleve.

They were looking pale and shocked.

"There! Honor is satisfied," she said, slipping into her seat.

Rosa and Cleve exchanged looks.

"No," Rosa said, and leaned toward her, one hand on her forearm. "It wasn't Haligon you knocked down."

"It wasn't? But that's the fellow you pointed out to me. He's in brown . . ."

"So is Haligon. He's the one followed you across the dance floor. The one you were talking to, and I don't think you were giving him any what-for."

"*Oh.*" Tenna slumped weakly against the back of her chair. "I hit the wrong man?"

"Uh-huh," Rosa said as both she and Cleve nodded their heads.

"Oh dear," and she made a start to get up but Rosa hastily put out a restraining hand.

"I don't think apologies will help."

"No? Who did I hit?"

"His twin brother, Horon, who's bad enough in his own way."

"Quite likely, with the lewd look he gave me." Tenna was halfway to convincing herself that she had at least hit someone who needed a put-down.

"Horon's a bit of a bully and nice girls won't have anything to do with him. Especially at a Gather." Then Rosa giggled, covering her mouth with her hand. "He was sure looking you up and down. That's why we thought you'd hit him."

Remembering the force of her punch, Tenna rubbed her sore knuckles.

"You may have done someone a favor," Cleve said, grinning. "That was some punch."

"My brothers taught me how," Tenna said absently, watching the group across the Square. She was a trifle relieved when Horon was helped to his feet. And pleased that he staggered and needed assistance. Then, as the group around Horon moved about, she saw Haligon's figure striding up to the station. "Uh-oh. Why's he going to the station?"

"I wouldn't worry about that," Rosa said, standing up. "Torlo would love to remind him of all the harm he's been doing runners."

"Even if they weren't as pretty as you are," Cleve said. "Let's see about your leathers."

They took their empty glasses back to the refreshment stand. Tenna managed one more look at the station but there was no sign of Haligon or Torlo, though there was a lot of coming and going. There would be, on a Gather day. Would she have to knock Haligon down, too? To satisfy runner honor? It wouldn't be as easy, for he had been wary enough of her when he had caught up with her on the dance floor.

After a second round of the Gather stalls, they all decided to find out what prices were being asked. At the first tanner's stall, Cleve did more of the talking so that the real buyer was protected from the blandishments of the tanner journeyman, a man named Ligand.

"Blue for a harper singer?" Ligand had begun, glancing at Tenna. "Thought I saw you eyeing the stall earlier."

"I'm runner," Tenna said.

"She just happens to look her best in blue," Rosa said quickly in case Tenna might be embarrassed to admit she wore a borrowed gown.

"She does indeed," Ligand said, "I'd never have guessed her for a runner."

"Why not?" Rosa asked, bridling.

"Because she's wearing blue," Ligand said deferentially. "So what color is your delight this fine Gather day?"

"I'd like a dark green," and Tenna pointed to a stack of hides dyed various shades of that color in the shelves behind him.

"Good choice for a runner," he said and, with a deft lift, transferred the heavy stack of hides to the front counter. Then he moved off to the other end of his stall, where two holders were examining heavy belts.

"Not that trace moss leaves stains," Rosa remarked as Tenna began flipping through the pile, fingering the leather as she went along.

"We go for the reddy-browns in Boll," Cleve said. "So much of the soil down in Boll is that shade. And trace moss doesn't do as well in the heat as it does in the north."

"Does fine in Igen," Tenna said, having run trace there.

"So it does," Cleve said reflectively. "I like that one," he added, spreading his hand over the hide before Tenna could flip to the next one. "Good deep emerald green."

Tenna had also been considering it. "Enough here for boots. I only need enough for summer shoes. He wouldn't want to divide it."

"Ah, and you've found one you like, huh? Good price on that." Ligand was obviously aware of all that went on at his booth. He flipped up the hide to see the markings on the underside. "Give it to you for nine marks."

Rosa gasped. "At five it's robbery," Then she looked chagrined to have protested when Tenna was the prospective purchaser.

"I'd agree with that," Tenna said, having only four to spend. She gave the skin one more pat and, smiling courteously at Ligand, walked off, her companions hastily following her.

"You won't find better quality anywhere," Ligand called after them.

"It was good quality," Tenna murmured as they walked away. "But four marks is my limit."

"Oh, we should be able to find a smaller hide for that much, though maybe not the same green," Rosa said airily.

However, by the time they had done a third circuit and seen all the green hides available, they had not found either the same green or the same beautifully softened hide.

"I just don't have five, even if we could bargain him down to that price," Tenna said. "That brown at the third stand would be all right. Shall we try that?"

"Oho," Rosa said, stopping in her tracks, her expression alarmed.

Cleve, too, was stopped, and Tenna couldn't see

what caused their alarm until suddenly a man appeared out of the crowd and stood directly in their path. She recognized the tall, white-haired man from the morning's ceremony as Lord Holder Groghe.

"Runner Tenna?" he asked formally. But the expression in his wide-set eyes was pleasant.

"Yes," she said, raising her chin slightly. Was he about to give *her* what-for for punching his son Horon? She certainly couldn't admit to having hit the wrong one.

"Shall we sit over here, with your friends?" Lord Groghe said, gesturing toward a free table. He put a hand on her elbow and guided her gently in that direction, away from the stream of folk.

Tenna thought confusedly that neither his expression nor his tone were peremptory. He was unexpectedly gracious. A heavyset man with a full face and the beginning of jowls, he smiled to everyone as they made their way to the table, for there were many curious glances at the four of them. He caught the eye of the wineman and held up four fingers. The wineman nodded and hastened to serve them.

"I have an apology to make to you, Runner Tenna." He kept his voice low and for their ears alone.

"You do?" And, at Rosa's startled expression,

Tenna added courteously with only a short hesitation, "Lord Groghe?"

"I have verified that my son, Haligon, ran you down four nights ago and you were sufficiently injured so that you were unable to run." Groghe's brows met in a scowl that was for the circumstances, not her part in them. "I confess that I have heard rumors of other complaints about his use of runner traces. Station Master Torlo informed me of several near-collisions. You may be sure that, from now on, Haligon will leave the traces for the runners who made them. You're from Station Ninety-Seven? Keroon Hold?"

Tenna could only nod. She couldn't believe this was happening. A Lord Holder was apologizing to her?

"My son, Haligon, had no idea that he had nearly run you down the other night. He may be reckless," and Groghe smiled somewhat indulgently, "but he would never knowingly cause injury."

Rosa prodded Tenna in the ribs, and Tenna realized that she must make as much as she could of this opportunity, not just for herself but for all runners.

"Lord Groghe, I . . . we all," and she included Rosa and Cleve, "would be grateful to know that we may run the traces without interference. I had only the briefest warning that someone else was using the path. The hill hid his approach and there was wind, too, covering the sound. I could have been severely injured. Traces are not wide, you know." He nodded, and she went on boldly. "And they were made for runners, not riders." He nodded again. "I think Fort Station would be grateful for your help in keeping just runners on the traces."

Then she couldn't think of anything else to say. And just sat there, smiling with nervous twitches in the corners of her mouth.

"I have been well and truly told off, Runner Tenna." He smiled back at her, his eyes dropping for a split second to her bodice. "You're a very pretty girl. Blue becomes you." He reached over and gave her hand a pat before he rose. "I've told Torlo that the incursions will cease." Then, in his usual booming voice, he added, "Enjoy the Gather, runners, and the wine."

With that he rose and walked off, nodding and smiling as he went, leaving the three runners stunned. Rosa was the first to recover. She took a good swig of the wine.

"Torlo was right. You did it," Rosa said. "And this is *good* wine."

"What else would they serve Lord Groghe?" Cleve said, and surreptitiously eased the glass left

at the Lord Holder's seat closer to his. The level
of wine had not been much reduced by the sip that
Lord Groghe had taken. "We can split this one."

"I can't believe that Lord Holder apologized
to . . ." Tenna shook her head, hand on her chest.
". . . me. Tenna."

"You were the one injured, weren't you?" Rosa
said.

"Yes, but . . ."

"How did Lord Groghe know?" Cleve finished
for Tenna, who was puzzling such an answer.

"We all saw Haligon go up to the station," Rosa
said before taking another sip of the wine. She
rolled her eyes in appreciation of the taste. "But
Lord Groghe's a fair man, even if he usually thinks
women are half-wits. But he's fair." Then she
giggled again. "And he said how pretty you are,
so that helped, you know. Haligon likes his girls
pretty. So does Lord Groghe but he only looks."

The three runners had been so intent on their
own conversation that they did not notice Haligon's
approach until he unrolled the green hide from Ligand's stall in front of Tenna.

"In apology, Runner Tenna, because I really
didn't know there was someone on the curve of the
trace the other night," Haligon said, and gave a
courteous bow, his eyes fixed on Tenna's face.
Then his contrite expression altered to chagrin.

"The station master gave me what-for in triples. So did my father."

"Oh, didn't you believe Tenna?" Rosa asked him pertly.

"How could I doubt the injuries she showed me?" Haligon said. Now he waved for the wineman to serve their table.

Cleve gestured for him to be seated.

"Is . . . your brother all right?" Tenna asked, a question she hadn't quite dared ask Lord Groghe.

Haligon's eyes twinkled with merriment. "You have taught him a lesson, too, you know."

"I don't usually go around knocking people down," Tenna began, and received another surreptitious jab in her ribs from Rosa, sitting beside her. "Except when they need it." She leaned forward, away from Rosa. "I meant to hit *you*."

Haligon rubbed his jaw. "I'm as glad enough you didn't. When Master Torlo told me that you'd been kept from running for three days, I knew I was very much at fault. Then he told me of the other near-misses. Will you accept this leather in compensation, with my apology?"

"Your father has already apologized."

"I make my own, Runner Tenna," he said with an edge to his voice and a solemn expression.

"I accept, but . . ." She was about to refuse the leather when, once again, Rosa jabbed her. She'd have sore ribs at this rate. "I accept."

"Good, for I should have a miserable Gather without your forgiveness," Haligon said, his expression lightening. Lifting the glass he had just been served, he tilted it in her direction and drank. "Will you save me a dance?"

Tenna pretended to consider. But she was secretly thrilled, for despite their first encounter, there was something about Haligon that she found very attractive. Just in case, she shifted in her chair, moving her upper body away from Rosa to avoid another peremptory jab.

"I was hoping to be able to do the toss dance," she began and, when Haligon eagerly opened his mouth to claim that, she added, "but my right leg isn't entirely sound."

"But sound enough surely for the quieter dances?" Haligon asked. "You seemed to be walking well enough."

"Yes, walking's no strain for me..." and Tenna hesitated a little longer, "but I would enjoy having a partner." Which allowed him to ask for more than one dance.

"The slow ones, then?"

"Beveny asked for one, remember," Rosa said casually.

"When does the dancing start?" Tenna asked.

"Not until full dark, after the meal," Haligon

said. "Would you be my supper partner?"

She heard Rosa inhale sharply but she really did find him an agreeable sort. Certainly the invitation was acceptable. "I would be delighted to," she said graciously.

It was so arranged and Haligon toasted the agreement with the last of his wine, rose, bowed to them all, and left the table.

"Yo-ho, Tenna," Rosa murmured as they watched his tall figure disappear in the Gather crowd.

Cleve, too, grinned. "Neatly done. Do hope you'll be back on another Cross soon in case we have some more problems you can help us with."

"Oh, run off, will you?" Tenna replied flippantly. Now she allowed herself to finger the dark green leather hide. "Was he watching us, do you suppose? How'd he know?"

"Oh, no one's ever said Haligon was a dimwit," Rosa said. "Though he is, riding runner traces like he has."

"*He* must have told his father, then," Cleve said. "Owning up to all that shows an honest nature. I might end up liking him after all."

"Proper order," Rosa said. "Though he never admitted using the traces before when Torlo braced him on that." She grinned at Tenna. "It's sure true that a pretty girl gets more attention than a plain one like me."

"You are not plain," Cleve said indignantly and realized he had fallen into Rosa's neatly laid trap to elicit a compliment from him.

"I'm not?" she replied, smiling archly.

"Oh, you!" he said with the wordless disgust of the well-baited. Then he laughed and carefully split Groghe's glass between their glasses. "Much too good to waste."

Tenna returned to the station long enough to put away the beautiful leather. And long enough to get many requests for dances and to be supper partner from other runners who congratulated her.

"Told ya so, dinnit I?" Penda said, catching Tenna's arm as she was leaving. The woman was grinning from ear to ear. "Pretty girl's always heard, ya know."

Tenna laughed. "And Haligon's going to stay off the traces."

"So his father promised," Penda said, "but we'll have to see does he."

"I'll see that he does," Tenna promised airily and returned to the Gather Square. She'd never had such a marvelous time before.

The supper lines were now forming down the road at the roasting pits and she began to wonder if Haligon had just been funning her and had never intended, Lord Holder's son that he was, to honor his invitation. Then he appeared beside her, offering his arm.

"I didn't forget," he murmured, taking her by the arm.

Being partnered with a Holder's son allowed them to patronize a different line at the roasting pits and so they were served well before Cleve and Rosa. The wine Haligon ordered was more of the excellent one she'd sampled in the afternoon so Tenna was quite merry and relaxed by the time the dancing began.

What surprised her, because she'd given the first dance to Grolly—as much because he didn't expect to get any dances from such a pretty girl as because he asked her first—was that Haligon did not dance it with someone else. He waited at the table for a breathless Grolly to bring her back. It was a sprightly enough tune for dancing but not as fast or complicated as the toss was. The next dance was at a slower tempo and she held out her hand to Haligon, despite the fact that half the male runners at the Gather were now crowding about for a chance to dance with her.

He pulled her into his arms with a deft movement and they were suddenly cheek to cheek. He was only a little taller than she was so their steps matched effortlessly. One circuit of the room and she had perfect confidence in his leading.

Since they were dancing cheek to cheek—he was only a little taller than she was—she could feel his face muscles lifting in a smile. And he gave her a quick pressure with both hands.

"Do you know when you're running again?"

"I've already had a short leg, down to the port," she said. "Enough for a good warm-up."

"How *do* you manage such long distances on your own legs?" he asked, holding her out slightly to see her face in the light of the glowbaskets that lined the dance floor. He really wanted to know, too.

"Part of it's training, of course. Part that my Blood is bred to produce runners."

"Could you have done anything else with your life?"

"I could but I like running. There's a sort of . . . magic to it. Sometimes you feel you could run round the world. And I like night running. You feel like you're the only one awake and alive and moving."

"Quite likely you are, save for dimwits on mounts on traces they shouldn't be using," he said in a wry tone. "How long *have* you been running?"

He sounded genuinely interested. She had thought perhaps she had made a mistake, being sentimental about something as commonplace as running.

"Almost two whole Turns. This is my first Cross."

"And I was a dimglowed idiot who interrupted it," he said in an apologetic tone.

Tenna was almost embarrassed at his continued references to his mistake.

"How often do I have to say I've forgiven you?" she said, putting her lips closer to his ear. "That green leather is going to make fine shoes for me. By the way, how'd you know that was the hide I wanted? Were you following us about?"

"Father said I had to make amends in some way more personal than handing you marks . . ."

"You didn't give Tanner Ligand what he asked for, did you?" Her query was sharp, because she didn't want him to have had to spend more than she felt necessary. And she leaned away from his guiding arm enough so that she could see his face as he answered

"I won't tell you how much, Tenna, but we struck a fair bargain. Trouble was," and now Haligon's voice was rueful, "he knew just how much I needed that particular hide. It's the talk of the Gather, you know."

Tenna suspected that it was and she hoped she could tell it to her own station before they heard rumor, which always exaggerated.

"Hmmm. I should have expected that," she said.

"I shall be able to make two pairs of summer shoes out of that much leather and I'll think of you every time I wear them." She grinned up at him.

"Fair enough." Evidently satisfied by this exchange, he resettled his arms about her, drawing her just that much closer. "You didn't seem as interested in any other hide, you know. So I'd got off more lightly than I thought I might. I didn't know runners made their own footwear."

"We do and it's much better to make them for yourself. Then you've only yourself to blame if you've blisters."

"Blisters? They would be bad for a runner."

"Almost as bad as sticklebush slivers."

He groaned. "Will I ever be able to live that down?"

"You can try." Maybe she could get him to dance with her all night. He was possibly the best partner she'd ever had. Not that she ever lacked for them. But he was subtly different. In his dancing, too, for he seemed to know many combinations of the dance steps and she really had to keep her attention on her feet and following his lead. Maybe it was him being a Holder's son.

"Maybe it's being a runner," and his remark startled her, it being near what she'd just been thinking, "but you're the lightest thing on your feet." He reset his hands more firmly about her, drawing her as close as he could.

They were both silent, each concentrating on the complexities of the dance. It ended all too soon for Tenna. She didn't really wish to release him. Nor he, her. So they stood on the dance floor, arms at their sides but not with much distance between them. The music began again, a faster dance, and before she could say a word, Haligon had swung her into his arms and moved off in the rhythm of this tune. This time they had to concentrate not only on the steps but also to avoid collisions with more erratic dancers whirling about the floor.

Three dances to a set and Haligon whisked her off the floor during the change of musicians on the pretext of needing a drink. With glasses of chilled white wine, he guided her into the shadow of a deserted stall.

She smiled to herself, rehearsing a number of deft rejections if she needed them.

"I don't think you're at all lame, Tenna," he said conversationally. "Especially if the station master let you take a run down to the port. Care to have a go at the first toss dance after all?"

His expression dared her.

"We'll see."

Pause.

"So, will you run on tomorrow?"

"I'll be careful with the wine in case I do," she said, half warning him as she lifted the glass.

"Will you make it to the sea from here in one run?"

"Quite likely. It's spring and there'd be no snow on the pass trace."

"Would you still go if there were?"

"No one said anything about snow on the pass trace at the station."

"Keep your ears open, don't you?"

"A runner always needs to know conditions on the trace." She gave him a stern look.

"All right, I've got the message."

"Fair enough."

Pause.

"You're not at all what I expected, you know," Haligon said respectfully.

"I can quite candidly say the same of you, Haligon," she replied.

The new musicians played the first bar of the next song, to acquaint people with a sample of the dance to come.

So, when Tenna felt his arm about her shoulders, she did not resist the pressure. Nor did she when both arms enfolded her and his mouth found hers. It was a nice kiss, not sloppy as others had been, but well placed on her lips, as if he knew what he was about in kissing. His arms about her were sure, too, not crushing her needlessly against him. Respectful, she thought . . . and then, as the kiss deepened with her cooperation, she didn't think of anything but enjoying the experience.

Haligon monopolized her all evening, rather deftly, she realized. Always whisking her off the dance floor before any one else could find her. They kissed quite a bit between dances. He was far more respectful of her person than she expected. And said so.

"With the punch you can deliver, my girl," he answered, "you can bet your last mark I'm not about to risk my brother's fate."

He also found other chilled drinks for her to drink instead of more wine. She appreciated that even more. Especially when the music of the toss dance began. The floor cleared of all save a few hardy couples.

"Shall we?" and Haligon's grin was all the challenge she needed.

The ache in her right shin was really minor and her confidence in his partnering had grown throughout the evening; otherwise she would not have taken his dare.

During the pattern of the dance, the female partner was to be swung as high as possible, and if she was very clever, she would twirl in midair before being caught by the male. It would be a dangerous dance, but it was ever so much fun. Tenna's older brother had taught her and given her enough practice so that she was well able to make the turns. It had insured her partners at any Gather in the east once it was known how light she was and what a good dancer.

From the very first toss, she knew that Haligon was the best partner she'd ever had. There was great cheering for them when she managed a full two turns in the air before he caught her. In one of the rare close movements of the dance, he whispered swift instructions so that she was prepared for the final toss. And able to execute it, sure he would be there to keep her from crashing on the floor. She was close enough to being missed so that the spectators gasped just as he caught her half a handspan above the floor. Another girl was not so lucky but suffered no more than the indignity of the fall.

Cleve, Rosa, Spacia, Grolly, and most of the station crowded about them when they left the dance floor, congratulating them on such a performance. They were offered drinks, meat rolls, and other delicacies.

"Upholding the honor of the station," Cleve loudly proclaimed. "And the Hold, of course," he magnanimously added, bowing to Haligon.

"Tenna's the best partner I've ever had," Haligon replied sincerely, mopping his face.

Then Torlo reached through the crowd and tapped Tenna's shoulder.

"You're on the run list, Tenna," he said, emphasizing the warning with a nod.

"To the coast?"

"Aye, as you wished." Torlo gave Haligon a severe look.

"I'll escort you to the station, then, Tenna?" Haligon asked.

The harpers had struck up another slow dance. Rosa and Spacia were looking intensely at Tenna but she couldn't interpret their glances. She also knew her duty as a runner.

"This is the last dance then." And she took Haligon by the arm and led him to the floor.

Haligon tucked her in against him and she let her body relax against his and to his leading. She had never had such a Gather in her life. She could almost be glad that he'd run her off the trace and so started the events that had culminated in this lovely night.

They said nothing, both enjoying the flow of the dance and the sweet music. When it ended, Haligon led her from the floor, holding her right hand in his, and toward the station, its glowbasket shining at the door.

"So, Runner Tenna, you finish your first Cross. It won't be your last, will it?" Haligon asked as they paused just beyond the circle of light. He lifted his hand and lightly brushed back the curls.

"No, it's unlikely to. I'm going to run as long as I'm able."

"But you'll be Crossing often, won't you?" he asked, and she nodded. "So, if sometime in the future, when I've got my own holding . . . I'm going to breed runners . . . beasts, that is," he qualified hastily, and she almost laughed at his urgent correction. "I've been trying to find the strain I want to breed, you see, and used the traces as sort of the best footing for comparison. I mean, is there any chance you might . . . possibly . . . consider running more often on this side of the world?"

Tenna cocked her head at him, surprised by the intensity and roughness in his pleasant voice.

"I might." She smiled up at him. This Haligon was more of a temptation to her than he knew.

Now he smiled back at her, a challenge sparkling in his eyes. "We'll just have to see, won't we?"

"Yes, I guess we will."

With that answer, she gave him a quick kiss on the cheek and ducked into the station before she could say more than she ought right now after such a limited acquaintance. But maybe raising runners—both kinds, four-legged and two—in the west wasn't a bad idea at all.

Short Novels By Bestselling Masters

In Three Spectacular Volumes

"Microcosmic glimpses of broadly imagined worlds and their larger-than-life characters distinguish this hefty volume of heavyweight fantasy.... There's enough color, vitality, and bravura displays of mythmaking in this rich sampler to sate faithful fans and nurture new readers on the stuff of legends still being created." —*Publishers Weekly* (starred review)

Legends 1

Stephen King tells a tale of Roland the Gunslinger, in the world of The Dark Tower, with "The Little Sisters of Eluria."

Robert Silverberg returns to Majipoor and to Lord Valentine's adventure in an ancient tomb, in "The Seventh Shrine."

Orson Scott Card spins a yarn of Alvin and his apprentice from the *Tales of Alvin Maker*, in "Grinning Man."

Raymond E. Feist's *Riftwar Saga* is the setting of the tale of "The Wood Boy."

Legends 3

Robert Jordan relates crucial events in the years leading up to *The Wheel of Time*™ in "New Spring."

Ursula K. Le Guin adds a sequel to her famous books of *Earthsea*, portraying a woman who wants to learn magic, in "Dragonfly."

Tad Williams tells a dark and enthralling story of a haunted castle in the age before *Memory, Sorrow, and Thorn,* in "The Burning Man."

Terry Pratchett relates an amusing incident in *Discworld,* of a magical contest and the witch Granny Weatherwax, in "The Sea and Little Fishes."

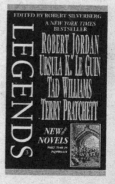